He smelle

wind. His hard body pressed the length of hers sent heat raging through Mariah's veins. Never in her wildest imaginings had she thought to be kissed like this, so all consuming, so full of passion—and by Silver Eagle.

Reveling in the strength of his lusty body molded to her softer curves, the familiar sounds of the woods—birds chirping, leaves rustling in a faint breeze, faded away. She brushed aside thought of the danger to them if caught like this. All she wanted, all she needed, was right here in Silver Eagle's arms, in his delicious kiss.

Her fingers sank into his thick, coarse hair as he slanted his head to gain better access to her mouth. She found her tongue boldly dueling with his and felt the evidence of his desire against her soft flesh. The stiff coils of the bullwhip anchored at his side rubbed her pelvic bone.

She gasped at the thought of making love with him.

Praise for Joyce Henderson...

Joyce Henderson's previous work has finaled in the National Readers' Choice Award.

"Henderson is at the top of her game. She knows what her readers want, and she delivers—a sexy hero you can't help but fall in love with and a spunky heroine who's his match in every way. *CAPTURE AN EAGLE* will capture your heart!"
~Lynnette Hallberg, multi-published author

To Larry...

Enjoy!!

Joyce Henderson

Capture
an
Eagle

by

Joyce Henderson

Capture an Eagle

COPYRIGHT © 2009 by Henderson Family Trust

Cover Art by *Nicola Martinez*

The Wild Rose Press
PO Box 706
Adams Basin, NY 14410-0706
Visit us at www.thewildrosepress.com

Publishing History
First Cactus Rose Edition, 2010
Print ISBN 1-60154-630-0

Published in the United States of America

Dedication

As always I offer my undying gratitude
for the unselfish support and insightful critiques
by fellow writers, Diane O'Key and Lynn Hallberg.

My thanks to Western artist Ron Scofield
for answering questions about the Old West,
obscure information I might not find elsewhere.

To my children, Vonda, Mark, and Coleen,
thanks for your support from a distance.

My love to Bob
for his never-ending love and encouragement.
We've traveled a long trail together.

Prologue

Central Texas, 1837

"Ward, our baby will die if we don't do something!"

"What can we do, darlin'?" Ward watched his beloved Sarah try in vain to coax his precious four-day-old son, Tanner, to accept her breast. His little face flushed, his body limp, Tanner wouldn't even open his mouth when she nudged his lips with her nipple.

His whimpers had gradually subsided to ominous silence. No strength left. Ward feared his first born would likely meet the angels in a day or two.

Sarah's lovely hazel eyes beseeched him. "Dr. Cartwright said he must have liquid!"

Ward squatted beside his wife's rocking chair and caressed the little mite's cheek. Help existed, but Sarah would likely fight him.

He pulled a chair from the dining table and settled next to her. "Uh, Sarah darlin', one person might know how to break Tanner's fever."

Ward swallowed and took her hand in his. "I've heard talk about the shaman in the Indian encampment down by the river."

He barely got out the last word before Sarah wagged her head.

"Holy Mother, you would likely be killed if you approached that band." She squeezed his fingers. "No. There must be someone—"

1

"Dr. Cartwright says the shaman is gifted, and she's a woman."

Poor, but it was all he had. Sarah's prediction might be right. Maybe he wouldn't get within a mile of the scattered tipis before those redskins were on him like a pack of wolves.

But Cartwright, who practiced what medicine he knew down near Burnett Station, vowed they were a peaceful bunch. He'd patched up one of their braves after he got shot up trying to rustle a steer.

"I could lose you, too!"

Ward caressed Sarah's damp cheek. "If I don't try, little Tanner is a goner for sure." Afraid to give her false hope, he added, "There's no guarantee the old woman can help Tanner, but she's the only one who might know somethin' Cartwright don't. Tell you what. I'll take Samuel with me. He's right smart at signin' with them Indians."

****

One hour of steady riding later, Samuel Tucker at his side, Ward headed toward the river that bisected his property to the northwest. Actually, if he wanted to press the issue, the Indians camped inside his property line, but he had no intention of runnin' 'em off. And if Wings of a Dove healed his son, he never would, by gum. He'd protect them from now until Doomsday.

"Mista Ward, y'all think this be a good idea?"

Ward glanced at Tanner bundled in two blankets, cradled against his chest. "I don't know, Samuel, but my boy is dead if this shaman can't work some magic."

"Magic?" Samuel's dark eyes rounded in his equally round face.

Jehoshaphat! Not a good choice of words. Samuel harbored a belief in voodoo and witch doctors. Before she died on the same plantation where Samuel was born, his old grandma had done

2

her work well. Too well.

"I mean a medical miracle, Samuel. No hocus pocus. If Wings of a Dove has a gift for healin', I suspect God Almighty had a hand in her learnin'."

Rolling his eyes, Samuel said, "Mebbe so. She ain't scary like no voodoo queen I remember; no, she ain't. An' that be a good thing."

At that moment a brave stepped into their path, an arrow nocked in his bow, though carried at his side rather than pointed at them.

Both men's mounts shied and danced sideways.

"Whoa." Ward quieted his horse with a steady hand.

Before he could say anything, Samuel made crude signs, pointed to Ward, then his own mouth, and pantomimed why they were there. Ward was impressed. Samuel, undoubtedly as uneasy as he, showed no fear before this Indian who could let that arrow fly in a second.

Of medium height, the Indian stood very straight and gravely watched Samuel's hand signals. When he nodded in understanding, two feathers attached at the crown of his midnight hair swayed gracefully. He signed back to Samuel, turned, and walked away.

"We is to follow him, Mista Ward."

Ward stared in astonishment. "Just like that? No palaverin'?"

"Falcon Wing say we see Wings of a Dove. She decide if'n she help Masta Tanner."

Samuel nudged his horse ahead, and Ward followed, gray eyes narrowed on the Indian's bare back as he walked lightly, his feet seeming to skim the ground. 'Course, the fellow wore moccasins rather than boots.

Shortly, they crossed a narrow section of river and stopped before a tipi nestled near the water. Others rose here and there, maybe a dozen in all. A

3

small band. Other than the occasional theft of cattle, they kept to themselves, so even the Rangers had stopped harassing them.

The Indian disappeared into the tipi.

"We best not get down until told, Mista Ward. These folks turn on you in a blink."

Ward didn't have to be told twice. Several braves had gathered near another tipi, heads nodding as they spoke among themselves. He swiped his damp forehead. Yeah, it might be hot, but nerves caused him to sweat.

The Indian reappeared and motioned them down. As Ward neared the tipi, the Indian eyed his hip piece and frowned, but allowed them inside. Another surprise. Ward would have bet the Indian would want him disarmed.

It took a moment for his eyes to adjust to the dim interior. A woman sat near a small fire in the center of the swept ground. Even in this heat, she was shrouded in a blanket, only her dark face visible.

No way could he judge her age. While her face was lined, her black eyes were clear and piercing. A work-worn hand snaked from beneath the blanket and beckoned him forward. She pointed to the skirt of the blanket spread around her. He looked at Samuel.

"Lay your boy there."

Hesitantly, Ward knelt and placed his infant son near enough for her to touch him. He stayed put, and so did she. After a second, she glared at him and motioned him back.

"I don't think—"

"She ain't gonna do nothin', you sittin' on top o' her. She leery, Mista Ward."

"No more than I am, Samuel." He studied the woman's sober countenance and reminded himself he had come here of his own free will. Since she'd

4

probably sit there forever if he didn't comply, he rose and moved back. One step.

She laid her weathered hand on Tanner's blanket, closed her eyes, and sat motionless so long that Ward began to fidget. After a time, she pulled the blanket back from Tanner's pinched little face, leaned down, and turned her ear to his mouth.

A movement at the back of the tipi caught Ward's attention. A younger version of the woman before him cradled a baby in her arms no bigger than his own son.

"Who is she?" he asked.

Samuel murmured something in a singsong voice. Her attention on Tanner, the shaman responded with a couple of signs.

"Her daughter. Little bundle is her grandson," Samuel said.

Ward's attention refocused on the older woman, who spoke in a hushed voice as she covered Tanner's face. His heart sank. She wouldn't help.

Motioning to Samuel, she nodded once as her hand disappeared beneath the blanket.

"She be sayin' you's to leave him. Come back afore sun sleeps tomorrow."

"Leave him?" Alarm sizzled through Ward. This heathen couldn't be serious! Leave his precious son, not knowin' what the devil she'd do?

"Mista Ward," Samuel touched his arm, "she ain't gonna harm him. She'll do all she can in her ancient way. My grandmammy always said, 'Leave the healin' to the womenfolk.'"

Envisioning the horror on Sarah's face if he returned without Tanner, Ward looked into the old woman's eyes. She didn't flinch.

"Tell her if she heals my son, she and her people will be safe on this land for all the days of their lives." He focused his eyes on hers. "And if Tanner dies, I'll trust she did all she could. My pledge is the same."

Before Samuel signed or said a word, she nodded.

Ward's brow creased. Had the old woman understood him?

Chapter One

Central Texas, 1865

"Tanner!"

Mariah Kelly hung out the coach window, waving madly when her brother walked out of Hawkins' General Store, a sack of supplies over his shoulder.

Home! Glory be, how wonderful! Not even the crushing heat diminished her joy. After two years in Maryland, days spent at the girls' school, even longer nights in the hospital caring for wounded soldiers, she felt like she'd been released from prison. For one instant she relived the nightmare—screams, smiles, prayers. Benediction.

The coach jolted to a halt; her body slammed against the wood. "Ow!"

Rubbing her elbow, she steadied herself, pushed the memories from her mind and the feathered hat from her brow. This latest fashion would be the first thing to go. Give her a broad-brimmed Texas hat any day.

She retreated into the coach and fell against the hard seat. The matron next to her, whom she'd done her best to ignore these five long days, harrumphed at Mariah's unladylike display. But the three men facing her grinned.

Too eager to wait for the outrider to open the door, Mariah bolted out and nearly pitched to her knees, staggering to catch herself.

"Whoa."

She'd nearly forgotten that male voice. Her brother caught her forearms in strong gloved hands.

The darn hat dipped over her brow again, so she couldn't see his face, but oh, how she loved him. "Tanner."

"I thought Pa paid that fuddy-duddy school to teach you ladylike manners, Mariah."

She pulled one arm from his grasp and slammed her fist into his unyielding chest, then shoved back the hat.

"Worked real well." Laughter rang in Tanner's voice. His smile was as wide as the sky, his green eyes the color of high-summer clover.

Her own eyes teared with joy as she threw her arms around his neck. "It's so good to be home!"

In years past Tanner would have pushed her away, embarrassed by her affection. But he'd grown up. And now she found it such a blessing to embrace a man whole in body.

He hugged her back fit to crack her ribs. Then he unwound her death grip and held her at arm's length. "Let's get a look at you, darlin'."

Glory, how she'd missed that drawled endearment. Only Pa and Tanner called her that. Well, when she behaved. She glanced past him, searching for the enigmatic Silver Eagle. Surely, he was here, too. During the years of growing up, Tanner and his shadow never went anywhere without each other.

"Hey, you've...grown." Tanner ruffled her hair. "Not up, but out."

She let go of the longing to see Silver Eagle and focused on her mischievous brother again. "What do you mean, *out*? I'm not fat!"

He grinned. "Didn't say that. You left a scrawny girl; now you're, uh...womanly, sort of."

She gave him a saucy smile. "I'll take that as a compliment."

A portmanteau banged onto the ground next to their feet, spewing dust over them. Mariah whirled, eyes widening when her trunk began to slide off the top of the coach.

"Don't you dare drop that trunk!" she ordered. "I've got breakables in there."

The coachman grunted and braced his boot heel on the luggage rail as he pulled on the large black case, barely managing to keep it from going the way of the smaller one. Sweat popped on his face. "I can't get it down any other way, woman!"

"Hold it." Tanner stepped close to support the unwieldy metal trunk. "I've got it."

Amazed, Mariah watched the trunk settle on his shoulder. Tanner bent his legs and lowered it to the ground without jarring it one bit. She hated to be a fussbudget, but she cautioned, "Not on the end. Set it down on the bottom."

He complied, then straightened, brushing sweat from his brow. "What've you got in that thing? Gold bars?"

"Of course not," she said, distracted by her first real look at her brother. Her *big* brother. Tanner sported wide shoulders, muscled forearms, and a narrow waist. *He* had certainly filled out over the past two years, too. He'd become a man, and no doubt one to be reckoned with. But she didn't say so. No sense giving him a swelled head.

"Is this all you have?"

Mariah raised her arm. Her reticule dangled from her wrist. "And this."

"Okay. Let's wrestle this thing over to the buckboard and get you home. Ma and Pa weren't expectin' you for a couple days. Pa's in Fort Worth at a bull auction."

Again glancing toward the ranch wagon, she fished for information. "Maybe Silver Eagle could help you."

He pointed at the trunk and huffed. "With this? No need."

Well, shoot. That didn't work. Of course, Tanner was totally unaware of where her interest lay regarding Silver Eagle. Interest that, after two long years, still surpassed what any white woman should feel for an Indian. What she'd ever felt for any other man.

Rather than lift the trunk again, though, he grabbed the end strap and began to drag it across the uneven ground. Mariah closed her eyes, praying the beautiful crystal bowl she'd brought for her mother would make it home in one piece.

He hadn't taken two steps before the woman who'd harrumphed every hour on the hour all the way from El Paso demanded, "Young man! Now that you have ceased making a spectacle of yourself, I need assistance departing this wretched stage."

"Patience," Mariah muttered and turned to face the dour-faced matron.

His expression questioning, Tanner lowered the trunk to the ground and doffed his hat. "Ma'am?"

"Are you deaf?"

"Mrs. Crump—" Mariah reined in her hostility. "My *brother* will help you if you'll curb your tongue."

"Sis—" Tanner stepped toward the woman adorned in unbecoming puce. "She's obviously upset."

Once upon a time, Mariah would have lost her temper. And though she'd had a gullet full of this obnoxious woman, she held her tongue, shot a glance at Tanner, and spoke for his ears only. "Help the biddy down, and let's go home."

As she presented her back to the horrible woman, Mariah's pulse skittered. A man every bit as muscular and tall as her brother dropped a heavy barrel from his shoulder into the Broken Spur's wagon bed.

Hair as black as a cave hid his face. He wore a buckskin shirt, jeans, and dusty boots. Unlike Tanner's pistol, this man favored a wicked-looking knife in a sheath that dangled from the right side of his belt and a bullwhip coiled against his other hip.

Silver Eagle. The world faded away.

Handsome as ever, he, too, had matured into a formidable specimen. Tall, lean, somehow dangerous. She glimpsed the silver-tipped feather that had adorned his shoulder-length hair since earliest memory.

Her breath stopped altogether when he looked across the dusty road, pinning her with polished-onyx eyes. Fleeting though it was, she knew he recognized her.

"Sis, you shouldn't have been so rude." Tanner once again curled his fingers around the trunk's handle.

She glanced over her shoulder at the woman who now tongue lashed the man atop the coach. "Brother, you don't know what rude is until you've ridden five-hundred miles cooped up with that woman."

"Maybe so, but—"

"Where's Silver Eagle going?"

"Home," Tanner said, not missing a beat. "He came in to help load supplies. He works for Pa full-time now but refuses to live in the bunkhouse. You remember how he is. Sticks mighty close to his people."

That was true, but he'd spent a prodigious amount of time with Tanner, as well. Man and horse passed the opening between the store and Sheriff Tate's office.

"He's still riding that big black and white pinto," she said as if her heart weren't lodged in her throat. "Glory, how old is that stud?"

"Not more than eight, I'd say."

"I see he's given up his Indian way and uses a saddle now."

Tanner shrugged. "Depends. Still more comfortable bareback, but if he needs a saddle horn for tether, he rides a saddle."

Dadburnit, she had to know. "Is he married yet?"

Brow creased, Tanner stared at her.

"Just wondered why he's in such an all-fired hurry to leave. He could have at least welcomed me home." She tried to cover the blushing heat that had blossomed under her brother's scrutiny. "He hasn't changed one bit. No wonder I never liked him."

Tanner gave her a "you don't think I believe that tall tale" look. But he didn't argue, didn't say anything. Simply hoisted the trunk into the wagon bed.

"Gotta settle up with Mr. Hawkins. Back in a minute." He disappeared into the store again.

Shoot. Why did she have to ask if Silver Eagle were married? She could have bitten off her tongue as each word escaped her mouth.

She hadn't fooled Tanner, at least about not liking Silver Eagle, and she couldn't deny the truth to herself. She rubbed the ache in her chest. Of all the men she'd met these past years—*too* many—the numerous marriage proposals she'd received, some serious, some lighthearted, why did she have to yearn for *this* man?

When Ma and Pa finally sent her off to a finishing school, they had not realized the danger they'd exposed her to. They had no idea Baltimore was practically a battle ground in the War between the States.

Sure, just as Ma remembered, Maryland, her girlhood home, was green, lush with oak, myrtle, dogwood. Glorious in the fall when the leaves changed color—now soaked in soldiers' blood.

Mariah winced. She'd missed her home every minute of every day. Foolish, maybe, but there it was. A dyed-in-the-wool Texan right down to her boot soles.

And Silver Eagle, dang his stiff-backed pride, was a part of that life. A bigger part than she cared to admit. Seeing him now was like a kick in the gut.

"Oh!" Reality returned with a jolt as Tanner lifted her to the buckboard seat.

At one hundred twenty pounds, she didn't consider herself a lightweight. Glory be, her brother had developed into a strong man. But she shouldn't be surprised. He roped and threw cattle for a living or mended fence when the cattle or horses broke through. Heavy, muscle-building work.

As he climbed up beside her, she gazed up and down the dusty street. Not much doing in the middle of the day with most folks home for their noon meal. Even Crabapple's saloon was quiet. No boisterous yells, no tinny piano. She arranged the hot walking-suit skirt on the hard seat.

"Hang onto that silly hat, Mariah. It'll scare the horses if it blows off."

"It is silly, isn't it?" She reached up and pulled out the two hatpins holding the veiled confection. In short order she released her titian hair to tumble nearly to her waist.

"Holy smokes, that mop has grown a foot since you left home." He tugged a curl. Something he'd done just to annoy her when she was little.

"Yeah." She slapped his hand. "I'm going to talk to Ma about cutting it. The school matrons absolutely forbade any of us to cut our hair." She glanced at him. "So, what's happening at the ranch? All the details, brother dear. Don't leave out a thing."

Including what's happening with Silver Eagle. Would she ever get Tanner to open up about his lifelong friend?

"First things first, Mariah." He pulled two coiled sticks of licorice from his pocket and handed one to her.

She grinned. "Oh, you remembered!" Every time Tanner had returned from town when she was growing up, he'd brought her the chewy licorice.

Sticking the other in his mouth, he tore off a bite as she did the same. In moments, his teeth were shaded black. She laughed as he snapped the reins over the horses' backs.

"We just returned from a drive to Cheyenne. Time now to begin the long season of roundin' up strays and findin' calves for brandin'."

"How many in the herd this year?"

"We delivered just under fifteen hundred. Pa and McAllister combined stock for the trip. Nine hundred ours, and we managed to get nearly that many to the railhead. McAllister only lost a half dozen. Good weather most of the way, too."

"I want to go on the drive next spring."

Tanner laughed. "Whistle in the wind on that one, sis. Pa flat out won't let you, and Ma would have a heart attack at the thought."

Mariah's brow scrunched in a frown. Same old arguments. She'd begged until her throat was sore her last year home. To no avail. Pa was adamant, and Ma had threatened to lock her up if she didn't change her tune. So she had.

Now, though, she was twenty-three-years old. Old enough to make decisions for herself. On the other side of the country, she'd been doing just that for two years, and she was still alive and whole for goodness sake! Watching men suffer and die had matured her. Ma and Pa had yet to know the details.

Now was not the time to argue, though, and Tanner wasn't the one she needed to convince. She glanced sideways at him and reconsidered. He'd probably be just as difficult as Pa. Taking a deep breath, she pushed the desire to the back of her mind.

She'd have seven or eight months to wear them down.

****

His thoughts awhirl, Silver Eagle rode at a comfortable lope. One glimpse of Mariah Kelly at the stage office was all he needed. He had thought himself prepared to see her again, but his pulse quickened at the sight of the fiery curls beneath her hat.

Two years past and all the years before, though tempted, he had kept her at a distance, telling himself she was his best friend's sister. He would never do anything to jeopardize his friendship with Tanner.

But now she had returned, more enticing than before. More of a woman than he was ready to face, *could* face, without betraying his desire.

Heat shimmered on the prairie as he rode toward the river.

His people had lived there for all the seasons of his life, for two generations before he'd opened his eyes to the world.

Grandmother Wings of a Dove had often told stories of how she had saved Tanner when the boys were but a few days old.

Ward and Sarah Kelly did not know that his mother, Sparrow, had nursed their child for a day, but Silver Eagle treasured that brotherhood.

Ward Kelly had honored his promise to Wings of a Dove. To this day, no white man threatened the band without Ward Kelly coming to its defense.

Of course, none of his people strayed far from the small village except him, for his daily rides to the Broken Spur.

Long ago his father, Falcon Wing, had quit raiding cattle herds for meat, and for many years had done odd jobs for Mr. Kelly, too. In return, Tanner's father supplied the band with a couple steers each year, more if hunting season proved bleak.

Sarah Kelly traded needles and tin cookware with his mother, though she never showed her face in the village. Mrs. Kelly sent the items home with him, and he returned with herbs or blankets made by his grandmother and aunt, and Sparrow's beautiful woven baskets. The arrangement had worked well for many years.

And in payment? He lusted after Ward and Sarah Kelly's daughter. If he overstepped with Mariah Kelly, all could be in jeopardy. No white man, even Ward Kelly, would countenance an Indian courting his daughter.

He slowed his mount to a steady *clop clop* as he rode into trees that bordered the narrow river. Ahead, he saw his sister kneeling at water's edge, pounding a shirt with a rock.

He scowled to find her alone.

Quiet Bird, mute since birth, was easy prey for a man bent upon doing an unprotected maiden harm. If attacked, she could not scream for help. However, she could hear, and she looked around now at his approach.

"*Ni nami?*, why are you alone?"

She made signs that even the Kellys and other white people understood.

A smile crinkled her dark eyes as she signed that Sparrow was skinning a steer brought to the village. Talking Woman needed Grandmother. Her time had come. The birth of another papoose would bless the tribe this day.

No one questioned his grandmother's abilities. As the band's shaman, she was right more often than not with foretelling the future, be it the sex of an unborn child or changes in the weather. And her healing herbal decoctions were sought by Indian and white man alike.

"A boy child or girl?" he asked.

Boy, Quiet Bird signed by extending two fingers behind her crown. She would have clasped one of her braids to signify a girl child.

She settled back to washing clothes as he dismounted. He was hungry, but that could wait. His slender sister was nearly finished. He would keep watch over her.

He tethered the pinto close enough to the water downstream so the stallion could slake his thirst. When Silver Eagle drew his canteen from a saddlebag and offered it to Quiet Bird, she refused, continuing her industrious pounding.

Seated beside her, forearms resting on bent knees, he watched her for a time and listened to birds twitter overhead.

Peaceful. Quiet Bird loved the river, and like him, enjoyed the solitude of her own company. Nothing to muddle the mind.

Today, his was running like a crazed buffalo. No doubt, he would see Mariah again tomorrow. He glanced at his sister. "Mariah Kelly is home."

Delight lit her features as she sat back. Water dripping from her hands, she signed her pleasure and asked if he was glad she had returned.

He shrugged, squinting over the water to hide his eyes from her. Quiet Bird could read a person's thoughts almost as well as Grandmother Wings of a Dove. "Tanner will be happy his sister is home. Pest that she was, he missed her."

Quiet Bird laid wet fingers on his buckskin sleeve. He gave her his attention. Expression grave, she signed, *And you, ni pabi?, my brother?*

He might hide his desires from others, but never from his sister or grandmother. Still, he tried. "I am pleased for her. She is not happy away from her family and the Broken Spur."

Though she signed nothing, Quiet Bird's deep sorrow shone in her eyes. She patted his arm, then turned back to her laundry. She knew as well as he that having his heart's desire would never come to pass. He was accepted on the Broken Spur as Tanner's friend, but never as a family member. Never as their daughter's mate.

Shortly, Quiet Bird finished the washing. He helped her gather the wet clothes to dry on rope lines in the village. When he offered her his horse, she put her hand to her belly and chided him with silent laughter. White men coddled their women, but Indians would laugh at him if they saw him offer such courtesy. She did allow him to carry her basket while she walked beside him.

As he rode toward home, one thought drummed in his mind. He would never find a mate of his own blood who he could love as fiercely as he loved Mariah Kelly.

Chapter Two

On horseback, Mariah could make the trip from town in less than two hours. The wagon, however, required patience. She and her brother settled into companionable silence as the wagon creaked toward the ranch.

She didn't really mind, though. It was heaven to gaze at this prairie she'd missed so much while in the East. She'd walked the hospital's corridors, heard the men's moans, held the hands of more than she cared to remember as they died calling for their mamas or sweethearts. The Civil War hadn't ended soon enough for them. They'd never go home.

She inhaled deeply, remembering the times she had tried to bring back this spot, the smell of sage and wind-whipped dirt. Sometimes thoughts of home were all that saved her sanity. God willing, she'd never have to leave Texas again. Ma always said, "Home is where the heart is."

So true.

"Oh, look! There's McCallister's place."

Her brother slanted an eye at the gated entrance to Jessup's spread. "You're right, sis, the place hasn't moved one inch in thirty years. Been there nearly as long as the Broken Spur."

"Of course it has, smart britches, but I haven't seen it in forever! It's just wonderful to see, that's all."

Tanner would never understand. Determined not to leave home, he'd sweet talked Ma until she agreed. And when Ma wanted something, Pa always gave in. So Mariah'd gone off to school while her brother got to stay home. And thank the good Lord. Pa needed the help. Life on the prairie was precarious.

And worse, had Tanner been in the East, he'd have surely been in the thick of war. The war she'd felt guilty to leave behind. No, not the war, the boys. That's what so many were—boys, mere children forced to do dreadful things, suffer dreadful things.

"Are the McCallisters any easier about Silver Eagle and his people living so close?"

Tanner snorted. "Doubt that old man Jessup will ever understand those folks ain't no threat."

"Well, you have to admit they're much different from most Comanches we hear about."

"Yep, but unlike those who roam the *Llano Estacado*, they'd perched right where they are today long before any of us moved here. They ain't movin', and they sure as shootin' ain't causin' trouble.

"Miz McCallister is doin' poorly. Heard tell she's got cancer."

Though she had reason to worry about Mr. McCallister, she sure didn't wish ill for his wife.

Mariah settled down to eat dust for another few miles, squirming uncomfortably on the hard seat. Boy, when she got to the house, this darn heavy walking suit would go the way of her ridiculous hat. Maybe Ma could make curtains out of the skirt material.

Up ahead, she spied a man working along the fence that separated the two ranches. Max Stoddard, Pa's foreman. "Max!" Waving, she stood up.

Tanner grabbed a fistful of skirt and yanked her down to the seat. "You tryin' to spook the horses, Mariah? Holy smokes, you forget how to handle yourself around stock?"

"No! I'm just glad to see an old friend."

"Well, dammit, wait until we come abreast of

him."

Though Tanner appeared to have perfect control, she sat until he hauled back on the reins and the wagon rattled to a halt.

Max's brow crinkled as he stared at her across the fence.

"Miss Mariah? Good Lord, you've grown into a right purty gal."

Oh, dear. Max had called her "Miss" from the time she was able to trot around and cause trouble. Obviously, nothing had changed. Smiling, she clambered down from the wagon and walked over to grab his hand through the fence. She pulled, and he obliged, leaning closer.

She planted a smacking kiss on his sun-toughened cheek. "Thank you, Max. It's so good to be home."

Her show of affection brought a flush to his weathered face. Respectful-like, he whipped off his sweat-stained hat. Glory, was he now going to give her a wide berth like he did Ma, so shy he could hardly string two words together in a grown woman's presence?

"Your folks will dance a jig when they see you."

Her brother said, "Yeah, they sure will." Then he hiked his chin. "That corner post looks rickety."

Max glanced at the fence he'd been inspecting. "Yup. Wouldn't happen to have a post or two in the wagon bed, would you? We had a half dozen left after the last mendin' job."

"'Fraid not. I stacked 'em behind the barn just this mornin' afore I drove into town."

"Figures. Guess I'd best ride this fence line a bit and see if others need replacin'."

"Samuel and I can come out tomorrow and fix any you find," Tanner said. "Pa wants you to take some hands south to begin collectin' unbranded stock."

"Yeah, I know. Won't you be goin' with us?"

Tanner looked at Mariah. "I'll catch up in a day or two."

Flabbergasted, she stared at him. Her brother wanted to stick around for a bit? It warmed her heart, but she said not a word to embarrass him.

Instead, she hiked her skirt, planted a foot on the wagon's running board, and extended her hand for his assistance. Settling on the seat, she turned to Max. "See you at the ranch later?"

"'Spect so." He clamped his hat over tousled brown hair, mounted his sorrel, and rode off.

Another fifteen minutes took them to the always-open gates of the Broken Spur. Her father considered this open range, but Jessup McCallister had insisted they separate their land.

In the distance the barn and outbuildings stood beneath a blazing sun. On a slight rise, surrounded by old oaks and a couple of pecan trees, the ranch house rambled wide and low as if haphazardly thrown down to take root.

Home. At long last. Mariah swallowed the emotional lump in her throat and sighed at the sight. As Tanner brought the wagon to a lumbering halt near the barn, the screened door slammed in the midday quiet.

"Tanner Kelly, where in billy heck have you been?" Her mother's mouth dropped open, gold-shot hazel eyes wide. "Mariah?"

She jumped from the wagon and ran to embrace the woman who had petted and protected her as she grew up. "Ma!"

Ma hugged her back as fiercely, then set her at arm's length. The sweetest smile this side of the Rockies wreathed her face as her gaze wandered over Mariah. "We didn't expect you for a couple more days. Your pa will be fit to be tied when he finds you home. He so wanted to meet the stage."

"The coachman drove after dark most nights, so we got here sooner."

"After dark?" Her mother's brow creased. "That's so dangerous."

"Ma," Tanner called, "you want the sack of beans in the house or the bunkhouse? And the flour?"

She gestured to Tanner. "Let's get Mariah's things in the house; then I'll bring out containers for both. Most will go to the bunkhouse."

He groaned. "You want me to heft that trunk by myself?"

Both women grinned at his theatrics.

"Do I look like a pack horse, son?"

Tanner called Ma "squirt" behind her back. Mariah, only three inches taller than her mother's five-foot-two, provided fodder for him to lord it over her forever and a day, too.

At that moment, Samuel led a horse out of the barn.

"Samuel," Tanner called, "after you pen that beast, come over and give a hand."

"Yes, suh. Be right there."

"What a pantywaist." Mariah grinned and waved at the black man she'd always considered part of the family.

He paused, looked hard, then a smile spread across his round face. "I declare. Welcome home, Miss Mariah."

Tanner regained her attention. "You want to heft one end, sis?" He gestured. "Have at it."

"Children," Ma scolded through her smile. "Have either of you grown up yet?"

"No," they said in unison. Devilment glinted in Tanner's eyes.

****

Two days later, barely past daylight, Silver Eagle attached his lariat to the headstall of Mariah's seven-year-old mare and coaxed her into a trot. With little effort from him, she responded spiritedly.

When Mariah had claimed the buckskin for her own, he had been the one to gentle her, having seen too many horses with low spirits after the white man's brutal taming methods. While the Kellys did not abuse their stock, they broke horses in their age-old way. He had heard Horace McCallister say, "Father's horse wrangler rides the fire and spit out of green stock. Shows 'em who's boss."

Horses were sociable animals. With patience Silver Eagle taught horses who their leader was, but left their spirits intact.

Since Mrs. Kelly drove a buggy and did not care to ride, he had taken over Nutmeg's daily exercise on the lunge line to keep the mare fit rather than have a man ride her. The buckskin was good natured, and Silver Eagle had determined to keep her that way. Now that Mariah was home, today would be his last day with her horse. The last day of this connection that had helped him feel Mariah's presence.

Drawing Nutmeg in, he murmured in Comanche, "Work well for Mariah."

The horse nodded as if she understood. Dark eyes watching him, her ears twitched. He scratched her pole. "You have not felt a body's weight for many suns. Do not shy when she mounts."

Still rubbing the mare's fine coat, he looked to where the sun would rise. His favorite time of day. So still. He often wondered if the Great Spirit held His breath awaiting the sun's first peek over the horizon. A cock crowed. He smiled. Behind him a voice shattered his peace. Hot desire seared through him.

"Do you always talk to horses, Silver Eagle?"

Surprised she had arrived without his knowledge, his body tightened. He had thought to have this one last morning workout with no one the wiser. Still not prepared to face her, he now had no choice.

Giving himself time, he removed the lariat and coiled it with callused hands. After a deep breath, he turned to the woman who had filled his thoughts for so many suns and dark nights. Unwise of him, but truth.

"Welcome back to Broken Spur, Miss Mariah." Thank the Spirits his voice did not betray his thudding heart.

"Miss? Sounds strange coming from you."

He kept his counsel rather than respond to her taunt. "You could have welcomed me yesterday."

Did he hear hurt in her voice? Surely not. He had chosen not to greet her. Cowardly, perhaps, but he had needed, still needed, more time to mask his desire. Somehow he must find a way to go about his business on this ranch while staying as far from Mariah Kelly as possible.

Long ago he had known she would be a beautiful woman. Her glorious hair was caught at the nape with a rawhide strip similar to those his sister coiled through two braids. As Mariah's spring-grass eyes inspected him from dark hair to booted feet, his member threatened to betray him. A muscle ticked in his jaw; his teeth clenched in an effort to suppress the wayward flesh.

"You and Tanner have grown to manhood in my absence."

"Boys grow." Could she not speak of something else? He was a man, all right, one who would gladly throw her to the ground and take her right now.

She lifted the gate latch and stepped inside the corral. Nutmeg backed away and trotted to the other side, then turned to watch her.

Mariah smiled. "She's forgotten me. Will I have to repeat the get-acquainted process you taught me, Silver Eagle?"

He shrugged. While he did not think so, he could not be sure. The horse was intelligent and would surely remember her scent. The scent that teased him now.

"Where Tanner is?"

"Finishing breakfast. I was anxious to see Nutmeg. I plan to ride with you and Tanner today."

His heart clenched. *Not a good idea.*

Before he could object aloud, she continued, "Ma said I may. Pa won't be back until this evening about suppertime." She smiled. "I still don't do house chores very well."

Unconventional to a fault, Mariah had donned attire similar to that she had worn as a young girl— a boy's shirt, jeans, and boots. Her long legs, encased in tight denim, did nothing to cool his blood. She carried a broad-brimmed hat in gloved hands, and a canteen hung from a shoulder strap.

Stalling as best he could, he asked, "What Tanner think?"

She laughed, a pleasant sound that rippled over him like water spilling over rocks.

"I don't know. He has nothing to say about where I go, what I do."

"Gone two day, maybe. Round up stray take time. Sleep on ground, eat hardtack."

"Oh, I think I can manage." She grinned. "I've been sleeping on little better than a cot for a couple years at school. The ground might be a welcome change."

"Ground hard." *Like my body!* Before his thoughts ran away with him, he said, "Horse no seasoned. Most day she penned, no long ride."

"But Tanner says you've exercised her every single day since I left."

Thank you, my friend. She did not need to know that. He shook his head. "No same."

"Maybe, but I'm going to get my saddle and test

her while you're here. If she doesn't buck me off, I'll ride along." She shrugged. "Maybe not all day. I'll see how she goes."

"She no buck. Better see she let you near, Miss Mariah." The Spirits knew the mare would respond to Mariah. So did he, but it had not stopped him from voicing the excuse. Having her along did not fit his plan of distancing himself from her.

She turned on her heel and headed for the barn, her hips swaying enticingly. As the sun broke over the horizon, her hair lit to a fiery hue before she disappeared through the open double doors. *What would it be like to release those curls, feel them spill through my fingers*?

The screened door slamming shattered his lingering desire. At the same time that Tanner loped toward the corral, Max Stoddard stepped out of the bunkhouse on the barn's far side. Samuel and two other hands followed. The workday on the Silver Spur would now begin in earnest.

****

Mariah paused inside the barn and took several deep breaths, fanning her face with her hat. The man was gorgeous—and hostile as a rattler. Unchanged in attitude, for sure. A challenge to even carry on a conversation with him.

His dark brooding eyes were the most unsettling. She swore they saw into her mind. She sure hoped that was her unease talking rather than reality. Now that she'd seen him again, her fantasies erupted as they often had before she went away. To be honest, they'd never ceased.

But those notions could bring nothing but heartache. He Indian, she white, never the twain could meet. Ma and Pa would have conniption fits if they knew her feelings were deeper than friendship. Pa might even bar Silver Eagle from the ranch. She couldn't do that to him or the people who depended on him. He and Tanner were as close to brothers as either would ever have in the flesh. And she wouldn't see him, be near him, accidentally brush against him. Her heart skipped a beat.

These one-sided feelings infuriated her. He didn't want her near. He made that apparent in every word, every glance directed her way. She rubbed her temples to soothe the ache caused by those thoughts. She'd have to settle for her relationship with Quiet Bird and renew the fledgling one with Sparrow. Maybe tomorrow.

Before she pulled her saddle from the rack, she brushed her hand over the smooth leather. How she had missed this tack. At school, when given a few hours free time, she and her friends had ridden in the park, sidesaddle, like ladies, and always with companions. She hadn't been allowed to tear off on her own. Oh, no! One must ride sedately, smile prettily at passersby, and return to the stable as decorously as one left. "Ack!"

Returning to the corral, she found her brother talking earnestly with Silver Eagle. Before he realized she was behind him, Tanner said, "She won't last, Sil. Grin and bear it."

"I heard that, dear heart."

Not the least bit contrite, he laughed and faced her. "What do you bet I'm right? You haven't ridden rough terrain for a long time, sis. Your butt will be numb before noon vittles."

Silver Eagle's gaze arrowed to that butt, and Mariah's face flamed. Did Tanner have to make reference to her bottom? Better to ignore him. "Open the gate, please."

She entered the pen and propped her saddle on its fenders and horn, then looked to Silver Eagle for some sort of guidance. When he simply gazed at the horizon, she roped in her irritation.

"Uh, Silver Eagle, do you think she'll come to

me?"

He shrugged. "Find out."

Seething at his indifference, she moved toward Nutmeg, hand extended. "Come, girl. Remember me?"

The mare loped to the far end of the corral. Mariah wondered if she even understood English. Earlier, Silver Eagle had spoken in his tongue. Now he did so again. Nutmeg pricked her ears toward him, then looked at Mariah. After a moment, the buckskin began a slow approach, chocolate-colored ears forward, eyes darting between her and Silver Eagle.

Rather than press the skittish horse, Mariah raised her hand and crooned, "Come, girl."

Nutmeg stopped a long pace away, stretched her neck forward, and blew. Another short step brought her close enough to lip Mariah's fingers. Blowing again, she nodded, and then ducked her head for Mariah to scratch her forelock.

Mariah's delighted laughter sent the horse back a nervous step. "I won't hurt you. Promise."

Nutmeg stood still, allowing Mariah to run a hand over the sleek neck. She molded the deep chest, noting how well the mare had muscled out in the past couple years.

Mariah smiled. She had chosen well. This mare possessed a lot of heart and stamina in her beautiful form.

While Tanner went to the barn to get his horse, she tacked up. Upon mounting, she waited a tense moment, expecting Nutmeg to explode beneath her. But the mare stood as stoic as a packhorse. Good thing. For though Silver Eagle watched, black eyes intense, he didn't offer to help. Blast his indifferent hide.

Foregoing spurs this first ride, a few minutes later Mariah touched boot heels to the mare's sides.

When the men left, she followed without a hitch.

****

By eleven o'clock Mariah reluctantly agreed that Tanner had known what he was talking about. Her butt was numb, and her thigh muscles burned from gripping the saddle leathers. Weary, she longed for a nap. But she had to get home first. The men still rode south, and she suspected they would continue after lunch.

She knew where she was. Much longer, though, and she might lose the trail on the return ride. She couldn't ask her brother to escort her after she'd pushed herself on him and Silver Eagle.

Both men rode ahead. Mariah wasn't the least surprised they ignored her. Tagging along today was reminiscent of past times when she'd badgered them until they threatened to bury her head in the nearest stream. Tanner had, anyway.

She'd never been adept at reading Silver Eagle's expressions and certainly not his thoughts. Her only consolation was watching him work, his body one with his horse. And, of course, the beautiful day. The sun overhead warmed her back, but it wasn't so sweltering she felt wilted.

"Tanner."

Looking over his shoulder, he reined in. "Yeah?"

"I'm turning back."

"Come on, Mariah. We can't knock off for the day."

"I'm not asking you to. I know the way home."

He frowned. "Probably, but times have changed, sis. It's not wise for a woman to ride alone anymore."

"Don't be silly. We're on Broken Spur land."

"Yeah, but there's no fence out this way. And even if there were, anyone can ride onto the ranch. Sometimes 'anyone' can be a lowdown cur."

"Glory be, your vocabulary has broadened!"

"Oh, shut up," he said with a grimace. "Dammit,

if you start for home, I have to go with you."

She narrowed her eyes and stroked the rifle butt jutting from the scabbard. "Oh, pshaw. I know how to use this. I'm not afraid to ride alone, big brother."

"Maybe not, but Pa would have my hide if I let you—"

"He won't know! Ma doesn't expect him home until tonight. Stop carping at me. I've lived and worked on my own for a long time, Tanner. I'm a grown woman!"

Exasperation darkened his features. "That's the problem, Mariah. Some saddle bum comes along, you'll be in big trouble in a heartbeat."

"Ma drives her buggy alone."

Tanner glanced at Silver Eagle. "Not often."

She didn't understand that look, knew some secret passed between them, but she was determined to have her way. "You can sit here arguing until the steers find *you*, for all I care. I'm going."

He glared at her a moment longer, then sighed. "Promise to go right home? Not stop anywhere?"

"Oh, for— Where would I stop?" She swept her arm. "There's nothing between here and the house but trees and brush."

"Promise?"

She expelled an exasperated breath. "If that makes you happy, yes. I promise!"

After another moment, he nodded. "Okay." He glanced skyward. "It's early. You should be there in less than two hours if you don't tarry."

True. This morning they'd meandered all over hell's half acre. But she could ride practically a direct line and be home for a late lunch. "I won't. Stop nagging."

"Uh-huh. See that you do."

She let him have the last word. No skin off her nose. He'd taken male protectiveness to a new level, but she'd let it pass. This time.

****

Silver Eagle watched Tanner gaze after his sister. While there had been no recent problem, a year ago Amelia Pickett had narrowly escaped a bunch of cowhands looking for trouble—and a little fun—on their return from a long drive. Since then, he had taken it upon himself to follow Mrs. Kelly whenever she left the ranch.

As Mariah disappeared behind a stand of trees, unease roiled in his gut. "You go. I follow her."

"She won't like it, Sil."

"She not know."

Tanner stewed a moment, then nodded. "Okay. Catch up with me by nightfall. I should make it to the south line shack if I haven't spotted stock. We can bed down there, then look farther south tomorrow. If we cover this area now, maybe we won't have to come out this way again until spring."

With a nod, Silver Eagle nudged his horse to a lope and took out after the stubborn woman of his dreams. He could catch up with Mariah soon enough; she had left at an easy canter. He pushed his stallion a bit harder, then slowed when he caught a glimpse of her past some distant boulders. Her hair shone in the sun as bright as lantern light.

He smiled. Tanner was right. She would be hot as the fire in her hair if she discovered he shadowed her.

His smile faded. Tanner spoke truth about women not riding alone. His sister occasionally slipped away unprotected, but never ventured too far. Quiet Bird, well aware of the danger, usually honored his and their father's wishes.

His eyes narrowed when he again glimpsed Mariah. She had stopped to look back along her own trail. He reined his horse behind some trees and brush. Apparently, she had heard his stallion's hoof beats.

He dismounted, ventured a bit closer, and peered around the foliage. When she stepped down from her horse, he wanted to shake her. But as she rubbed her beautiful backside and started forward, relief flooded through him. He realized why she'd left the saddle. Unaware of him behind her, sore from the entire morning spent riding and obviously weary, she was taking a break from the saddle. Not that she would ever admit it. He bit back a chuckle.

Mariah walked along an open stretch, so he would wait until she dropped from sight over the rise. He scratched his stallion's jaw. "We follow soon." The pinto nudged his shoulder and lipped his buckskin shirt.

Out of the corner of his eye, Silver Eagle caught movement. Scowling, he stared hard at the eastern ridge. "What is he doing here?"

Silhouetted against the cerulean sky, Howling Coyote sat his mount. Painted Woman, though not a blood relative of Silver Eagle's, had grown up in the band and mated with this outsider. Howling Coyote had been nothing but trouble in the years since he joined the band. Devious, he stole from white people long after it was necessary for survival. More than once he had put the entire band at risk. The last time, he had stolen a rifle from the Picketts five miles to the north. Silver Eagle confronted him, then gave the rifle to Mr. Kelly to return to Carl Pickett.

Silver Eagle had not wished to hand the sheriff an opportunity to ride into the village with a posse. No telling what calamity would have befallen his people had that occurred. Silver Eagle wished his father would call a council of the elders and banish Howling Coyote.

More than a year had passed since he'd offered for Quiet Bird as his second wife. Thank the Spirits, she had refused. She had witnessed the warrior's abuse of Painted Woman and wanted no part of him.

Though Painted Woman would be called simpleminded by the white man, she was sweet natured and did not deserve a man like Howling Coyote. Still, he did treasure his two small children.

Howling Coyote started down the ridge directly toward the trail Mariah walked. Glancing quickly in her direction, Silver Eagle chanced showing himself. He mounted, spurred his horse into the open, and reined in.

Howling Coyote was nothing if not alert, and sure enough, he reined his horse, as well. The warrior sat for endless moments facing him, then finally turned and disappeared over the ridge.

Silver Eagle looked ahead to find Mariah now out of sight. He signaled his horse to a steady walk. Soon, she would be in view of the ranch, but he would follow a little longer.

He wondered what Howling Coyote had been up to. While he did not believe the man would be foolish enough to harm Mariah or any white woman, he coveted the white man's firearms, and he would undoubtedly steal her rifle if he could.

Shortly after the time of the Great Darkness, when only Spirits had roamed Mother Earth, his Indian ancestors began hunting for food. While he was yet a babe, Mr. Kelly convinced his neighbors the band would mind their own business and hunt when game was plentiful. But they needed more than snares, bows and arrows, spears, and knives. Grudgingly, the town council had agreed that Mr. Kelly purchase two rifles for the band. Two, but no more. He had gifted them to Falcon Wing and his brother, Crow Dog.

Silver Eagle doubted not that Howling Coyote would continue to seek a way to have his own rifle. But the troublesome warrior was unknown to Mariah Kelly. Silver Eagle determined to keep it that way.

What might have happened had he not insisted on following her home today? Upon his return to the village, he would question Howling Coyote.

Perhaps it was time to request his own council.

Chapter Three

Sore as the dickens, Mariah remounted, knowing it wouldn't do to walk into the ranch. Ma'd probably try to limit her riding. And by glory, she intended to regain her stamina and ride when and where she darn well pleased.

Not safe to ride alone, my foot. She couldn't argue the point that she'd been away a long while, but Ma and Pa would just have to come to terms with the fact that she now made her own decisions. She knew how to protect herself, and she knew how to ride.

She might be sore this first time out, but she'd ride again tomorrow. Not with Tanner, though. And for sure, not with Silver Eagle. If the folks would allow her a smidgen of loose rein, maybe she'd collect Amelia Pickett and ride down to the creek for a picnic and a swim or visit Quiet Bird.

Of course, she *should* offer to help Ma. She would—eventually, but not these first few days home. All she asked was a short time to savor her freedom after being cooped up in that darn women's dormitory. Time to deal with the haunting memories of that stifling army hospital, though she would never begrudge the time spent writing letters by lantern light, wrapping bandages, or simply talking to lonely, injured men.

Shaking herself out of the heartbreaking reverie, she decided Amelia would know all the gossip from Burnett Station to Waco. She and Amelia, two years older and a homebody right down to her toes, had grown up together. Mariah had talked her friend into some great adventures when they were younger.

She grinned at the memory of the first time she'd coaxed the blue-eyed blond to climb the oak down by the creek. Glory, Mariah hadn't courted total disaster for her friend. True, Amelia lost her footing and tumbled to sit hard on her rump, but no broken bones.

Those were the days when Amelia was plump and she like a rail. About a year before Mariah left for school, Amelia had begun to lose what her mother kindly called baby fat. Mariah couldn't wait to see her again. Amelia, much prettier than she, didn't seem to realize it, bless her.

Though it made no sense, Mariah felt eyes on her. Pausing, she glanced around. Not a soul anywhere. In the distance she could make out the barn roof. Almost home, she thought with some relief. Nutmeg danced beneath her, and Mariah let her have her head.

"Ow! Ow! Ow!" She bounced before settling into the horse's motion. She'd welcome a good soak in Epsom salts after supper. Maybe before. She tugged her hat tighter on her head. Tanner wouldn't be home so he'd never know.

When she led Nutmeg into the barn, Samuel and a younger man she didn't recognize were mucking stalls. She breathed deeply, savoring the smells of horseflesh and hay.

Samuel straightened, his large teeth glistening in his coffee-colored face. "Y'all didn't last long, Miss Mariah."

"No need to remind me." She smiled back. "I'll do better tomorrow, you just wait and see."

She turned to the new man, a runt next to Samuel. "I'm Mariah Kelly. You must have hired on after I left."

Respectful-like, the hand touched the brim of his dilapidated hat. "Ma'am. Ben Stewart. Been workin' on the Broken Spur a spell. Mebbe six months."

She began un-tacking Nutmeg. "Like it here?"

"Right nice, ma'am. Good grub and my own cot. Can't ask for more than that."

She guessed Ben Stewart was on the short side of his thirties. He'd probably worked a lot of ranches, so he'd know the Broken Spur was well run and her father an amiable boss.

In her travels she'd learned there were kind men aplenty, and a few downright mean.

"I can do that for ya, Miss Mariah," Samuel said.

She shook her head. "Nope. I haven't been allowed to take care of my own horse for a long time." She patted Nutmeg's sleek, sweaty neck. "Need to let this girl know who's boss."

"She's right smart lookin'," Ben said.

"Yeah," Samuel added, "and Silver Eagle's been workin' her ever' day."

A bolt of heat flashed through Mariah. Silver Eagle. His mature handsomeness took her breath. Annoyed that the mere mention of him had the power to unsettle her, she redirected her thoughts.

While the men went back to work, she stowed her gear, then brushed Nutmeg to a shine. A smile tugged at Mariah's lips when the buckskin's coat rippled. It felt so good to commune with the mare like this. If two years away had taught her anything, it was to savor the simple things, even the prospect of working cattle.

Finished with Nutmeg's grooming, Mariah strode into the kitchen, where it was so hot she felt like she'd dived right into the Franklin stove. Ma worked at the sink, slicing vegetables for supper.

The ravages of a hard life on a Texas ranch were beginning to show on her face. But Mariah thought the lines etched by love, the willingness to sacrifice for her man and the children she cherished.

Mariah moved up behind her. Despite the dust and dirt coating her clothes, she wrapped her arms around her mother's waist and laid her cheek against silver-streaked hair. "Ma, I need a bath; then, I'll help with supper."

Ma patted her hand. "I didn't realize you and Tanner were back."

"Uh, Tanner isn't. He and Silver Eagle are still searching for strays."

That got her mother's attention. *Uh-oh.*

Dropping the knife on the counter, her mother turned to face her, brow crinkled. "How did you get home?"

"I rode back." Feigning nonchalance didn't work.

Ma's eyes widened. "Alone?"

"Glory be, I can ride without someone watching over my every move."

"Sit down, Mariah."

"I need a bath."

"It can wait."

As Mariah reluctantly took a chair at the kitchen table, Ma sat across from her, folding work-worn hands on the yellow, oilcloth-covered table. "Times have changed, hon. It's too dangerous to ride alone like you did years ago."

"Tanner fed me that same ridiculous—"

"And well he should have!"

"I know my way around the Broken Spur." She bit her lip. Might as well get the telling over with. "Ma, in Maryland, I rode or walked all times of the day and night from the school to the hospital to tend dying men. Riding here in the open is not near as frightening as some of those late night walks on Baltimore streets. Besides—"

Her mother's eyes widened. "I can't believe the school's matron allowed you to do that."

"You drive into town alone."

39

Ma sighed and brushed at a strand of hair that had loosened from the braid that fell halfway down her back. "Honey, I haven't gone into town by myself for the past year or so."

"Excuse me? You mean to tell me you can't go anywhere without a man dogging your steps?"

"If your pa or Tanner aren't around, I inevitably catch a glimpse of Silver Eagle."

"Silver Eagle?" She stifled a snort. He wouldn't care if *she* fell and broke her neck.

"Yes. He's taken it upon himself to watch over me." She smiled. "That boy has become very protective. When he's not working alongside your pa or Tanner, he's close by in case I need a man's strength."

Mariah huffed. "He wouldn't protect me, that's for sure. He's annoyed I'm back."

Ma tilted her head. "What makes you think so?"

"Well, take this morning. He barely spoke. Then, when Tanner arrived, he ignored me. Acted as if I didn't exist as we rode south."

Before the words left her mouth, Mariah recalled the odd feeling that eyes followed her during the ride home. Nonsense, she assured herself. Probably some curious animal.

Ma chuckled. "Silver Eagle isn't gregarious."

Good heavens. She hadn't noticed her family's silver dollar vocabulary before she left for the East. Instantly, that thought made her contrite. To think she considered her parents uneducated shamed her.

"I know the boy is protective of Quiet Bird. I've seen them together."

"Quiet Bird is his sister and has a problem I don't have! Shoot, if threatened, I'd scream my head off."

"And if you were in the middle of nowhere, who would hear you?"

"I'd shoot the cur!"

"Mariah."

Her mother had a point. But now that she was finally home, Mariah had no intention of giving up her independence. While on school grounds in Maryland, she'd endured the dormitory matron's restrictions and hovering presence because she'd had no choice. Here, she intended to do as she pleased.

Within reason.

She grimaced. Pa would, of course, have something to say about her comings and goings. He always had.

"Well," she hedged, "I'll be careful. Promise. I don't intend to run wild, Ma."

Ma rose and resumed supper preparations. "See that you don't. The men who work on the Broken Spur and nearby ranches are, for the most part, trustworthy. Can't say that for cowboys passing through. Not anymore."

There it was again. Glory be, what had happened to people in the two years she'd been away? Of course, war had uprooted many, including undesirables who roamed the countryside.

"Mariah, there's plenty of hot water in the stove's reservoir." Ma paused and looked at the small watch fob pinned to her calico bodice. "You best put the tub in your room. Your father could come in anytime."

Carting water from the kitchen to her bedroom to fill the tub took a while and played havoc with her already sore muscles. But as Mariah stepped in, steam rising from the water, it was worth it. She sank slowly, relishing the heat. "Ahh." She scrunched a towel to cushion her head as she lay back. Though small, the tub was large enough to accommodate her long legs bent at the knees. She wiggled her toes, closed her eyes, and reminded herself not to drift into sleep.

The warm water soothed her muscles, and she

lingered longer than she should have. When she stowed the tub and walked back into the kitchen an hour later, she felt almost human.

Her mouth watered at the scrumptious fragrance of beef stew bubbling on the stovetop. As she arrived, her mother drew a pan of biscuits from the oven.

"I'm starved!"

"Supper is ready as soon as your pa—"

The screened door banged closed, and her father charged in like a force of nature. "Where is she?" he bellowed.

Chapter Four

Unable to prevent her wide smile, Mariah wondered if there'd ever been another girl born as lucky as she. "Pa!"

Confident he'd catch her, she launched herself into his waiting arms as she had when a small girl.

Pa was a strapping six feet tall and broad of chest. His bear hug took her breath. When he released her too quickly, she nearly tumbled backward.

"Jehoshaphat! You've turned into a great lookin' gal, daughter." He chucked her under the chin, gray eyes atwinkle. "How many hearts did you leave pinin' in Maryland?"

Discounting the patients who fancied themselves in love with her? she wondered. "None that I know of, Pa. And that's just fine with me. I'm home, by glory, and I never want to leave again."

"You will when you find the man of your dreams," her ever practical ma said.

"Not if I find him here." And to her despair, she had.

Her mother ignored her cheeky remark. "Ward, honey, supper is ready. You need to wash off about ten pounds of dust before I'll allow you at my table."

"We've got ourselves a lot of catchin' up to do, daughter. How was your trip home? Dadburn, I'm sorry I didn't meet your stage."

Before Mariah could answer, her father stepped aside to give his other girl a glad-to-be-home kiss. And like everything else he did, he didn't kiss Ma by half measure. No sirree. He scooped up her mother as he had her, and then planted one on her lips that could melt iron.

Mariah grinned. Her mother always looked dazed after his kisses. And sure enough, as her senses returned, a flush reddened her mother's cheeks.

"Ward Kelly, you carry on in front of the children something awful!"

"Do not. I love my wife. I love my kids. Ain't one damn thing wrong with expressin' it for all to see."

"Well, you two can talk while you eat."

"Mr. Kelly!" The sound of running feet was followed by pounding on the screened door. "Mr. Kelly!"

Pa strode to greet the foreman. "Max?"

"It's Tanner!"

"What about him?"

The foreman drew in a labored breath. "He's hurt."

Following her mother, Mariah rushed up behind Pa, and he opened the screen for Max.

"I ran across Sil takin' him to his grandmother."

"Holy Mother!" Ma's hand slapped against her chest, and she turned white as dense fog.

"They run across old Beelzebub. That darn rogue gored him."

"Oh, Jesus!" Pa swore. "If Tanner's hurt, Silver Eagle should have brought him here!"

"That's what I said, but Sil insisted it was too far. Lost a lot of blood. Couldn't get it stopped. Said his village was closer. That his grandmother could help Tanner better than anyone else."

Her father grabbed his hat from the peg. "Better go see how bad he is."

"I'm going, too!" Ma reached back to untie her apron.

"Now, honey—"

"Don't, 'now, honey' me, Ward Kelly. He's my boy as much as yours."

"Of course he is, darlin', but—"

"That shaman helped Tanner once before, and I'm grateful." As she spoke, she removed her apron and flung it over the back of a chair. "But I'll see for myself this time."

Her father cast a pleading glance at Mariah.

"I'll drive her, Pa. I need to go, too."

Giving Ma a quick kiss, her father said, "It'll be okay."

Mariah motioned to Max. "Get Ma's buggy ready."

Already out the door, Pa didn't look back. Max ran after him. Mariah grabbed her mother's arm. "Get a shawl while I change."

"Change? But, Mariah—"

"I'm not going out there in this blasted skirt, Ma." She flipped the material with an impatient hand.

In less than five minutes, Mariah hopped into her mother's two seater while Max helped her mother into the other side. Mariah took up the reins and slapped them on the gelding's haunches. He took off like fire scorched his tail, pinning a white-lipped Sarah back against the seat. The fact that she didn't utter a word of caution told Mariah plainer than day exactly how upset she was.

The beautiful evening blurred as Mariah kept the horse at a gallop. She was anxious to see Tanner for herself. For heaven's sake, she'd just come home. *Please, dear God, let him be all right.* She couldn't stand it if— Shoving the unfinished bleak thought from her mind, she concentrated on her driving.

Though she'd never been to the Indian village, Mariah knew where it was. Everyone did, though no one but Tanner visited. Slowing at the river, she drove the horse across shallow water.

Crystal droplets sprayed from the wheels and splashed her trouser legs. Fearing if she slowed too much the wheels would sink in the wet sand, she snapped the reins and kept moving.

Shortly, Mariah pulled back to avoid crashing into trees on a barely-there narrow trail. Not for the first time, she wished her mother had learned to enjoy the speed and freedom of riding. On horseback they could already have been there.

"Is it much farther, Mariah?"

"I don't think so, Ma. The women regularly walk to the river for water and to wash clothes. That's where I've visited with Quiet Bird and Sparrow."

Directly ahead she glimpsed a tipi, then another and another as a clearing opened up before them. Spying her father's horse picketed beneath a tree near one dwelling, she turned in that direction and slowed to a walk just as Silver Eagle stepped from the tipi.

He straightened and threw up a hand, signaling her to stop. Beside her, Ma drew in a sharp breath. His buckskins were smeared with dark stains. Tanner's blood? Oh, glory!

Grim faced, Silver Eagle helped her mother alight. Mariah jumped down and ran around to join them, her legs shaking. "How is he?"

"He sleep. Grandmother Wings of a Dove stop blood, stitch wound."

Her mother's face drained of color again, eyes stricken. "Where is he? I must see him." Her voice came perilously close to breaking.

Silver Eagle swept his arm as invitation to follow. Several villagers stared at them, though they said nothing and came no closer.

Never before had the entire Kelly family intruded upon this village. Long ago her father had brought Tanner here, and her brother still visited, but she and her mother had never presumed to be welcome.

Ducking inside the tipi, she took a moment to adjust to the dimness. Her father hunkered down by Tanner, who lay still between him and a shrouded Indian woman. Undoubtedly, Wings of a Dove, Silver Eagle's fabled grandmother. Sparrow, Silver Eagle's mother, laid a wet cloth on Tanner's brow.

Her father glanced up at Silver Eagle. "You should have taken him home."

"No time."

Quiet Bird rose and extended her hand to Mariah's mother. As if in a trance, Ma rested her hand in Quiet Bird's and allowed the girl to lead her around to kneel at Tanner's head.

Tears blurred Mariah's eyes as she gazed down at her brother. *Please, God, let him live. Let him heal and regain his strength.*

The shaman lifted a light blanket from Tanner's chest, folding it back to reveal his side. A large bandage covered his ribs from a couple inches below his armpit to just above his belt line. No surgeon in the hospital could have done a better, neater job of bandaging Tanner.

Other than an indrawn breath, her mother didn't say anything, her expression as stoic as the old Indian's.

Wings of a Dove spoke at length in her own tongue.

His eyes unnaturally bright, Silver Eagle knelt next to her pa. "She say no muscle tear. Poultice draw bad Spirits. He sleep two suns, maybe, recover strength. Much sore." He nodded. "Tanner, he strong man."

Her father murmured as if talking to himself. "I should have been with you boys."

Which made no sense to Mariah. Those *boys* were men. Men who worked same as Pa. He hadn't had a father hovering over him. Besides, prudently, the men usually traveled in pairs. And Silver Eagle had been there to help Tanner.

"Ward." Ma stroked Tanner's pale cheek. "We'll need the buckboard to carry him home."

Even before she finished speaking, Wings of a Dove shook her head, spoke again in Comanche.

Through her fog of pain and disbelief, Mariah suspected the shaman understood English.

Silver Eagle also shook his head, but at his grandmother. Frowning, he exchanged a few words with her before translating.

"She say Tanner no can move, maybe three, four suns." He paused, cast a quick glance at Wings of a Dove, then sighed and extended an invitation of which he obviously didn't approve. "Mrs. Kelly, you like, you stay. Sleep here." He gestured to blankets neatly piled against the hide wall.

Ma's eyes widened. "But I—"

"You think that's necessary?" Pa asked.

"Grandmother Wings of a Dove see more than white man's doctor. She know when bad Spirits leave. No safe move Tanner now."

Standing out of the way, Mariah watched her mother stare into Wings of a Dove's fathomless eyes. She didn't want to leave Tanner here, but didn't want to put him at further risk, either, and must be suffering the agonies of the damned considering the choices. Mariah also knew her mother wouldn't be comfortable here overnight.

After long minutes her mother spoke directly to the older woman. "I trust you will do your best for my boy, as you did those long years ago. I will leave him in your care, but I will return each day."

Wings of a Dove nodded, then turned to her grandson rather than speak directly to white people. Silver Eagle translated, a slight tremor in his deep voice, a voice usually so strong and confident. "Grandmother say all welcome here. She show what she do. When take Tanner home, know how make poultice."

Mariah backed out of the tipi. Tears threatened as she walked to the buggy, leaned against the back painted a bright rooster green, and rubbed her forehead. How ironic. Tanner had worried she might be in danger, yet *he* was the one lying gravely injured.

She couldn't hold back the visions of other men injured as badly as Tanner. So many had died. Mother Superior of the Sisters of Mercy Convent had insisted the many deaths were from uncleanliness on the part of doctors more than from grievous wounds. Mariah wouldn't worry about that with Wings of a Dove tending Tanner.

"You brother, he well soon."

Mariah's head snapped up. She hadn't heard Silver Eagle approach. He stood a few paces away, his dark eyes still unnaturally bright and unsettling as ever. She suspected he was as worried about Tanner as she.

"How did it happen?"

"Tanner, he rope heifer. No see Beelzebub."

"Hidden in the brush?"

Silver Eagle nodded.

"Is that the rogue longhorn Ma wrote about that Pa chased off?"

Taciturn as ever, Silver Eagle nodded again.

"It's hard to believe that vicious bull is still alive. Pa should have shot him."

"He dead now." Silver Eagle traced his finger across his own neck.

"You slit his throat?"

He simply looked at her, his lack of response confirming she was right. He'd gotten close enough to that huge bull to— She closed her eyes. He'd risked his life to save her brother and been in more danger than he would credit.

Her glance ran over the stains on his buckskins. She shivered. He could have been gored as easily as Tanner.

Both could have died out there on the prairie, no one the wiser until found God-knows-when. For that matter, maybe he was hurt and just hadn't said so.

She looked again, more closely this time, heart in her throat. The buckskin shirt stretched over his wide chest was streaked with dark stains, one especially dark in the middle of his chest. "Did that bull get you anywhere?"

"No."

Quiet Bird joined them, sending Mariah a tentative smile. Then she signed to her brother. It was difficult to follow, but Mariah surmised she asked him about Mariah staying the night.

Silver Eagle cast a quick glance at her and shook his head. That didn't deter Quiet Bird. She smiled again, closed her eyes, and put her hands together against her cheek, then pointed once to Mariah and again at another close by tipi.

"I may stay?"

Quiet Bird nodded. Mariah looked to Silver Eagle, but he scowled at his sister, saying something in his native tongue.

The lovely Indian persisted, signing until he sighed heavily.

Reluctantly, he said, "Quiet Bird say you stay. Sleep her tipi."

He obviously didn't like the idea, but Mariah wasn't about to look a gift horse in the mouth. "I'd love to, Quiet Bird."

She didn't know what her folks would think, and she didn't care. Some member of Tanner's family should be on hand if needed. Why not his sister? But if she were honest with herself, she also wanted to stay out of curiosity about these people—and Silver Eagle.

"How Mrs. Kelly go home?"

"Ma can drive herself. Pa will be with her."

"How you go home?"

This man was a trial, as impossible as he was handsome. Why didn't he want her here? She'd stay out of his way.

She tamped down the hurt, let the building anger take over. "Look, Silver Eagle, I'm staying, so you might as well get used to it. Why don't you go change your clothes? It'll give you something to do other than give me grief!"

"How you go home?" he persisted.

"Pa can bring my horse when he comes back tomorrow."

"He welcome here, Mr. Kelly is."

"And I'm not?" Throwing caution to the wind, Mariah closed the distance between them and poked him in the chest. "Your sister invited me, so even if you have a burr up your—"

Was that a hint of a smile? Not likely.

Silver Eagle turned on his heel and strode off toward another tipi, his, no doubt, and only a few yards from Wings of a Dove's.

Tentatively, Quiet Bird touched Mariah's arm. She pointed at her brother, then put her hands on either side of her head and shook it.

"What? He's upset? Worried about Tanner? Well, so am I! It's my brother in there. Yours is certainly inhospitable. No question there!"

It stung. She shouldn't let the fractious man rile her, but he did. She found herself staring after him, watching his graceful strides before he disappeared into the tipi. No matter his behavior toward her, she still longed to know him better. Much better.

She blew out a breath. *You've lost your mind for sure.*

Quiet Bird beckoned her to follow as she started back to her grandmother's tipi. Time to tell her parents. Another confrontation. But dadburnit, she would stay—for her brother as well as for the adventure of a night in the Indian village.

"Ward, I suspect Tanner will sleep the rest of the night. Perhaps we should go on home and come back early tomorrow," her mother said as Mariah entered the tipi.

Without Silver Eagle there, Wings of a Dove remained mute.

Mariah decided she knew from whom he'd inherited his stubborn nature. The woman had wrapped Tanner in the blanket once more and sat motionless, only her gaze darting between Mariah's parents.

Maybe it wasn't stubbornness, Mariah thought. Although they'd lived in relative peace for many years, perhaps the presence of white people still made Silver Eagle's grandmother nervous.

Ma looked up at her. "It's time to leave, hon."

"I'm staying."

Her mother rose to her feet. "You're what?"

"Someone should be here if Tanner wakes." She gestured at Quiet Bird. "She said I could stay overnight with her." Seeing denial building in her mother, she rushed on. "I want to stay, Ma. I want to be here with Tanner. It's been so long. You and Pa can come back first thing in the morning. Pa can lead my horse, so I'll have a way home when I'm ready."

Her mother had never said much regarding the Indians, but now her expression was so troubled, Mariah wondered if there wasn't a measure of fear on her part.

"Darlin', that's not a good idea," her father said.

"Why not? Silver Eagle comes to the Broken Spur every day. I can certainly stay here and be just as safe as he is with us."

"That's not the point, Mariah."

"I might be able to help. I didn't sit night after night beside injured men and not learn something about doctoring." She frowned. "Or maybe it's because I'm a girl? Well, I'm not, Pa. I'm a grown woman now, able to take care of myself. "

"Maybe," he said tightly.

"You don't trust them?"

"Of course I trust them!" Pa blustered. "We wouldn't leave Tanner here if we didn't."

"Good. It's settled then." She hoped she'd gained the upper hand.

"You just got home," her mother said. "We haven't even had a chance to visit with you."

"Ma." Mariah put a consoling hand on her shoulder. "We won't visit tonight even if I go back with you. You and Pa will probably turn in the minute you get home, so you can be back here at daybreak. I'm home to stay." She put a smile in her voice. "We'll have plenty of time to visit once Tanner is out of the woods and in his own bed."

Her mother silently studied Mariah and then her father.

Mariah glanced at Wings of a Dove, but there was no help from that quarter. The old woman remained silent as a post. Sparrow wasn't any help, either, and Quiet Bird ducked her head. No way would she get into the fray, though Mariah thought she and her folks would understand her signs.

After several moments of indecision, Pa gave in. "All right. We'll see you early tomorrow. Don't cause any trouble, Mariah. Don't make me regret this."

He talked to her as if she were a ten-year-old! Though it galled her, she kept her mouth shut. He was understandably worried for Tanner, and no good would come from riling him at this point.

She'd won.

Both of her parents knelt again. Pa laid a broad hand on Tanner's forehead. Ma leaned close and

53

whispered something, then kissed both of her brother's closed eyes.

Tears blurred Mariah's vision as she stepped outside again.

"You brother, he well soon."

"From your lips to God's ear, Silver Eagle," she murmured to the echo of his prophetic words.

Chapter Five

For the umpteenth time, Mariah flipped to her
other side, wiggling on the robes Quiet Bird had
provided. Even though the skirts of the small tipi
had been rolled up a foot or so, no breeze stirred.

Amazing how quiet and still it was throughout
the camp. If anyone else was as restless as she, they
certainly didn't announce it. She turned onto her
back once again, sat up, and pushed hair back from
her sweaty brow before lifting it off an equally
sweaty neck.

Quiet Bird lay on the other side of the center
lodge pole, her breathing slow and measured. She
wasn't having one bit of trouble sleeping.

Mariah felt around until she found her socks
and both boots, tipped them upside down for a
shake, then slipped them on. A drink might help. If
Quiet Bird had a canteen, Mariah hadn't seen it, and
she knew the small bucket was empty. She'd already
checked earlier. Apparently, the river was the only
place to quench her thirst.

Walking as quietly as possible while watching
for snakes, she strolled toward the tributary she'd
crossed earlier in the day. The moon's faint light
didn't illuminate much beneath the canopy of oak
and cottonwood leaves. The odor of cooking fires
lingered in the air, but all remained quiet.
Amazingly so.

Mariah knelt beside the river, cupped her hands
together, and scooped up the cold crystal water. It
tasted wonderful, but drinking this way was

awkward as the dickens. If she had any sense, she'd have brought the bucket.

Peering along the embankment, she spied a rock that would make a dandy seat if she could nudge it a little closer to the river's narrow offshoot. After she checked that no water moccasins lurked around or beneath it, pushing the rock proved surprisingly easy. She sat down and removed her boots and socks, rolled up her pants legs, then swung around and immersed her feet.

"Ahh!" Leaning between her spread knees, she scooped up water a lot easier. She scrubbed at her face, cooling hot skin.

Frustratingly, Tanner slept on.

Silver Eagle showed complete faith in his grandmother's healing art. Perhaps he had a right to that opinion. Many times she'd seen him banged up while working on the Broken Spur. Unfailingly, after seeking Wings of a Dove's help, he'd returned the next morning no worse for wear.

As Quiet Bird drew her away, Mariah had prayed Tanner would wake soon.

If Ma had chafed at being overlooked for a shaman, she'd remained admirably quiet.

Forearms resting on her knees, Mariah idly watched the water eddying at her feet. Silver Eagle rose in her mind's eye, talking quietly to Nutmeg as he had early this morning. She smiled. Was that only this morning? Glory, one's life could change so much in such a short time.

Silver Eagle had a gift for breaking horses that no one on the Broken Spur had ever mastered. Actually, breaking was the incorrect word. He "gentled" a horse.

That certainly proved true. Not one horse he worked lost its spirit, from carefree kicking-up-its-heels to bridle and saddle work. Definitely a gift.

Night sounds penetrated her thoughts, not

obtrusively, but there, nevertheless. Small nocturnal animals ventured in all directions, looking for food. A rustling of leaves wafted on the hot air. Slight though it was, she welcomed the breeze.

Thankfully, the high humidity in Maryland didn't visit this part of Texas. She'd take this dry heat any day. The blessed quiet was far different from Baltimore, too. Even in the dead of night as she'd traversed the streets toward the dormitory, strident sounds had penetrated the still, humid air.

She shivered, remembering the last poor man she had sat with—and watched slip away. Blinded by a mortar, he'd lain helpless from the internal bleeding the shell had caused.

Compassion shining in his eyes, Dr. Gray had said, "Just sit with Corporal Haines and hold his hand, Miss Kelly. I reckon he'll meet his Maker before the night is gone."

Not long after, coughing, spitting blood, the corporal had squeezed her hand for the last time. "Be a good girl for your ma, Priscilla. I love you, daughter. Tell your ma I wish I coulda made it home."

Tears clogging her throat, Mariah had answered him as if she were the precious daughter he'd sought to comfort. "I will, Pa."

And then he was gone.

Mariah's senses refocused when she realized all sound had ceased. She peered up at the glittering stars. Uneasy, she scanned the darkness, the deeper shadows. A familiar figure stood not ten feet away.

"Silver Eagle?"

"You no should be here alone."

He hadn't moved, hadn't looked her way. Simply stared at the heavens. Lord, he was a beautiful man! Practically naked, only a breechclout covered that part of a man's anatomy that had roused her curiosity for years.

Observing propriety even in the midst of blood and gore, Dr. Seamus Gray had made sure the girls helping at the hospital never saw his patients completely naked.

Shoot, she knew how animals mated. What went where. But a man was different from a horse or a bull. Smaller, for sure. At least, she certainly hoped so. She bit down on her lip to suppress a chuckle.

Dang, if *she* could strip down to her camisole and drawers like men could, she'd be much cooler. Not at all fair. "Couldn't sleep."

"Tanner, he well. You see."

He'd nailed her misgivings, but her brother wasn't the only reason she couldn't sleep. The magnificent man standing a few feet away also contributed to her sleeplessness. But she'd cut out her own tongue before she'd admit it aloud.

Silver Eagle had made it abundantly clear he considered her nothing more than a nuisance. Because she dogged Tanner's and his steps years ago? That didn't seem fair, either. But changing his mind wouldn't be easy.

Did she really want to? Of course she did. She couldn't hornswoggle herself into thinking otherwise.

"I'm sure he will be," she finally retorted into the long silence. "It's just that I want to talk to him." She shook her head. "No. I want *him* to talk. Until he does, I'm left wondering how he really is, how he feels."

"Wings of a Dove give Tanner pain decoction when he wake. No need suffer while heal. He no talk much. Most time in dreamland. Three suns, maybe."

Mariah pulled her feet out of the water, shook them, and spun about to pull on her socks and boots. "Maybe so. But I intend to be there when he wakes."

Starting for Quiet Bird's tipi, she suddenly turned back. Silver Eagle bumped into her. He had moved so quietly and swiftly, she hadn't heard him. His strong hands clasped her forearms, preventing her from tumbling backward. Now he was within a hairsbreadth, touching her. His body heat added to her discomfort.

Discomfort? No. Admit it. *Awareness*. She looked into his shadowed face. Mesmerized by his overwhelming presence, his heat, she gulped in an effort to suppress her racing pulse.

He released her and stepped back. "What?" He sounded irritated.

"I...I was going to ask you to come get me if Tanner wakes when I'm not there."

"I no there, either, Miss Kelly. Wings of a Dove send Sparrow."

Odd how he spoke of his mother and grandmother as though they were mere acquaintances. Mariah wondered if, when speaking directly to them, he called them Mother and Grandmother. In her short time here, she'd learned these people dealt quite formally with each other. Not a single sign of overt affection between them, unlike her family.

Although, Quiet Bird often touched her kin. But that was probably to get their attention.

"Get sleep, Miss Kelly."

"Stop calling me Miss Kelly!"

His lips kicked up in the first genuine smile she'd seen since her return. "I say Tanner's sister?"

"Dang it, Silver Eagle, why won't you use my Christian name? You did when I was younger."

"No my place call grown white woman Christian name."

"Oh, for heaven's sake! I've known you since I was knee high."

His lack of response affected Mariah like fingernails on a chalkboard. And that was ridiculous.

59

"Okay, be that way! See if I care." She whirled and stalked toward Quiet Bird's tipi, grumbling under her breath, "The man's impossible!"

And I'm being childish. As she ducked into Quiet Bird's tipi, she sighed, hoping sleep would come.

****

Silver Eagle watched until she was safely inside. Then he swiveled and headed back to the stream. Howling Coyote stepped into his path.

"She is an interesting white woman."

"You stay a league away from her."

He had known the warrior lurked nearby, but he had not alerted Mariah to that fact. She would not meet Howling Coyote, not if he could help it.

Even though Howling Coyote cuffed his own woman, he was a cunning warrior, and Silver Eagle did not believe he would harm a white woman. But he would certainly give her a fright. The warrior had survived a pox, which had left deep marks on his face. In an attempt to disguise the disfigurement, he painted his face white.

"You are not chief. I will speak with her if I wish, Silver Eagle."

"In her tongue?"

Howling Coyote stepped back, his belligerent manner somewhat subdued. "You know I do not speak the white man's tongue."

Silver Eagle nodded. "You would do no more than frighten her. So stay away."

"While you earn money, I am forced to remain in this village. I can work as well as you, Silver Eagle."

"Yes. But you do not speak their language. You do not understand their language. You refused my offer to teach you what I know of the white man's tongue."

"I could work *with* you! You could tell me what I need to know."

Silver Eagle sliced his hand in the air. "No. I have no time when I ride with Tanner."

"You do not want me to earn money."

True. With money, Howling Coyote would figure out a way to buy a rifle. No telling what mischief he would get into then, what trouble he would cause the band. Chief Falcon Wing could not watch him every moment.

"You provide the band with much meat, Howling Coyote. You are needed here."

He spoke truth. No matter that Silver Eagle would never trust him. Howling Coyote was a good hunter with bow and snare. And upon his return from buffalo hunts, he shared his bounty.

For the second time in almost as many minutes, Silver Eagle watched someone stalk off in a huff. Come morning, he would speak with his father regarding the troublesome warrior.

As he stripped off his loincloth and stepped into the stream, his thoughts returned to Mariah Kelly, and he smiled ruefully. Dealing with her presented an even greater challenge, from hiding his desire to her pigheadedness.

****

Mariah started awake when a hand shook her shoulder.

Groggy, she sat up quickly and just missed bumping heads with Quiet Bird. The girl motioned that Tanner was awake.

Mariah readily understood the maiden's signs. They were clear enough that one need not understand Comanche *or* English. A school in the East specialized in teaching the deaf how to speak with their hands, but Quiet Bird didn't need that training, not a bit.

Scrambling from bed, Mariah again pulled on her socks and boots and followed her friend. Wings of a Dove and Sparrow sat either side of Tanner. His eyes were closed, but he opened them when Sparrow laid her hand on his shoulder. He grimaced and sucked in a breath.

When Sparrow made room for her, Mariah fell to her knees. "Glory, Tanner, you almost got yourself killed."

"I...know," he whispered. "Didn't look before...I rode in." He glanced at Wings of a Dove. "I'm...in good hands."

Though stoic as an imposing butte, the old woman's eyes crinkled. A smile? Yeah. Even if she refused to speak, the old shaman understood English.

"When can I...go home?"

"I don't know. I suspect not for several days. Silver Eagle said you'll sleep most of three days."

Even as Mariah spoke, Sparrow slipped her arm beneath Tanner's neck and raised his head. Wings of a Dove lifted a cup to his lips.

"What is it?"

Mariah grinned. "I don't know that, either. Probably something to make you sleep."

"What if I don't...want to?"

Mariah patted his shoulder and chuckled. "I don't think you have a say in the matter, brother dear. No doubt, Wings of a Dove can heal you, but I've got a sneaking hunch she'll do it her way."

Tanner turned his face from the cup bumping his chin. That slight movement caused him to suck in another breath. "Where're Ma and Pa?"

"Right here, son." Her father stepped into the cramped tipi.

"Oh, Tanner, you're awake!"

Mariah shifted to give her mother room to kneel next to Tanner. Ma brushed his tumbled dark blond hair off his broad forehead.

Mariah figured it was her mother's sneaky way of checking to see if Tanner was feverish. His eyes were glassy, so he could be. Or, it might be the effect of the potion the old lady had fed him and wanted to pour down him again. Patient as a cat poised at a mouse hole, Wings of a Dove held the cup close to Tanner's mouth.

"How do you feel?"

"Like I was dragged behind a runaway wagon."

Mariah jumped when Silver Eagle spoke behind her. "Wings of a Dove give medicine, Mrs. Kelly. Tanner sleep more."

Her brother stared at his friend. "I'd like to stay awake awhile, Sil."

Silver Eagle didn't argue; instead, he spoke to his grandmother. Her response was terse and guttural.

"You body rest, well soon."

Tanner hitched a breath and smiled weakly at the woman who once again cared for him as she had so many years ago. He turned his attention to Ma and Pa. "You don't need to stick around."

"Maybe not, son, but we'll stay until you drift off," Pa said.

As Tanner drank down the potion, his gaze roamed to Mariah backed against the tipi wall. If he intended to say something, it never came. Sparrow lowered his head, and immediately he exhaled a long breath and closed his eyes.

Within moments his breathing was measured in deep sleep.

Mariah had no idea what that concoction was, but it must be potent as the dickens. They could have used it on the patients she'd been forced to watch suffer. Most days morphine had been scarce as hen's teeth, and laudanum was not available in large supply, either.

Inexplicably, tears pricked her eyes. Silly, now that she was fairly sure Tanner would be all right, yet she couldn't seem to stop them. Rather than have anyone see her weakness, she ducked out of the tipi and walked away from the village.

With no particular destination in mind, she paused now and then. She scrubbed at her cheeks, a futile attempt to rid herself of leaky tears. Tanner would be perfectly fine. She knew that, but it scared her to see her strong brother helpless and hurt.

She hadn't gone far when she heard a man's voice, loud and agitated. Rounding a clump of trees with more than usual dense underbrush, she came in view of a man as he slapped a woman hard enough to send her to her knees.

Shocked, Mariah watched her stubby fingers cup the side of her tattooed face. Dark eyes wide with fear, the little woman never uttered a sound.

"Stop that!" Without thinking, Mariah marched forward and helped the little Indian woman to her feet. Then, anger sparking, she rounded on the man. Though his appearance sent her back a step, she was mad as a drenched cat.

"Why don't you pick on someone your own size?" She and he were very nearly the same height, although he had her by quite a few pounds, and his face was white as a ghost's. Gulping in a nervous breath, she nevertheless held her ground. "Shame on you! Hitting a defenseless woman!"

He said something in Comanche, and the shockingly tattooed woman at her side cringed as if at another imminent blow.

"If you hit her again, I swear I'll slug you to the other side of eternity!"

Her rage had *him* backing up a step; then his lip curled in a sneer. As he reached for her arm, another voice erupted from behind her in a torrent of Comanche. The man withdrew his hand, retreated, and dropped his gaze. But not before casting a vicious glance at Mariah.

She whirled around to confront an older, stern

faced Comanche. Silver earrings dangled to his shoulders. A bone breastplate adorned his bare chest, his burly shoulders draped with a long piece of hide. The man stood about five-feet-ten. His stance was wide, legs encased in buckskin.

She blinked into his midnight eyes and recognized him for who he was—chief of this small band. Silver Eagle's father. She gathered the little Indian woman close to protect her from both men and spoke with more bravado than she really possessed.

"He was hurting this little lady. Do you allow such to go on in your village, Chief?"

If he understood her, he didn't respond. Instead, he spoke in a harsh voice to the other male.

Beside her, the little woman, no more than a girl as far as Mariah could tell, walked slowly toward the man who had abused her and hung her head as if *she* had done something wrong.

"Just wait a cotton pickin' minute here!" Mariah strode to the young woman and tapped her on the shoulder. "You don't have to put up with that kind of treatment."

The girl shied from her and shook her head.

"Idiot," she muttered to herself. These people couldn't understand her, not a single word. But they understood signs, and Mariah slapped herself on the cheek, pointed in turn to the girl and the younger man and said, "No!" She shook her head and repeated her words as she slapped her own cheek again.

"Surely you understand me, Chief!" Mariah dragged the girl in front of her and put her arms protectively around her. "He has no right to abuse her!"

Other than her own agitated, harsh breathing, not a sound intruded. Nothing, until Silver Eagle spoke. Mariah closed her eyes and heaved a sigh of relief. Though she hadn't heard his arrival, she thanked her lucky stars he was here. He could make the chief understand. But the man she thought would support her didn't. His words only angered her further.

"Painted Woman belong Howling Coyote. His woman."

Mariah glared at him. "No one *belongs* to another, Silver Eagle. She may be his wife, but that doesn't give him the right to hurt her."

Painted Woman? It fit. Tattoos of flowers, a serpent, even two birds adorned both her arms and her cheeks.

"She accustomed."

"And that makes it right?" Incensed beyond belief, Mariah shouted, "That's just dead wrong! How can you stand by and allow it to go on?"

She caught the quick frown Silver Eagle sent his father, yet he answered her calmly enough. "No my place interfere."

Mariah's eyes narrowed on the chief. "What about him? Can he stop it? Show this girl a little compassion?"

****

He could, Silver Eagle thought, but his father stayed out of domestic business. It was beneath a chief to step into squabbles between mated individuals. Yet Silver Eagle wondered what he would think about this white woman ranting in his face. His father understood Mariah's every word, though, like Wings of a Dove, he pretended not to.

"Chief Falcon Wing say nothing. Painted Woman ask assistance, she have." He shrugged. "No ask, no get."

"Does she know this, Silver Eagle?"

Maybe not, he thought. If slow thinking Painted Woman had ever known, she had probably forgotten.

"Does she?" Mariah persisted.

66

He sighed. His father wouldn't say anything, so he had to bring this confrontation to a conclusion and pray to the Spirits he could talk Mariah Kelly into going home. She would be nothing but trouble as long as she stayed in his village. He was more sure of that than ever. And not only to assure the order his father maintained over the band's warriors. Just looking at her, Silver Eagle's member stirred, and his heart raced.

"I know not, Miss Kelly. But I speak to her, she listen."

A moment passed before he realized Mariah's expression meant that she expected him to enlighten Painted Woman right now. *That* he would not do. No need to antagonize Howling Coyote further.

Silver Eagle would speak with his father first. If Falcon Wing would not help Painted Woman, then *he* would be forced to speak to her. But both conversations would be private.

"Miss Kelly, go back to village. Now. Painted Woman no in danger."

Mariah eyed Howling Coyote. "I don't know about that."

"She go with you."

He spoke to Painted Woman kindly, telling her to follow Mariah, but the girl looked at Howling Coyote with apparent distress.

"Go now," Silver Eagle insisted. "Everything will be all right." Painted Woman obeyed, but kept casting fearful glances back at her mate.

Perhaps it would be advisable to speak to his father with Howling Coyote present. It might be the only way to spur Falcon Wing to action. With no one else in the tribe near, the entire incident would remain among the three men.

He sighed, then swung about to confront his father.

Chapter Six

"*Ni ahpï?*, what would Mr. Kelly do if he discovered Howling Coyote had struck Miss Kelly?" Silver Eagle captured his father's attention. Gratified, he continued, "Would our peaceful existence here be in peril?"

"No harm befell the white woman."

"This time."

"You challenge my judgment?"

Before Silver Eagle could answer, Howling Coyote spoke. "The woman interfered between me and my mate. She deserved to be punished."

"Certainly not by you!"

"Silver Eagle!"

He wanted nothing more than to beat Howling Coyote to his knees, but that would not gain his objective.

Respectfully, he nodded to his father. "I am sorry. Perhaps you were about to explain to Howling Coyote that the trouble caused by his actions would not go unnoticed by white men—by Mr. Kelly."

Falcon Wing shook his head. "Do not put words into my mouth, *nï tua?*."

At least his impertinence had not distanced him so far that his father no longer recognized him as his only son. Yet. He cautioned himself to tread lightly. As chief, Falcon Wing might banish *him* rather than Howling Coyote. However, he must be sure his father entertained sending the troublesome warrior whence he came.

"I cannot speak for you, *nï aphï?*. The great chief

of our band deliberates with wisdom from the ages. I fear not that you will consider all possibilities. Perhaps you, my wise *ahpï?*, will choose to reprimand Howling Coyote. Perhaps you will banish him if he continues to chastise his woman as he intended to do to Miss Kelly."

"You have no right—"

"Silence, Howling Coyote!"

Every living thing seemed to heed Falcon Wing's command. For long moments the quiet was absolute. Leaves did not rustle; birds did not sing. As if frozen, even the skitter of small animals stilled.

Though Silver Eagle deferred to his father's authority, he had planted the seed. He did not back down, but remained arrow straight, awaiting his chief's next words.

Intense eyes narrowed upon Silver Eagle, undoubtedly daring him to utter another word. Falcon Wing finally shifted his stern regard to Howling Coyote.

"You will keep your distance from all white people, Howling Coyote. I trust you will deal justly with Painted Woman. You are a strong warrior. The band would not fare as well without your hunting skills."

Though his father's too mild rebuke vexed, Silver Eagle had to accept Falcon Wing's approach.

Howling Coyote stood his ground for a moment longer, then nodded to his chief. "I will be about my business." Casting a smirk at Silver Eagle, he left.

Far from satisfied, Silver Eagle watched him go. Well, his father *had* insinuated that Howling Coyote teetered on the brink of a more stern reprimand. Silently, he vowed to make it his business to keep an eye on the man.

"You would do well to avoid confrontation with Howling Coyote, *nï tua?*."

Now that it was just he and his father, Silver

Joyce Henderson

Eagle ventured further with his concerns. "He is dangerous. He should be banished for his abuse of Painted Woman. Howling Coyote will take liberties beyond his station in the band if you choose not to act."

"You will cease further accusations and innuendos. These choices you speak of are mine alone. I shall think on these matters. If I decide to invoke further sanctions against him, I shall do so in my good time—and privately. Unless one is prepared to do battle with a seasoned warrior, authority should be prudently applied, *nï tua?*."

"He has already watched Mariah Kelly when he should have been nowhere near. Had I not interfered, I do not know what calamity would have befallen her and the band."

His father frowned. "When did this happen?"

"The day Tanner was gored."

"I shall remain vigilant, Silver Eagle."

Not what he wanted, but what he would have to settle for. His father knew his concerns. Perhaps his chief would, as promised, watch Howling Coyote more closely.

Silver Eagle knew *he* certainly would.

****

As the day wore on, Mariah filled the hours studying the village people as they went about their chores. She assisted Quiet Bird with gathering wild onions for supper's stew, which Sparrow oversaw at a fire pit between Quiet Bird's and Wings of a Dove's tipis.

While gathering wild berries, Mariah ate until her belly ached. Dang, they were tasty, though.

She spied her mother as she stepped from the tipi to stretch, leaving Tanner's side for the first time since arriving that morning. "You must be weary to the bone, Ma. How is Tanner?"

She probably sounded overanxious since she had

70

looked in on her brother little more than an hour past. Shoot, he might look like he slept peacefully, yet the size of the bandage indicated a large wound. If infection set in...

"His brow remains cool, Mariah. That's all I can say." Her mother propped her hands on her waist and bent one way, then the other.

"My back doesn't take kindly to sitting on the ground hour upon hour. I don't know how Sparrow and Wings of a Dove do it."

"Doubt if either one has ever sat in a chair, Ma."

"Hmm." Her mother gazed about at the activity.

In the center of circled tipis, half a dozen children, the smaller ones stark naked, gleefully played a game, kicking a bladder ball back and forth. They crashed into each other, fell, squealing with laughter, then scrambled to their feet, vying to be first to kick the ball again.

Painted Woman stood on the sidelines as if guarding the play. Mariah didn't want to be caught staring, but she couldn't help it. Others in the village sported tattoos, but none as extensive as Painted Woman's.

Perhaps Painted Woman had no say in the matter. Maybe she'd been forced to endure the defacing. Some Indian women were treated like chattel by the likes of that vicious brute this morning. Mariah bit down hard on the expletive she wanted to scream at the top of her lungs.

Quiet Bird approached with a bowl of fragrant stew. Lifting it to Mariah's mother, she hiked her chin toward her grandmother's tipi.

Ma simply stared at her.

"Uh, Ma, I think she wants you to take that to Tanner. If he's awake, I bet he's ravenous."

"More than likely." Ma smiled at Quiet Bird as she took the bowl. "He was asleep when I came out, but he's been awake off and on the past couple of hours."

"Then he must be better."

Her mother shook her head. "Don't know about that. But he refused to drink Wings of a Dove's potion the last two times she tried to give him a dose."

Mariah chuckled as Quiet Bird filled another bowl. "What happened?"

"Tanner didn't win the battle of wills the first time, but the second—" Ma smiled. "I'd say he's better, or the shaman wouldn't have allowed his stubbornness to prevail." Her mother sniffed the steamy ingredients. "Smells delicious. If he's able, Tanner will surely eat every bite."

While offering Mariah a bowl, Quiet Bird motioned with her free hand as if doffing a hat, then raised her hand high.

"My father?" Mariah asked.

Quiet Bird nodded, a smile lifting her lips.

Hah, Mariah thought; though rusty from long absence, she was getting back into the hang of talking to her friend. And Quiet Bird had apparently learned a lot of English in the intervening years. She understood much more of what was said to her.

When Mariah entered the tipi, she found her father seated to one side of her brother, her mother kneeling on the other. Sure enough, her brother was taking bites of the food.

"Hey, sis," he said, his voice weak.

She stepped closer. Tanner's eyes were much clearer, but shadowed with pain. At the same moment his gaze shifted beyond her shoulder, the hair rose on her nape.

"Beelzebub get you, Sil?"

"No. He no get another."

Tanner chuckled, then grimaced.

"My friend, you rest. No talk."

Tanner didn't have to be cautioned twice, pain

evident in his stifled groan.

"Mr. Kelly, horses and buggy ready when you be."

Pa glanced at Silver Eagle. "Thanks. As soon as we finish eatin' we ought to head back home, Sarah." His gray-eyed gaze settled on Mariah as she pressed the bowl into his hands. "You best go home with us, girl. Don't want to be over stayin' our welcome."

"That's for sure, dear," her mother agreed.

No help for it. She would have to leave, and maybe that was for the best. Silver Eagle didn't want her here. And she sure as shootin' hadn't made friends with Howling Coyote this morning. The chief, either.

"Okay." Turning, she spied the relief on Silver Eagle's face. Her chest constricted.

On the other hand, she wouldn't let Silver Eagle dictate her comings and goings where her brother was concerned. She knelt and planted a gentle kiss on Tanner's forehead. "Sleep well tonight. Maybe you'll be fit enough by tomorrow evening to travel home in the wagon."

"Maybe," he said just above a whisper.

It grieved her to watch him valiantly try to hide his suffering, particularly from Ma. A vain attempt. Yet men would be men. And women needed to humor them so they believed they had the upper hand.

"Don't fret," she murmured. "We'll be back tomorrow and decide then."

Determined to keep her feelings from Silver Eagle, she brushed past him and left the tipi. Her parents hadn't brought Nutmeg for her to ride. Instead, a gelding stood in the traces of her mother's buggy, patient as a predator on the hunt.

Resigned, Mariah hopped onto the seat and waited. A few minutes later, perched beside her, Ma left the driving to Mariah. As they headed toward home, she refused to look back for fear Silver Eagle watched.

After they were out of earshot of the village, her mother asked, "Mariah, what is wrong with you? Where are your manners?"

Distracted by thoughts of the magnificent warrior, Mariah glanced at her mother. "Manners? What—"

"You failed to thank Wings of a Dove or Sparrow for their hospitality. Quiet Bird was sorely perplexed, too. I saw it in her face."

"I'm sorry. I wasn't thinking. I'll apologize the next time I see them."

She couldn't say what she really felt. *I'm hurt. Silver Eagle can do without my presence.* Glory! Even to her, that sounded downright childish and pathetic. Not to mention it would alert her mother to the fact she was attracted to a man who lived in a different world.

She'd had a glimpse of him the last couple of days. While parts of it intrigued her, she knew if she spent more time there, she'd again be in heaps of trouble with Silver Eagle's father.

And that vicious Howling Coyote! Even now her blood boiled. It was downright awful that he'd cuffed his poor wife. The red imprint had stayed on her cheek for a long time. No doubt his slap had been hard enough to bruise.

It was undoubtedly fortuitous that Chief Falcon Wing had arrived when he did. Howling Coyote would probably have slapped her, too. And sure as shootin', she wouldn't have stood for it. Nor would her father.

Mariah shivered. She had to have misunderstood Silver Eagle's acceptance of such treatment.

Chapter Seven

Two days passed before Wings of a Dove pronounced Tanner well enough to travel. Mariah had been on edge all morning, not permitted to go with her father and Samuel to bring him home.

But now, at last, her brother was here, resting in his own bed. She peeked in. Finding Tanner sound asleep, she stood quietly and watched his chest steadily lift and fall beneath the sheet. Pa said Tanner never uttered a sound of complaint, but the strain of traveling still showed on his face.

Her mother's hand fell on her shoulder. "Come, honey, let's have a little chat. We haven't had any time together since your return."

Mariah stole another look at her brother.

"Wings of a Dove sent some of her medicine home with your father. I dosed Tanner about half an hour ago. He needs to rest." She pointed. "I left your grandma's old bell close, so Tanner can ring when he wakes."

Her mother found an infinite variety of chores to keep herself busy all day, every day, and today, the noon meal over, she walked into the sparsely furnished parlor and sat in her rocker beside the dead hearth. She picked up scraps from the basket beside the chair and began piecing them together for a quilt top.

Mariah followed her and flopped into the big old brown mohair chair her father usually occupied. Inept at household chores, she was absolutely pitiful when it came to sewing. She admired her mother's deft fingers weaving the needle through the black cloth, attaching it to a red square.

"You have anyone special in mind for that quilt?"

Ma shook her head. "Just making it." She glanced up, a sudden blush reddening her cheeks. "You'll think I'm daft, but I wait for whatever I make to speak to me. If it doesn't, then I store it in a trunk and eventually use it myself."

Mariah caught her lip between her teeth, suppressing a burst of laughter. She couldn't hide the grin, though, no matter how hard she tried "Speak to you?"

Ma chuckled. "I didn't expect you to understand." She hesitated a moment, then asked, "Do you miss your friends in the East?"

"I made few friends while I was away. I think I bored everyone to death talking about home." Wearing her favorite jeans, Mariah swung the leg she'd draped over the chair arm. "I'll be the first to admit I didn't take full advantage of seeing the sights in the East. It was—" She shrugged. "I don't know. I just wanted to be home."

Her mother paused, dropping her hands to her lap as she looked Mariah over. Though she smiled, her words spoke her thoughts clearly. "You apparently missed the lessons in ladylike demeanor as well."

Her folks had spent a ton of money to send her to that school. Mariah knew that, but—dang it. Dang it, nothing. Time to straighten up and conduct herself in a more mannerly fashion. After all, she claimed to be a grown woman. Best act like one.

Swinging her leg down, she pushed back in the seat and put her knees together like a prim miss. Not the least bit comfortable; nevertheless, she'd make an effort for Ma's sake.

"In your letters you glossed over working in a

hospital. Did you spend much time there?"

Mariah's eyes clouded as she thought back to the last day she trudged down the few steps to the dusty street and left the suffering inside those dreary halls and rooms.

Her mother didn't need to know that, in an effort to reduce fever, she had bathed men too delirious to help themselves. Often, though, they didn't know she was there ministering to them. More than one doctor welcomed the help from the nearby school.

"I rotated with other girls two days a week." She looked down at her hands, hands that had clasped weakened ones, hands that had folded in prayer as each man prayed for release from the pain, or breathed his last. "So many died, Ma. It was—hard." *Hard?* Impossible to put into words how heartbreaking.

"I regret the timing we chose to send you to school, hon. I suppose your father and I closed our minds and eyes to the War."

"I'm thankful Tanner didn't go, Ma." She bit her tongue, loathe to relive those nights of anguish and death.

But Ma gazed at her expectantly. So she chose to tell her about the men who had survived. One in particular made her smile. She watched her mother's busy fingers as she spoke.

"I discovered that men in pain tend to look upon those administering to their wounds as more than they are." She chuckled. "One young man, a boy really, called me his angel." She glanced up to find her mother's sweet smile on her.

"You think you weren't, Mariah? How many of the girls at the school declined to help at the hospital?" When she failed to answer, her mother added. "Most, I'd wager."

True. Still, her motives for helping were not

77

altruistic, not by a long shot. At first, she was simply glad to shed the oppressive environs of the dormitory. She hadn't counted on men suffering and dying to take its place.

Shaking herself from those memories, she said, "I'll have you know I had more than a few proposals." She laughed, remembering the last, recalling his face so vividly. "Timothy Witherspoon was all of seventeen, I think. The poor boy had carrot red hair. Worse than my color if you can believe it."

"Your hair is gorgeous, Mariah!"

"Pshaw." She flicked her hand and continued. "I called him *Mr.* Witherspoon. He was one of the lucky ones. A ball went right through his arm, but no bones were shattered, and when he left, he was sporting only a sling."

"Where was he from?"

"Um, Green...something."

"Greensboro?"

"Yes, I believe so. He was very concerned that his folks were all right. He hadn't seen or heard from them for three years."

"And he was only seventeen? That means he started fighting at fourteen? That is so sad." Ma looked out the window, her mouth bowed in a frown. "And what was gained, I wonder, from all the killing."

It wasn't necessarily a question, and at that moment the bell rang from the back of the house. Mariah jumped to her feet.

"I'll see what Tanner wants." She'd have to thank him sometime for saving her from dark thoughts.

Pausing at his door, she blinked, then narrowed her eyes. "What the dickens do you think you're doing, Tanner? You can't get up yet."

His bare legs and feet dangled off the side of the

bed, the sheet barely covering his manly parts. The bandage on his side left a good portion of his broad chest uncovered.

He sucked in a quick breath, a telltale indication he was pushing his luck to even sit. But Tanner was nothing if not stubborn.

"I need to walk, sis. I feel weak as a starved coyote."

She strode into the room and stood before him, which forced him to tilt his head back to look up at her. And that was enough to send him backward to the bed.

"Damn!" He groaned and planted his hands to push himself up again.

She leaned over and pressed on his bare shoulder. "Don't be a danged fool, Tanner. You traveled half the morning. That's enough moving around for today."

Before he could protest, she continued. "If you're going to compare yourself to a mangy coyote, remember that those varmints have enough sense to lie low to regain strength."

He scowled. "Get out of here. I'm naked."

"For heaven's sake. I've bathed naked men." Tanner didn't need to know she'd only seen bare chests and legs. Bending, she clasped his ankles and lifted them up and onto the mattress.

He grabbed for the slipping sheet, face reddened. "Mariah! You're goin' to get an eyeful if you don't skedaddle!"

"What is going on here?"

Mariah glanced over her shoulder at her mother. "Tanner's trying to get up. He's too weak."

"Get her out of here, Ma."

"Out," Ma said, then she turned her glare on him. "Your sister is right. You, young man, will stay in that bed until I say you may get up."

"But, Ma—"

"Supper. If you feel up to it and if your father is here to catch you if you fall, you may join us at the supper table."

Mariah retreated to the door and turned to watch the battle of wills. She grinned when her mother pulled a spoon from one apron pocket and a small crock from the other. Saying nothing, she measured liquid into the spoon, then held it to Tanner's lips. Like a fractious child, he clamped them shut.

"Open." When he just looked at her stubbornly, she said, "Open your mouth or I'll have Mariah tickle you. You know how ticklish you are."

Mariah laughed. "Happy to oblige, Ma."

"I'll bet you wou—"

Ma slipped the spoon between his lips and upended the contents into his mouth. He sputtered but swallowed.

"What *is* that nasty tastin' stuff?"

"I don't know," her mother said, "but it will keep you abed for another hour or so."

Grumpily, Tanner straightened the sheet over his legs. "I don't want any more, Ma. Don't try to force it on me again. It won't work."

She lifted a brow. "Maybe, maybe not." Stoppering the clay pot, she dropped it and the spoon back into her apron pockets. "Right now, I want you to lie back and allow your body to heal."

****

Long since resigned to Mariah's lick-and-a-promise housework, Ma sent her outside to find something useful to do. Something she was good at and could enjoy.

The moment Mariah stepped out the backdoor, she spied Silver Eagle across the clearing, leading Tanner's favorite dun into the work ring. Since the man didn't want her around, she deliberately sauntered that way.

He released the lead rope and hung it on the fence, then vaulted into the saddle. While Silver Eagle oftentimes rode in the ring without tack, today the horse mouthed a snaffle, and Tanner's saddle graced his broad back.

He gathered the reins in one hand, and at the lope, began putting Dandy through cutting exercises—dodging one way, then the other, sliding stops, wheeling in place. He was mesmerizing, music in motion.

Mariah rode well. She knew she did, as did Pa, Tanner, and most of the hands. But none compared to Silver Eagle's grace, a superb horseman by any standards.

He slowed, patted Dandy, and let him stand quiet for a moment. Hands resting on his thighs, Silver Eagle spoke in Comanche. Dandy leaped into a lope. With leg pressure alone this time, he urged Dandy through the same maneuvers. Then, whirling 'round and 'round in place, the horse finally came to a stop, facing Mariah. She glanced up into Silver Eagle's smug face.

"You're showing off."

He arched a brow, shrugged, and slid from the saddle to land on moccasined feet. Turning around, he hooked the stirrup on the saddle horn and began to loosen the cinch.

"How Tanner is?"

Distracted by the view of his broad shoulders and tight, buckskin-clad butt, it took a moment to focus on his question.

Cheeks heating, she stammered, "Uh...um...he wanted to get up, but Ma gave him a dose of your grandmother's medicine with the idea of keeping him abed at least until supper."

"Is well." He pulled the saddle and blanket off the horse and tossed them atop the fence. Dandy stood quietly while Silver Eagle brushed his broad hand over damp hair where the saddle had been. He slipped the bridle from Dandy's head and gave him a light slap on the rump. "Walk off nerves."

Amazingly, Dandy did just that, clopping to the far side of the corral, then turning to mosey along the fence.

"How do you do that, Silver Eagle? Horses respond to you as if they understand language."

He nodded. "Do understand. No is hard. Talk, critters listen."

Mariah shook her head and *tsk*ed. "That's a load of bull. If I simply talk to Nutmeg, she goes her merry way. I have to assert authority with the bit and my knees or spurs." She scowled. "I've *never* seen you apply spurs *or* pull hard on your stallion's hackamore."

"No need." He eased through the slats, and curling his fingers to catch the blanket beneath, pulled the heavy saddle off the fence.

She fell into step with him as he headed toward the barn. "Come on, Silver Eagle. It wouldn't kill you to share your secrets." Besides, she liked the pleasurable vibrations that seeped through her at his deep voice.

"No have secret. Spend time, show horse you leader. He follow."

Was it really that simple? Well, yes. His ability to handle any horse given into his care was proof of the pudding. Now all she had to do was convince him to teach her how.

As she followed him into the shade of the big barn, strong smells of horseflesh, leather, and hay swirled through her.

Oh, yes. This was what she had missed while away. Down home smells soothed her like nothing else could.

She admired Silver Eagle's loose limbed gait, the swing of his well-toned body, as he strode away. But it was galling the way he seemed to wall himself up in another realm where she was not welcome. Heat flushed her veins. Well, there was *something* else that would soothe her. *Wouldn't it? Of course it would.* Unfortunately, that particular something was forever denied her.

He, Indian, she, white—and all that folderol.

****

Gnashing his teeth, Silver Eagle left Mariah as quickly as he dared without appearing to run like a frightened rabbit. She could be in the house and still he fancied he could smell the womanly scent that was hers alone. Walking beside her? Torture.

Perhaps he should stay away from the Broken Spur for a time, though it would not dull his desire for Mariah Kelly. A two-year separation had not done that, but he could at least work in peace. With an imperceptible nod, he warmed to the idea.

Mr. Kelly had asked him to train two recently acquired horses. The cleared meadow where he communed with his Sachem Spirits would make a good place to work the horses as well.

Rounding the end of the bunkhouse where he had left his mount, he found the pinto cropping dry grass beneath pecan trees. The stallion raised his head and whiffled a welcome. Silver Eagle brushed a hand over the horse's soft nose. "Wait for a short while, my friend. I shall find Mr. Kelly and tell him we will take the two young ones home with us."

Silver Eagle smiled when his favored mount nodded and blew in answer. As the animal moved away to sink his muzzle into the tree-shaded trough, Samuel approached.

Having lived about the same number of seasons as Mr. Kelly, the black-skinned man was kindhearted. For as long as Silver Eagle could remember, Samuel Tucker had been welcome in his village. Other than Tanner, Samuel was the only man not of Indian blood that his people would welcome into the band.

"Silver Eagle, y'all ready to work one o' them horses penned up behind the big barn? They's gettin' mighty frisky. The bigger one's feelin' his oats and kickin' the sorrel. Gonna leave marks if'n we don't separate 'em."

"Take both my place. Work better."

Samuel doffed his hat and wiped sweat from his brow. "You is free to try leadin' 'em home, but mebbe you do better takin' one and come back for t'other."

Responding to a soft whistle, the pinto trailed behind when Silver Eagle moved toward the barn, Samuel by his side.

"Miss Mariah say she can help—"

"No!"

Samuel's eyes widened at the outburst.

More calmly, Silver Eagle said, "No need help."

Having Mariah Kelly home on the Silver Spur was distraction enough. Having her in his village for two long days, and even longer nights, had been slow torment. He must avoid her as best he could, and he would start by training the Kellys' horses as far from her as he could get.

Chapter Eight

"Tanner!"

Mariah's exasperated voice had him swinging around, socks clutched in one fist. He slapped his free hand over the edge of the bureau drawer to steady himself.

"Dammit! You startled me."

"Startled is mild compared to what I'd *like* to do to you." Her gaze raced over his clothes. "Does Ma know you're up and dressed? Did she give you leave?"

"No. Ma doesn't know," he mimicked in falsetto. "I feel much stronger today. Time I got back to work. I don't need Ma's permission."

"Yes, you do, son."

He rolled his eyes and muttered something under his breath.

Their mother walked up to him and cupped her hand against his forehead.

He reared back. "Ma!"

Mariah chuckled. Tanner should know by now that no matter how old they got, Ma would treat them both like the children they would always be in her eyes.

Matter-of-factly, her mother said, "You feel normal, no temperature. But you will *not*—" She paused and scowled at him as he sat in the chair to don his socks. "Are you listening to me, Tanner Kelly?"

"Do I have a choice?" He tempered the smart-mouthed remark with an endearing grin, which got

Ma every time.

She laughed. "Tanner, you will be the death of me."

"Better him than me," Mariah said, but not quietly enough.

Ma looked back and forth between the two. "Oh, you will both undoubtedly have a hand in my early demise."

Tanner finished pulling on his socks, stomped into his boots, and stood, towering over both women. He patted Ma's cheek. "You couldn't get through a day if we weren't cause for worry, Ma, and you know it."

"That's the Lord's truth." She sighed. "But it's love for you children and your father that gets me up every morning to face another day."

For a moment Tanner held Mariah's gaze. Like her, he cherished this blessed woman, and like her, he was just as thankful. She knew he didn't know how to express it without embarrassing himself, other than to give Ma a squeeze fit to take her breath. Then he strode to the door, clipped his brown hat from the horseshoe hook, and left the room.

"Don't overdo, mind you," Ma called after him, shaking her head. "Guess I was lucky to keep him down four days. I just hope Wings of a Dove's stitches don't break open."

"He'll be all right, Ma. I'll ride with him today and keep an eye on him." She grimaced. "That is, I will if Silver Eagle doesn't slice me up with dagger looks."

Her mother began straightening the sheets and the harlequin-patterned quilt on Tanner's bed. "Mariah, I don't know that Silver Eagle thinks of you enough to care what you do. And why are you so intimidated by what he thinks, anyway? You don't have to run from him as if he's a bear. He's only a man; he certainly won't bite you."

The thought of Silver Eagle biting her in the throes of passion sent Mariah's temperature rising. She turned away, her cheeks flaming. "You're right. See you later, Ma."

Glory, she had to get a handle on her thoughts and feelings. Besides, even though she'd seen Pa nip Ma's ear on occasion, what did she really know about lovemaking?

In the barn she saddled Nutmeg quickly, determined to keep up with Tanner. When he was of a mind to, her brother could hightail it faster than a six-team coach flying across West Texas. She found him behind the barn, jawing with Pa and Max.

"You sure you're up to ridin'?"

"Don't you start, Pa. I wouldn't be here if I wasn't. Ma hovers worse than a hen settin' on her eggs."

"How 'bout the stitches?"

"I cut 'em out this mornin'."

"You what?" Mariah and her father exclaimed in unison.

Max just shook his head.

"Holy smokes, it ain't as if I did any damage. The gut wasn't any thicker than Ma's darnin' thread. I snipped the stitches with her scissors and pulled 'em out."

Pa glared at him. "Lift your shirt so I can see for myself, son."

"Oh, for—" Though he groused, Tanner pulled the shirttail from his pants and lifted it far enough to bare his side.

Mariah leaned past her father to get a view for herself. Though red as the dickens, the healing wound was clean and no blood seeped.

"You prob'ly shoulda robandaged it," Max said.

"Nothin' handy, and I sure didn't want to ask Ma for anythin'." Tanner stuffed in his shirttail.

"And why is that, Tanner?"

Ignoring her, he said, "Let's get to work, okay? Ain't plannin' to do much today, anyway. Figured I'd tail after Sil."

Mariah schooled her features not to betray her delight at that prospect. She had the perfect excuse to follow along. "Pa, why don't I stick with Tanner? If I notice any blood, or he starts looking peaked, I'll nag him home."

"Don't do me any *favors*, sis."

She grinned. "I aim to please."

Tanner turned his back on her as he mounted. "Max, where's Sil workin' today?"

"He took them two range horses to his place yesterday. Told Samuel he'd just as soon work 'em on his turf."

Ooh! Even better, Mariah thought. She'd keep her eyes peeled and maybe figure out some of Silver Eagle's tricks without badgering him. He wouldn't stand for her nagging as Tanner would. Although her brother could get mighty testy if riled, he really didn't have a choice. Silver Eagle did.

She mounted and followed a few paces behind Tanner.

Already the heat was settling in for the day. July afternoons were hotter than a just-fired pistol. It would be a few months before rain slaked the thirsty land, and scrub grass was brown and dangerously desert dry. Prime for heat lightning strikes to set off prairie fires.

One blessing, though. The air moved enough to whirl the windmill's blades. As they passed, she heard the creak of the pump drawing precious water from below. And that reminded her. "Hold up, Tanner. I forgot to fill my canteen." She reined in and unclipped the metal container.

She ground tied Nutmeg and walked over to the pump to fill the canteen.

Tanner shook his head "Might as well fill mine

while you're at it." He tossed it to her. "You don't have to dog my tail, you know. I'm fine."

"Maybe. But your welfare isn't the only reason I'm sticking with you this morning, brother dear. I want to watch Silver Eagle train those horses."

He frowned as she handed the filled canteen up to him. "You've seen him work horses dozens of times."

"Uh-huh, but it's been awhile. I didn't pay enough attention before. There are other ways of training than riding a horse into the ground, and he knows them."

"Yeah, Sil does a better job than anyone I know." He patted Dandy's withers. "I'm proud he trained this fella."

She mounted, gathered her reins, and moseyed along beside Tanner. No need for hurry. Another crystal-clear-sky day to be savored. And she would, by glory.

****

Silver Eagle tugged on the right rein as he stepped sideways. The horse shied, then pricked his ears forward at the calm voice speaking Comanche.

"Easy, boy, that was not uncomfortable. You will soon learn to turn from slight pressure."

Today he had chosen to plow rein his commands. Separated reins presented the horse with less confusion.

He glanced toward the logs laid end-to-end forming a makeshift barrier on one side of the meadow. Quiet Bird perched comfortably on a blanket, her back resting against a log. His sister had always been a bit fearful of horses. Drawing no pleasure from riding herself, she preferred to watch him train.

At the sound of approaching horses, Quiet Bird turned. Silver Eagle quickly pulled the reins through his hand for a firmer hold on the gelding.

He smiled when he recognized Tanner. The pleasure died when he saw Mariah Kelly behind his best friend. His body tightened. The Spirits appeared to laugh at his paltry attempts to avoid her.

"Hey, Sil, mind us watchin' you school the horses?"

Silver Eagle noted Tanner's wince as he stepped down. His mouth went dust dry, and his member throbbed just watching Mariah Kelly's long, shapely legs and lithe body as she gracefully dismounted.

Not good.

"Is no problem." The lie tasted sour on his tongue, her presence sure to destroy his concentration.

Tanner doffed his hat. "Hello, Quiet Bird."

She ducked her head, cheeks flushed.

Silver Eagle focused on her, his brow creased. Did his sister also long for someone she could not have? Suffer from the same kind of futile wish that burned in his own chest?

The Kellys secured their mounts' reins around trees.

Gathering his wits, Silver Eagle refocused on the task at hand. He again led with double reins, coaxing the horse forward with a gentle tug and release, tug and release, until the sorrel realized he was expected to continue walking until stopped.

The sun had climbed halfway into the sky before the gelding finally followed without hesitation. Every time Silver Eagle put up his hand and quietly said, "Whoa," the horse kept walking until he pressed his nose into a cupped hand.

Silver Eagle shook his head and murmured in Comanche, "We will try that again." He signaled the horse to walk. He repeated the command a half-dozen times before the horse stopped, but still he failed to stand quietly.

"You are not paying attention, my friend."

Neither was he. Every time he passed by his sister and the Kellys, his gaze shifted to Mariah. And every time he wanted to kick himself in the butt. Though he only gave her a fleeting glance, the horse sensed his divided attention and faltered every time.

This would not do.

But how could he persuade Mariah to leave without divulging his disquiet at her presence? He could not, so he led the horse to the far side of the meadow.

Finally focused, he led and stopped the horse with the patient attention he had acquired long ago. Each time the horse responded as commanded, Silver Eagle gave praise, "*tsaati*," and a pat to the jowl or the neck.

As the sun had dipped to near the treetops, the time had come to quit for the day. In English he said, "Is good." He scratched below the horse's ear and combed his fingers through the long mane. "*Tsaati*," he repeated in Comanche and rubbed the shoulder.

The sorrel stood quietly as he gathered the long reins and looped his arm over the gelding's neck. "Tomorrow we try obstacles, my friend."

Silver Eagle had never examined his habit of speaking to the Kellys' stock in both Comanche and English. His own mount and those of the band responded only to Comanche because that is all they ever heard. Now, he congratulated himself that he had focused so well on the training exercises that he had not thought of Mariah Kelly for quite a while. He had his body under control, thank the Spirits.

That is, he did until he turned to lead the horse across the meadow and spied Mariah leaning against the log, her long legs stretched on the ground before her. She was alone.

Chapter Nine

Did the Spirits bear him ill? It certainly appeared they intended to send him into his ancestors' hunting grounds on the receiving end of a bullet or with his neck in a noose.

"I've done nothing to provoke you, Silver Eagle," Mariah said. "Why are you scowling at me?"

Clearly, his expression gave away too much. He assumed he had perfected the indifferent, even bored, appearance over time. Many moons ago, when he had placed the barrier logs here, he had never considered Mariah Kelly would use one as a comfortable backrest. Though he might wish to, he could not banish her from this spot; it was, though on the fringe, Broken Spur land.

"I no scowl."

"Could have fooled me."

Realizing he could not win this argument, he changed the subject. "Where my sister is? Where Tanner is?"

"Quiet Bird was ready to go home. Tanner accompanied her." Mariah gained her feet as she spoke, brushed off her backside. "Besides, he wanted to thank your grandmother for her care."

"No need." He barely got the words out, so distracted was he imagining his own hand brushing the leaves from Mariah's trousers.

She grimaced. "Maybe you don't think so, Silver Eagle, but Ma would have our hides if either of us was less than courteous to your elders. Not only will Tanner thank her with a small gift, so will I."

Bewitched by the floral, womanly scent that was uniquely Mariah's, he barely heard what she said. His member pulsed. When his fingers involuntarily tightened on the leads, the green-broke horse tossed his head in protest.

Silver Eagle turned enough to hide the evidence his body betrayed and brushed a soothing hand along the sorrel's neck. Mariah did not help the situation at all. Out of the corner of his eye, he saw her approach, extending an entreating hand to the horse.

"He won't bite, will he?"

It is not the horse you should be concerned about, woman.

Steeling himself, his body rigid, he faced her. "Horse no is danger." He extended the leathers. "You want, you may lead."

She cocked her head, ignored his offer, and asked, "Silver Eagle, why do you dislike me?"

Her thick, fiery mane framed that unforgettable face, and her voice echoed as if in a dream.

Spirits, kill me now.

He could no longer remain aloof and distant. No one would know how hard he had fought his forbidden attraction to the woman gazing up at him with such bewilderment, such distress.

For the first time in his life, Silver Eagle abandoned his duty and dropped the reins of a halter-broke horse. One that did not belong to him.

Focused on Mariah's grass-green eyes, he willingly stepped into the path of that bullet, the one that would surely find him if Tanner or Mr. Kelly discovered the passion so long hidden in his heart.

"I no dislike, woman." He reached out and swept her supple body against his.

Though startled, her beautiful eyes wide, she did not struggle. No, she waited and watched as he slowly lowered his head and claimed her lips.

Her gasp of surprise fueled his desire. He deepened the kiss. She did not pull away. She did not stop him. Instead, her arms circled his neck, and she kissed him back. The tiny sound in her throat mingled with his own moan of pleasure.

****

He smelled of leather, wild sage, and prairie wind. His hard body pressed the length of hers sent heat raging through Mariah's veins. Never in her wildest imaginings had she thought to be kissed like this, so all consuming, so full of passion—and by Silver Eagle.

Reveling in the strength of his lusty body molded to her softer curves, the familiar sounds of the woods—birds chirping, leaves rustling in a faint breeze, faded away. She brushed aside thought of the danger to them if caught like this. All she wanted, all she needed, was right here in Silver Eagle's arms, in his delicious kiss.

Her fingers sank into his thick, coarse hair as he slanted his head to gain better access to her mouth. She found her tongue boldly dueling with his and felt the evidence of his desire against her soft flesh. The stiff coils of the bullwhip anchored at his side rubbed her pelvic bone. She gasped at the thought of making love with him.

She rode his thigh, which intimately caressed her mound. Deep in her core, sensations new to her tightened, and she moaned.

Her slight sound apparently triggered Silver Eagle's better judgment. God knew *someone* needed to exercise restraint. He jerked his head up and stepped back, holding her at arm's length, dark eyes stormy. His wide chest heaved, as did hers.

"Go. Find Tanner. Go home."

Before she could even muster breath to utter a word, he whirled and stalked away. It was then she saw the horse peacefully cropping grass at the meadow's edge. She watched Silver Eagle catch up the trailing leads, and without breaking stride, coil the long leathers in his hands and walk into the woods.

She stood as if planted, swallowing hard. Gradually, nature's sounds intruded. Fingers to her kiss-swollen lips, she relived the feel of his hard body crowding hers, her body singing with heated sensation. The tingling warmth of his lips lingered on hers.

Thoughtful, she walked back to the log and scooped up her hat. Were the kiss and his interest merely lust, or was there more to his terse words? *I no dislike, woman.*

What were his feelings, then? Deeper than mere liking?

She untied Nutmeg and mounted. The horse whiffled companionably as Mariah squeezed her knees against her barrel. Perhaps she was making a huge to do about nothing. Still, she couldn't let go of the consuming feelings she'd had while they kissed.

But that kiss had been from Silver Eagle, not just *any* man.

And for certain, not just *any* kiss.'

Maybe one day they *would* make love.

She'd been kissed once before, long ago, by Henry McCallister, but that had been a child's peck. And one or two of the men in the hospital caught up in gratitude had kissed her. But nothing compared with the intimate melding of lips to lips, body to body she'd just experienced.

Silver Eagle's kiss made her long for the impossible. His kiss was possessive, as if she *belonged* to him and him alone. She shivered at the thought.

At the edge of the clearing, some distance into the trees, she saw the colt frisking by Silver Eagle's side. He paused to open a makeshift gate designed to hold the two green-broke horses in a brush corral. Indian-trained stock mysteriously stayed in one locale even if free to roam, but not this pair. Not yet.

Though she was certain he'd heard her approach, the bullheaded man closed the gate and left.

"Silver Eagle," she called.

He didn't acknowledge her, just strode on until lost in the trees. *The nerve!* She urged the mare to follow. Before she had ventured very far, she spied him, now mounted, weaving through the trees toward her. She pulled up to wait.

His face might have been hewn granite. He drew rein and stopped beside her. "No should have happen. I sorry."

"I'm not." She blinked at her own bold reply. Well, dang, it was the truth. If she had her druthers, they'd kiss again—right now. Glory, they'd do *more* than kiss. But staring at his stony expression, she figured that wasn't going to happen. Not soon, anyway.

She tilted her head, unable to let it go. "Why *did* you kiss me, Silver Eagle?"

He remained silent for so long, she didn't think he would answer. But she'd be boiled in lye water before she'd beg for an explanation.

"Loco, maybe," he finally said.

"Loco," she repeated, frowning. "No, I don't think so. Your kiss was too—scorching."

Wryly he asked, "You experienced?"

Heat flared in her cheeks, sluiced through her body. Though definitely inexperienced, she could grow to crave *his* kisses.

"You're my first," she admitted. Though not exactly true, she couldn't compare that single time behind the barn episode, or the misguided, gratitude-induced, spur of the moment ones from injured men.

His dark gaze sent a chill slithering down her spine, which abruptly changed to scorching heat.

"No wise. What Mr. Kelly say he know I kiss you?"

A question she would rather not consider, but one she couldn't ignore as inconsequential. Ma and Pa would doubtless lock her up and throw away the key.

Not waiting for her reply, he said, "Is certain *my* people no like. Danger for them. Say again, I sorry."

He was really saying his kiss had been impetuous. And that brought her back to the original question. "So, why did you, then?" She knew she hadn't been the only one affected. Had seen it in his face. Had felt it in his body.

Silence, broken only by a squirrel's scolding, stretched between them. Silver Eagle's heated gaze roamed her body. He reined closer and raised his hand, his fingers capturing strands of her long hair. Gently, he rubbed the tresses between his fingers. She searched his unreadable expression.

"Find out what know long time, many moons." He shook his head. "Must no touch. Ever." He dropped his hand and took off at a trot.

Down deep, Mariah reluctantly agreed. Their attraction could be disastrous for both.

Clearly, Silver Eagle wished to distance himself from her. And for the next three days, Mariah avoided *him* by avoiding her brother.

Today she'd set out to help Max mend the fence that separated the Broken Spur from McCallister's spread. She had to agree with her father. The fence sliced through ideal pasture that both ranchers should be able to utilize without feeling threatened by each other.

She pounded a nail, securing a crossbeam at the top of a gatepost. Grudgingly, Jessup McCallister had consented not to use barbed wire. Far too dangerous to weanling cattle. And if horses got tangled in the wire, barbs could rip deep gashes in bellies and legs.

"That'll do it for today, Miss Mariah." Max straightened, doffed his hat, and wiped sweat from his brow on a cotton sleeve. "Gettin' near suppertime." He shoved a hammer into his tool belt.

Though no one on the range went without firepower, Max wasn't one to carry a handgun. He retrieved his rifle leaning against the gate, walked back to his tethered horse, and slipped the Winchester into the boot.

Working her shoulders, Mariah stowed her own hammer in a saddlebag. She smiled at the foreman as she mounted. "You don't have to tell me twice, Max. I've whipped up a powerful appetite, and my arm and hand ache."

He shook his head. "Fence mendin' ain't no job for a woman, missy."

What could she expect from a man who put women on a shelf as if exotic curios? They sure as shootin' shouldn't get their hands dirty with what he considered men's work. As far as she knew, he'd never pursued settling down permanently with the fairer sex.

As she kneed Nutmeg to follow, she studied Max's broad, lean, back. Surely he sought the company of a light skirt now and then. He was on first-name basis with Barney, who tended bar at the saloon in town. As was Tanner.

The rooms above the saloon were home to some hard-looking women. Women who kept their distance from the ranchers' wives and daughters when they shopped at the general store.

While in the East, plenty of Mariah's acquaintances gossiped in breathless tones about brothers who thought it their God-given right to bed scarlet women. A couple girls had even revealed that their fathers kept mistresses. As long as their mothers didn't know, or pretended not to know, it seemed perfectly acceptable.

Worry lines creased between Mariah's brows. She hoped the occasional hour her father spent in Mr. Crabapple's saloon was passed having a drink, jawing with Barney or other ranchers, or on games of chance, but nothing more. Picturing the kisses he gave Ma every evening when he came in for supper, the worry lines eased.

No doubt about it, Pa's passion for Ma was real. Besides, Ma would have his head boiled in a kettle if she caught him fooling around on her. Mariah suppressed a chuckle as she rode into the barn behind Max.

After bedding Nutmeg for the night, she approached the house, her gaze traveling over the home she had missed so terribly for so long. She paused when she thought of what might happen if she let on to her loved ones that she was interested in Silver Eagle.

Face it, Mariah, you're more than interested!

She sighed. Silver Eagle was right. No one would look kindly on either of them if they pursued a relationship. Well, anything other than the friendship that had been accepted for years. Though his Comanche blood stuck in some folks' craws, Silver Eagle worked for Ward Kelly, and he was Tanner's friend. By gum, nobody should forget that, or they'd have both white men to answer to. But if she and Silver Eagle were foolish enough to take kissing to a deeper, more intimate level—

"Mariah?"

Startled from her reverie, she focused on her mother, who stood in the doorway, holding the screen open. Mariah's cheeks warmed when she realized she'd been lingering in one spot for God only knew how long, staring into space.

Pulling off her hat, she made a production of knocking off dust as she slapped the felt against her leg and continued on across the clearing.

"Are you okay, hon?"

"Yeah. I was just thinking about how wonderful it is to be home." That wasn't an out and out lie. It had been her first thought.

Ma chuckled. "While you're woolgathering, supper is getting cold."

She hastened toward the house. "Pa and Tanner are home already?"

Letting the door slam behind her, Mariah followed her mother into the kitchen. She pulled up short when she came face to face with Silver Eagle's intense eyes. He stared at her from across the table. Astonished to see him here, she couldn't find her voice. Blindly, she reached out to steady herself on the chair's wooden back.

"Silver Eagle's joinin' us for supper," Pa needlessly observed. "It ain't often we have this pleasure."

Mariah blinked a couple times, collecting her wits, and started toward the bedrooms. "I need to wash up. Don't wait for me."

As she left the kitchen, she dimly heard her mother's amiable conversation. Entering her room, she slapped her hat on the hook, poured water in the basin on the washstand, and submerged her hot face.

During the years she was growing up, Silver Eagle had steadfastly refused to enter this house. Apparently, a lot of things had changed around here.

Chapter Ten

The next morning, eager to renew her friendship with Amelia, Mariah donned her best shirtwaist. Maybe her old chum would be the one person she could share her inner thoughts with. Or maybe not.

Feeling a little guilty about shirking chores, she found her mother on the back porch working the pump. Water gushed into a large washtub. Clothes and bed linens separated into piles dotted the plank floor. Mariah's mouth gaped when her mother proceeded to pick up the full tub.

"Glory, Ma, what do you think you're doing?"

The handles slipped from her mother's hands; the tub thudded to the floor. Water splattered her skirt. "You startled me!" She looked down at the once-full tub and shrugged. "It's wash day, Mariah, and I have to set this water over the fire pit."

"By yourself?" Mariah's voice rose in consternation. Good grief. Ma must have done this chore a million times. And *she* had been nowhere in sight to help her prior to going away to school.

A half smile kicked up her mother's lips. "And who else do you see here to do it? Of course by myself, hon."

Mariah stuck her gloves in her back pocket. "I'll get one side, you get the other." The weight of just one handle cut across Mariah's hand as she lifted. "Dang, Ma. You should ask for help carrying something this heavy. You're going to ruin your back."

A few steps from the screened porch, they

settled the tub on iron bars stretched across an open blaze. Mariah scowled. "Shoot, the damage is probably already done."

Her mother straightened and put a hand to her side. "Honey, my back stopped yelling long ago." She gave a weak grin. "About the same time my feet stopped barking."

Mariah glanced down at the high-buttoned ankle boots her mother favored. If they felt anything like those forced upon her in Maryland, they pinched and left a body's feet smarting long into the night. Enough to hinder sleep.

She couldn't help her hangdog expression when she thought today might not be the best time for visiting. Ma really did need another pair of hands.

"Umm," she hedged. "I was heading over to see Amelia." She shrugged. "Think maybe I better stick around and help with the wash."

Her mother rolled her eyes. "Don't be silly. I don't need help, Mariah."

"But—"

"No buts." She pulled a handkerchief from her apron pocket and swiped it across her already perspiring forehead. "Before you know it, you'll be joining the hands' roundup, sorting, and branding. Enjoy yourself for a few more days. Besides, I'm sure Amelia expects you about now. She'd be mighty put out if you didn't show up." She flicked her fingers. "Shoo."

Relieved, Mariah turned away, wondering if she could ever settle down with a man and do a woman's chores like Ma.

"Mariah," her mother called, "you let Samuel or Max know where you're headed. Remember what we said. A woman traveling alone is no longer as safe as she used to be."

She waved. "Yes, Ma." In her head she chided, *Yeah, yeah. Ridiculous*, but gripped her rifle, reassuring herself she was a crack shot. It would fall on deaf ears to point that out to Ma, though.

****

Setting Nutmeg to a ground-eating canter, Mariah came in sight of the Picketts' place in less than an hour. Two hounds bayed, announcing her arrival long before she got close enough to be recognized.

As she reined Nutmeg to a walk, both dogs bounded around the horse's hooves, making such a racket the mare laid back her ears.

"Git!" Mariah's order went unheeded.

"Jupiter!" a male voice bellowed.

The larger of the two dogs dropped to his belly as if shot. The other looked around at its companion and whined. He sat down and cocked his head.

Mariah laughed. She couldn't help it. The younger dog looked for all the world like a person bewildered about why his companion quit having so much fun.

"Mariah? Mariah Kelly?"

She looked down on Gordon Pickett. Four years older than Amelia, he was a hard-looking man. No doubt for good reason. He worked the farm side of the Picketts' ranch while his father and younger brother handled the cattle.

This ranch, much smaller than the Broken Spur, only supported a couple hundred head of cattle in any given year.

"Gordon." She dismounted and extended her hand.

He shifted the shovel he held, looked at his own wide palm, dirt in the creases, and gave her a lopsided grin. "Don't think that's a good idea. But good to see you."

She didn't care a fig if his hand was dirty. The grime was there from honest work, but she didn't argue. "Is Amelia about?"

Joyce Henderson

"Yeah, she and Maw is cannin'" He grimaced. "Tomatoes. I growed a bumper crop of 'em this year. She's gonna have to sell some to Mr. Hawkins if he's in the market to buy."

Although her folks had planted an orange tree and a lemon tree, and pecan trees grew wild on the ranch, her mother refused to get involved in growing their own vegetables and canning. She bought canned goods at the general store or purchased fresh gown tomatoes from her friend, Callie Pickett.

"Commerce" her mother called it. The Picketts needed the money, and Ma avoided digging in the dirt.

"Be sure to let Ma know, Gordon. We eat a lot of canned tomatoes at our house."

He nodded and called to a tall, scrawny man leaning on another shovel some distance away. "Kyle, get Amelia."

Mariah's eyes popped wide in surprise. "Kyle? That's your little brother?"

Gordon grinned, the scar on his cheek cutting deeper than other lines on his face. He'd tangled with a bear some years ago, lucky to come away with only the one defacing scar. "He's almost taller than me. When he fills out, I probably won't be able to wrestle him to the ground anymore."

From the house Mariah heard a shriek of delight, followed a moment later by a flurry of skirts sailing off the porch, headed her way. "Mariah!" Amelia called, and the next instant her friend had Mariah in a crushing hug. "Oh, my God, my God in heaven! It's so good to see you!"

You haven't seen me yet, Mariah thought wryly, and pried herself from Amelia's grasp. Pushing her to arm's length, Mariah said, "Let me look at you!"

Her first thought was she wouldn't have recognized her old friend. Her hair. Well, yes, Amelia still had glorious hair, though covered by a scarf. Understandable when working over a hot stove.

Her face, so rosy and fresh-looking two years ago, was now lined. Her hands were red; the nails stained. Undoubtedly, Amelia worked right along with her mother and brothers in the garden.

Mariah wanted to cry for her friend, but she didn't think it would be appreciated. Fortunately, she didn't have to say anything.

"My goodness, Mariah, you've surely gotten prettier than I remembered." She glanced at her brother. "Don't you think so, Gordon?"

That was Amelia. Always ready with a compliment for others, but Gordon was saying nothing. And Mariah was glad.

"I thought maybe you and I could steal off down to the creek for a little chat, Amelia."

Her baby blues, as shy as ever, clouded now. "I can't leave Ma to do the rest of the tomatoes, Mariah. She's been feelin' kind of poorly the past couple weeks. The baby is due—"

"Your mother is pregnant again?" erupted before Mariah could stop herself.

Fortunately, Gordon had gone back to his shovel work, and Amelia didn't take offense. Instead, she laughed. "You should have heard the tongue lashing she gave my father when she found out. As if she had nothing to do with it!"

Though Amelia blushed, those were bold words coming from the friend Mariah knew from years gone by. Mariah stood for a moment, and then switched the reins, ready to mount. "Well, I better get out of your way. I'll come back another day."

"You certainly will not, Mariah Kelly." Amelia clasped her arm. "You come right in and have a glass of sweet tea with me and Ma. Landsakes, we can take a short break. Ma needs to get off her feet for a while, anyway. This will be a good excuse."

Mariah cut a glance at the house, then back to her friend. "Well, if it wouldn't be a bother. I'd like to say hello to your mother."

When they started walking toward the house, the dogs jumped up. Tongues lolling happily, they whipped around their feet and Nutmeg's.

"Jupiter, Zeus!" Amelia said. "If you don't get out from under foot, I'm gonna take a stick to the both of you! Go on. Shoo!" She flapped her apron. "Under the house. Now!"

Mariah laughed at the hounds' hangdog expressions as they both slunk away and crawled under the porch. The smaller one, Zeus, turned around and dropped his long snout on his paws, eyes so woebegone. Mariah laughed again. She realized she missed dogs nosing around, getting underfoot more often than not. They hadn't replaced old Vinegar when he died more than six years ago.

She spent the better part of the day with Amelia and her mother. Even pitched in to remove jars from the steaming water kettles. Though she hadn't intended to stay so long, fortunately, Mariah had thought to loosen her saddle's cinch when she tied Nutmeg to wait in the shade.

Mariah accepted what she already knew, though. Prying her old friend away from home for even a few hours would never happen. Sweet as could be, Amelia was still a contented homebody and a cautious girl to the core.

****

Twilight was upon them when Silver Eagle and Tanner got to the creek not two miles from the home barn. Silver Eagle dismounted, lay flat on the ground, and stuck his head in the cool water. Beside him, his stallion lowered his head to drink.

Black hair plastered to his head, wet ends trailed over his buckskin work shirt. Beside him, hair dripping, water running down his face and soaking his cotton shirt, Tanner grinned.

"Hot today. I 'spect no relief for quite a spell."

"*Haa*," Silver Eagle agreed. They had found two dozen strays and herded them into the makeshift corral Ben Stewart and a couple other hands had built as a holding pen some three miles from the main compound. Once they were established as belonging to the Broken Spur and Mr. Kelly decided they had enough to fill the home corrals, they would drive them one at a time through the dipping chute, then brand them.

All hands turned out for those long hard workdays. Silver Eagle frowned, realizing Mariah would be in on that chore for the first time since she had come home. No doubt she would be soft after so long away. She would be tuckered by nightfall.

Silver Eagle scowled. "Tanner."

His friend glanced up at the urgency in his voice. "What?"

He pointed beyond Tanner. "That Nutmeg. Why mare loose?"

"Huh?" He swung around, his scowl matching Silver Eagle's. "Holy smokes, that ain't right."

Silver Eagle scanned the area, spied something white. Alarms clanged in his head when he recognized Mariah lying near the creek several yards away. He sprinted past Tanner, spouting a string of Comanche that Tanner probably could not follow. He knelt at her side. "Mariah!"

She moaned and uttered an unladylike, ear-scorching curse as he slipped an arm beneath her shoulders and eased her up. Tanner dropped to his knees.

She rubbed the back of her head. "Glory, something walloped me."

"You hear no one? You see no one?" Silver Eagle asked as he withdrew his arm. Her white shirtwaist and the side of her face were smudged with dirt.

Joyce Henderson

"No, I..." She blinked. "I stopped to get a drink, and... Well, I don't know." Gingerly, she stuck her fingers in her thick hair, then winced. "Shit!" she snapped. "That hurts."

Tanner grinned. "You learned some colorful ways of expressin' yourself while in the East, sis." He pulled her hand from her hair. "Let me take a look."

"Ow!"

"Hush. Stop bein' a baby." He parted her hair and peered at her scalp. "Yup. You got a jim-dandy goose egg there."

Desperate to hide his worry, his feelings, Silver Eagle walked away to retrieve Nutmeg. As he led the horse back to them, he scowled.

"No rifle?"

Mariah jerked away too fast and moaned again.

Tanner helped her to her feet. "Take it easy."

"But I had my rifle. I *always* carry it."

Silver Eagle slapped the empty boot. "No here now."

Mariah put her hand to her forehead. "I've got one hellacious headache."

Silver Eagle handed the reins to Tanner and walked a little distance away, dividing his attention between what was said and searching.

He heard Mariah ask, "What's he doing?"

"Lookin' for sign," Tanner said. "Some*one*, not some*thing*, whacked you a good one, sis. Is anythin' else missin'?"

She spread her arms. "I don't have anything with me." She inclined her head toward Nutmeg, appearing to regret it when she again clamped a palm against her forehead. "My canteen, but it's there."

A few feet away, Silver Eagle inspected her more closely. Finding her still buttoned and belted, he breathed a sigh assuring himself she had not

108

been otherwise assaulted.

"Look at me, Mariah," Tanner said.

She squinted. "I am!"

He clasped her chin and studied her eyes.

And Silver Eagle wished it were he touching her soft flesh.

"What?"

"You may have a concussion. You think you can sit a horse to get home?"

"Of course. Why couldn't I?"

"Yeah, why," Tanner muttered. He circled her waist and set her in the saddle before she could utter another word. "You start feelin' woozy, you'll ride with me."

"I'm all right, Tanner. Stop fussing like a crotchety woman."

"Wait until squirt discovers somebody conked you on the head. You'll find out what fussin' is." He frowned. "What were you doin' out here alone, anyway?"

Silver Eagle wanted to know that too. It was unsafe for a woman to travel alone on the prairie.

"I can take care of—"

Tanner laughed when she trailed off. "Yeah, you best rethink that before you finish it."

"Well, usually I can. Someone sneaked up on me. And why, I'll never know." She harrumphed. "I had been over to visit with Amelia." Gathering her reins, she shook her head. "Amelia isn't like she used to be, Tanner. She never was adventuresome, but boy howdy, now she hardly leaves the porch swing."

Silver Eagle wished, just for a moment, that Mariah could be more cautious like her friend. Then he looked at the coppery mass of curls and knew that would never be. Mariah was the fire to her friend's smoke.

"We best get home. The folks will begin to worry. You comin'?"

Still searching the underbrush, Silver Eagle said, "No."

As they rode away Mariah looked back at him. "If you find my hat, bring it to work tomorrow." She brushed a hand over the back of her head. "I had my hair tied with a blue ribbon. It's gone, too."

He raised his hand in acknowledgement.

Silver Eagle watched them out of sight, his gut still churning. He sucked in a breath, tamping down the fear that had swept through him like a roiling black cloud when he had seen Mariah on the ground.

He knelt for a closer inspection. Moving farther, he noted broken grass and impressions in the dirt. Finally, surrounded by foot and hoof prints, he found Mariah's crushed hat. Eyes closed, he pressed the felt to his nose, inhaled the scent that was uniquely hers.

Forcing from his mind futile longing for the woman he could not have, he scanned the area again. The assailant wore moccasins, and the horse was unshod.

His stomach sank.

Settling back on his heels, he pulled up grass and stuck a stem in his mouth. Eyes narrowed, he tracked the prints' direction.

His horse idled close by, cropping grass.

The man could have killed Mariah. It would make no difference if someone in his village had done the deed or not. No white man within a hundred miles would think twice before blaming his people—*all* of his people—for the attack if the Kellys spread the news.

Would they?

He discarded the stem, stuffed Mariah's hat inside his shirt next to his heart, then fluidly rose and mounted. The Spirits must surely be laughing at his hope that Mr. Kelly would remain quiet.

If anyone came out here to investigate, there

would be no doubt where the tracks led. *He* certainly was not in doubt.

He must convince his father to investigate the situation now, not days from now. His venerable father would be forced to invade another man's privacy, which he was loathe to do. But one man jeopardized the entire village.

An ache took root in Silver Eagle's heart.

He leaned forward. His mount responded to his master's urgency, his stride lengthening to eat up the ground. Like an eagle in flight, they flew toward home.

Chapter Eleven

"I told you it wasn't safe, Mariah," her mother scolded as she chipped slivers of ice from the block in the icebox safe. Finished, she slapped the pick on the table, wrapped the small chunks in a towel, and handed it to Mariah, who sat at the kitchen table with her father and Tanner. "Hold this on that bump. The skin is going to break if we don't get the swelling down."

Gingerly, Mariah laid the pack on her crown, hissing when the cold hit the swollen tissue. "Dang. That smarts!"

"You didn't see anyone?" her father asked for the third, or was it the fifth, time.

"No. I didn't, and I didn't hear anyone, either," she added before he could repeat the next question. "Whoever it was sneaked up on me quieter than the dead."

"Mariah, could you use another metaphor?" her mother said. "I don't know what you were hit with, but had the impact been on your temple or at the base of your skull, you might be talking to the angels right now. I almost lost one child this week."

"Oh, Ma, that's a bit dramatic."

"Oh, really?"

"Darlin'," her father soothed, patting Ma's shoulder. "She's gonna be fine. And she'll take our cautions to heart from now on. Won't you, daughter?" he said pointedly.

"Yes, Pa," she answered, acting the obedient child.

She caught Tanner covering his mouth to hide a grin. But he couldn't quite stifle the chuckle.

She reached beneath the table and pinched his forearm.

"Ow!"

"What's wrong?" Pa eyed Tanner.

"Nothin'." Her brother pushed back from the table. "I'm goin' to look up Sil. Ask if he found anythin'."

"We eat in about an hour, Tanner." Ma rose to chip more ice. "Maybe you should wait until tomorrow."

"Ma, if Sil didn't find sign, then I'm goin' back to see if I can. The longer we leave it, the less likely we'll find the culprit."

"Samuel will ride with you, son."

Tanner shook his head. "No. I'd as soon be on my own."

Mariah frowned. "It's just as dangerous for you to ride alone as it is for me." She threw up a hand when Tanner opened his mouth. "Don't you dare say differently! Dang it, yes, I'm a girl, but I can shoot as well as you."

Tanner crossed his eyes and stuck out his tongue, then started out the door. Mariah threw the wet towel. It splatted on his back and plopped to the floor.

Swinging around with a maniacal grin, Tanner strode toward her. She yelped, leaped up, and ran toward her room.

To the accompaniment of her mother's, "Children! Children!" Tanner's boots beat a heavy tattoo right behind her.

Mariah swung the bedroom door. Only it didn't close. Wouldn't have stopped him if it had. She whirled around and put up her hand, laughing as she backed toward the far wall. "Tanner, stop right there. I'm injured."

113

"No more damaged than me, sis."

Before she could dodge him, he grabbed her wrist and whipped her around. As he sat on the side of her bed, he forced her over his knees, and then gave her a flat-handed slap on the butt.

"Ow! Tanner! Ma!"

"You gonna behave?"

"I didn't—"

He spanked her again. "Yes, you did."

Though she couldn't see him, she could hear the humor in his voice.

"Don't you dare hit me again. I'll—"

Smack.

"Okay, okay! I give!"

When he eased his arm from her back, she scrambled to her feet. "No fair. You're bigger." But unable to resist his endearing smile, she burst out laughing.

"How's your noggin?"

She blinked and put a hand to her forehead. "Glory, the headache is gone." She wagged her finger at him. "Uh-uh, don't think you can take credit for curing my headache."

The springs squeaked as he rose. Chuckling, he asked, "Would I do that?"

"Are you two finished acting like ten-year olds?" Hands on hips, their mother stood in the doorway.

Tanner started out of the room, paused, and gave his mother a gentle pat on the cheek. "Until the next time, Ma."

She gave him a swat on his backside as he left.

Mariah shook her head. "He's a caution, that one."

And she wouldn't have it any other way.

****

Silver Eagle drew rein and dismounted, then forced himself to care for his horse before he approached his father. Bursting in on his chief like a buffalo gone berserk would not gain him what he wanted—Howling Coyote's dismissal from the tribe.

He stopped in his own tipi, and lifting the tail of his buckskin shirt, pulled out Mariah's beat-up hat. Again, he pressed the hat to his nose and savored her scent. He stowed the flattened felt in a trunk he had purchased in town long ago to hold clean clothes and valuables.

As he laid the hat atop a spare coiled bullwhip, a faint smile lifted his lips. A hat beyond wearing would not be considered valuable. Except, this one belonged to the woman he had loved for most of his years. He sighed for what could never be and left the tipi.

Gaining entrance to his father's lodge, Silver Eagle drew up short. Howling Coyote sat across the fire from his father and his uncle, Crow Dog.

"*Nï tua?*," the chief said, beckoning Silver Eagle to sit to his right. "We are discussing a hunt that Howling Coyote has scouted. A small herd of buffalo graze only two suns into the *Llano Estacado*."

Silver Eagle crossed his ankles and sank onto the spread robe where his father indicated. Gazing upon Howling Coyote, expression neutral, Silver Eagle asked, "When did you find this herd?"

With a mocking lift of his lips, he said, "As our great chief says, two suns past. I rode hard today to arrive with the news."

"Rode hard today," Silver Eagle echoed. "I wager you did."

Before anyone could comment on his cryptic remark, he asked, "How long have you been back?"

As the warrior shrugged an arrogant, dismissive shoulder, Falcon Wing said, "That matters not. We must gather our weapons and alert the women to be ready to move by the sun's rise. The buffalo will not remain close by for long."

That was true, but Silver Eagle did not wish to

put off telling his father about the danger that might threatened the band in a few days. His father needed to know that a thief was on the loose, and the entire band might be held accountable. And he did not wish to leave on a hunt until he assured himself that Mariah was truly unhurt.

Rather than bring Crow Dog into the discussion, and refusing to include Howling Coyote, Silver Eagle remained quiet as his father made plans for the hunt.

Sparrow was needed in the village to assist Wings of a Dove. Talking Woman would undoubtedly protest being left behind, but by all accounts, the recent birth of a boy-child had been difficult. With such a small band, Falcon Wing treasured all children brought into the world to carry on Comanche heritage, male children in particular.

Howling Coyote said Painted Woman would go, his children to be left in Sparrow's care. Crow Dog offered his two wives and niece. Four would be enough to skin the buffalo and prepare the meat to bring back to the band.

As Crow Dog and Howling Coyote rose to make preparations, Silver Eagle remained seated. Howling Coyote cast a narrow-eyed glance at him before ducking from the tipi. Though deceitful, he was not stupid. He knew exactly what Silver Eagle would discuss with his father.

"I sense that you do not wish to join the hunt, *nï tua?*."

Silver Eagle heard the censure in his father's voice, but he did not flinch. "*Nï ahpï?*, I believe Howling Coyote has lied to you. I believe earlier today he hit Ward Kelly's daughter over the head and stole her rifle."

Falcon Wing sat motionless for a moment. His father was nothing if not deliberate. He never jumped to conclusions or spoke hastily. Though this drove Silver Eagle over the edge of control at times, he managed to keep his council.

"The Kelly woman will recover from the attack?"

Silver Eagle nodded.

"That is good to hear. I would mourn the loss of Ward Kelly's child."

Silver Eagle would do more than mourn. He would kill Howling Coyote, for he was certain it was he who had attacked Mariah. And for what? A rifle!

"You believe Howling Coyote lies? There are no buffalo?"

"No, *ni ahpi?*. He would not lie about buffalo. I believe he lies about riding directly to the village to impart the news. Tanner and I found Miss Kelly by the stream that cuts across the northern corner of the Broken Spur. There are prints of an unshod horse and Comanche-made moccasins. They lead here, *ni ahpi?*."

His father picked up a pipe, and took his time filling the bowl. He stuck a slender stick into the coals of the central fire until it ignited with a small flame, and then lit the tobacco.

Tossing the stick into the fire, he spoke slowly. "You carry much enmity in your heart for Howling Coyote, *ni tua?*. That enmity often colors your judgment."

"*Ni ahpi?*—"

He lifted a staying hand. "Let me finish. We have lived in peace for many moons. Howling Coyote is aware of our arrangement with Ward Kelly and the white people in their village. The warrior is hot headed, but I believe he would think hard before jeopardizing the band, before putting his children in harm's way."

When his father again puffed his pipe, Silver Eagle waited a moment to assure himself it was his turn to speak. Forcing himself to relax, he unclenched his hands and gazed into his father's wise eyes. He knew in his heart that this time the chief was missing the point.

"Howling Coyote saw an opportunity to steal a much-desired rifle for himself. I believe that was his only thought when he came upon Miss Kelly alone."

Falcon Wing shook his head but said nothing.

"I followed the trail here," he said.

"*Nĭ tua?*, there are Comanche in the area other than this band. It grieves me that many of our brethren are hostile. They may be near. But we must thank the Spirits that whoever did this foul deed did not kill Miss Kelly."

He *could* thank them. In his heart he already had. He persisted. "My fear would be allayed if you would conduct a search of Howling Coyote's tipi."

Falcon Wing dashed his hope. "I will not condone invasion of a warrior's privacy without indisputable evidence."

"You do not trust my judgment."

The chief lifted a brow. "I *question* your judgment. There is a difference, *nĭ tua?*."

"That is true," he said grudgingly.

Despairing of convincing his chief otherwise, Silver Eagle sat in silence while his father puffed his pipe. The smoke drifted toward the vent hole in the center of the tipi. Silver Eagle enjoyed the sweet tobacco fragrance, white men's tobacco he had gifted to his father. Though he, himself, had never taken up the habit other than occasionally in council, it somehow soothed him to sit quietly with his father while he smoked.

After a time Falcon Wing knocked out the last of the tobacco into the fire ring. "We will leave at first light tomorrow, *nĭ tua?*."

"I prefer to stay here," he said. "If news of Miss Kelly's attack becomes known by their neighbors, we are in for trouble!" He tempered his tone. "It is my hope the townspeople would not know."

"Do you think Mr. Kelly will speak of this to his white friends?"

"Not intentionally. But the men who work for him will know, and they might talk."

"Ah." Resignation darkened Falcon Wing's features. "Then it is well that you remain behind to protect the family." He gave Silver Eagle a long, studied look. "If you are right, it would not go amiss with me if you spirited your *pia, cáco,* and *nami?* from the village."

"I will see to their safety while you hunt, *nï ahpï?.* Others will remain here to fight if need be."

Falcon Wing slowly wagged his head. "Fight? Let us pray to the Spirits it does not come to that. It would be a great breach of the trust between Ward Kelly and me if blood was shed."

It was not often that Silver Eagle thought his father's counsel unwise. But in this case, he believed the trust between the two men had already been shattered. One covetous warrior had placed the entire village in peril.

Still, he rose and bowed. "I will pray you are correct, *nï ahpï?.* Though, if my fear comes to pass, I will face the white men when they come."

Chapter Twelve

Silver Eagle stood behind the table beneath the oaks. Ever watchful, his dark eyes scanned the ranch compound. Max Stoddard and Ben Stewart walked out of the barn carrying tack. Both men had taken a bath, slicked back their hair, and donned clean clothes. Their banter carried on the soft evening air.

"Saturday night, and there's a shot of whiskey with my name on it at Crabapple's," Ben Stewart said.

After entering the holding pen, Max flung the saddle blanket over the sorrel he favored, then followed it with his saddle. "Uh-huh," he said. "Bet there's more'n one. I heard tell that redheaded hellion dealin' faro is mighty accommodatin', too."

"Uh, I wouldn't know," Ben retorted.

Silver Eagle smiled at the shit-eating grin on his face, and he heard Max's chuckle.

"Yeah. And my Ma was a preacher woman."

As the men rode away, Samuel waved good-bye from the bunkhouse doorway, and then carried a ladder-back chair from the bunkhouse. He sat, tipped the chair back, balancing on two legs, the wooden back rested against the clapboards. He began playing his Jew's harp. The pleasing notes drifted on the breeze.

Samuel was barred from entering into white men's evening pleasures just as Silver Eagle and his people were. Black people were just as much pariahs as Indians. While that didn't bother Silver Eagle, other than barring him from having his heart's desire, he had seen the sorrow Samuel suffered from the cold shoulders from many white people in Burnett Station.

****

Darkness had descended by the time Silver Eagle rode for home. There was no reason for him to stand guard after Mariah entered her house at twilight. He simply could not help himself.

The vision of her lying unconscious on the hard ground would not leave him. One day he would prove it had been Howling Coyote who hurt her. He would see justice done.

Riding into the village, he spied Howling Coyote seated cross legged on a robe before his tipi. As always, more an obedient servant than a mate, Painted Woman knelt before him and handed him a bowl. With no smile, no nod of thanks, Howling Coyote took it and began eating. Painted Woman remained where she was.

Silver Eagle knew the little woman would not eat until Howling Coyote had his fill and their children were settled for the night. That was the way of many of his people, but neither his way nor his father's. Thank the Spirits.

He supposed part of the reason Falcon Wing treated his women more kindly lay with Wings of a Dove's gifts. Though a woman, she possessed powerful medicine that rivaled the chief's.

After grooming his mount and washing up at the river, he strode toward his own tipi.

Sparrow intercepted him. "I have prepared buffalo meat with wild onions. Talking Woman and I made bread today, and there are berries. Would you care to partake with the family, *nï tua??*"

Since their discussion about Howling Coyote, he had avoided his father. Childish of him. He and his father had disagreed. But that did not make Falcon

121

Wing less a chief or less a revered father. Here was an opportunity to put an end to his silence.

"*Haa, nï pia.* Thank you." He followed her to where his father and grandmother sat near the entrance to his mother's tipi.

Quiet Bird served each of them, glancing up when he and his mother arrived. She signed her pleasure that he joined them for a meal, then proceeded to serve him and Sparrow. He waited until his sister filled her own bowl and took her accustomed place before he began to eat. He had long since noticed the Kelly men offered that minor courtesy to the women in their home. It was the least he could do for those who cared for him and his father.

As was usual, his grandmother finished eating before the others. Though she seemed well enough, he marveled at the little she ate.

"You arrive after the sun sleeps, Silver Eagle," Wings of a Dove said.

"*Haa.*"

"All is well in the Kellys' lodge?"

He nodded but refrained from speech. He had an idea where this conversation would lead, anyway. His grandmother would say her piece no matter what.

"The girl is well?"

"*Haa.* She works every day, *nï cáco.*"

"It is your duty to guard her?"

While he knew it would do no good, still, he evaded a direct answer. "I work with Tanner, *Cáco.* If his sister travels with us, together we watch over her."

Her frail body leaning against the hide-covered backrest he had made for her, she steepled her fingers before her mouth and studied him with those all-knowing, fathomless eyes. He had learned as a child not to attract their attention. Wings of a Dove could discern a lie or half truth behind every word.

"I will retire now," she said abruptly.

Silver Eagle did not believe he would get off so easily. Along with seeing lies or truth and being a gifted shaman, Wings of a Dove was a tenacious woman. And though she looked frail enough to blow away in a stiff breeze, she had a constitution of iron.

Falcon Wing started to rise, ever mindful of respect for both his mother and the shaman of his band. Placing a skeletal hand on his knee, she stayed her son's movement.

"Silver Eagle may assist me to my tipi this night."

With a straight face, he rose and offered Wings of a Dove his hand, then picked up the backrest and followed her. Ah yes, he had not heard the last of his grandmother's *wisdom*.

Cookfires glowed, casting dancing shadows on tipi walls, bathing tree leaves with an orange glow. High overhead, a half moon hung in the heavens, dimming the glitter of millions of stars, of other worlds inhabited by the Spirits.

Many voices pitched low in amiable conversation murmured on the air as his grandmother paused and gazed up through the leaves. "The Rain God draws nigh, Silver Eagle. Mother Earth will beat happy drums for the nourishment."

Though the air was bone dry and the breeze still warm, Silver Eagle reminded himself of another well-learned lesson—never question Grandmother's predictions.

After helping her settle close to the fire pit's glowing coals, he found her cob pipe and filled the bowl, then prepared to take his leave. "Sleep well with the Spirits on your shoulder, *nï cáco*."

She squinted in the dimness and patted the spread blanket. "Stay a moment, Silver Eagle."

Squelching a resigned sigh, he crossed his

ankles and sank down. It would do no good to protest or try to hurry her along. She would speak her mind, and in her own good time.

Wings of a Dove picked up a short stick from the tiny fire and touched the smoldering end to the tobacco in her pipe. Like his father, Grandmother seemed to find solace in this little ritual when contemplating a difficult situation. She drew deeply several times, the smoke escaping from her lips around the stem, until satisfied the pipe burned well.

She drew on her power to keep him seated a bit longer while she studied the near distance with unfocused eyes. He, however, was as patient, or maybe as stubborn as she. In years past, she had intimidated the village boys in this manner. Now, he waited her out, refusing to say a word.

If he owned a chained timepiece like Mr. Kelly's, he was certain the hands on the face would have signaled the passage of five minutes before Wings of a Dove finally spoke.

"Miss Kelly is a beautiful woman."

Though he agreed, he said nothing.

"She will find a man, a man who equals her high spirit."

Pausing again to draw on the pipe, Grandmother cast him a quick glance, but still he remained mute. What could he say? A white man would claim her? A white man with spirit to equal hers? He did not think so. *No, Silver Eagle*, he chided. *You do not* want *her to find a white man.*

"The white woman will bear a son with hair of night. A girl child—" Wings of a Dove shook her head. "No, two will have fire in their hair like their mother. And a fourth..."

Silver Eagle held his breath as his grandmother gazed into another world, perhaps.

Finally, she shook her head as if casting off a

dream. "I do not see the fourth child, but I know the gods will give her four babes."

He shivered beneath the gaze of her all-seeing eyes.

"Silver Eagle, proceed with care. What you want, you may have, but consider the price."

****

Seated at the same poker table with Ben, Max clamped a cigar between his teeth. Smoke curling from the stogie added to the stinging haze, smarting his brown eyes. He had steadily lost, two bits here, two bits there. This time he had a greenback on the scarred table, hopeful his two jacks would let him rake in the pot.

He was ready to ride after this hand but doubted Ben would leave. Picking up a whiskey, his third of the night, he downed it, set the glass aside, and studied Ben.

The ranch hand was well on the road to passin' out and had lost most of his pay. Lola Mae had quit dealin' for the night and perched on Ben's knee, eggin' him on.

As Ben flipped two bits onto the table to add to the three coins he'd already squandered on the hand, Lola Mae coaxed, "That's it, honey. Your luck is bound to turn on the next card."

"Yeah, well," Ben slurred, "mebbe there's enough money in that there pot for me to buy Miss Mariah a new rifle." He shook his head in an apparent effort to clear his vision. "If'n I do, she better not get walloped on the head and lose it again."

Except for Horace McCallister, who squinted at Ben with bloodshot eyes, the other men went still.

Lola Mae chided, "Hell, Ben, I thought you might buy me a pretty."

After a moment, Sheriff Tate asked, "What's he talking about, Max?"

Before Max could make up a lie, Horace, not quite as far gone as Ben, flourished his cards. "Call."

Grinning like a she-cat eyein' a chunk of raw beef, Horace sprawled his hand on the table. "Read 'em, boys. I gotcha, Ben. Three twos." He curled his loose-jointed arm around the small pile of money.

Standing behind his twin, Henry McCallister hooted. "Uncross your eyes, Horace. There aren't but two, not three."

"Huh?" Bleary eyed, Horace looked down at the surprisingly pristine cards scattered beneath his arm.

"Sorry," Max said, the last to lay down his hand. He hoped the sheriff would let his question pass about Ben's drunken spiel. "I've got you both. My jacks take that pot."

"Well, damn," Sheriff Tate grumbled. "I thought sure my tens would do it this hand."

He picked up the few coins left in front of him, as did Henry for his brother. A steady-eyed drifter Max didn't know leaned back and thumbed up his hat.

"Time for me to head home," Tate said. "Bessie will be waiting for me." As he stood, he pocketed his money. "Max, tell Ward I'll be out to see him in a day or two."

Oh boy, Max thought, the sheriff was worse'n a bloodhound sniffin' after a criminal. But he was smart enough to wait until he could talk to the right party. Ward might whap Ben a good one to sober him up, so's the young man'd understand the tongue lashin' he'd get for flappin' his gums.

Sure as God made little green apples, folks would lay the blame on the nearby Indians. Didn't matter a toot if they had a hand in Miss Mariah's head bashin'.

But, Max thought resignedly, what else could he do now but nod acknowledgement to Sheriff Tate?

His head now resting on his forearm, Ben snored softly as Max collected his winnings along with Ben's paltry pile of money. He grinned at Lola Mae, who had scooted from Ben's lap just before he passed out.

"I don't think you want him warmin' your bed tonight."

Her amply displayed bosom rose on a sigh above the black lace-trimmed bodice. "Ben Stewart has but few coins left to rub together." She laughed good naturedly. "My fee runs a mite high for a pillow to rest a drunken head on."

Lola Mae eyed the drifter, who had apparently availed himself of a bath before coming to the saloon. When he didn't so much as look up at her interested gaze, she shrugged and sauntered off, her candy-striped skirts sweeping the stained plank floor.

Horace, more than a little worse for drink, too, tried to stand, squinting when his brother lent a shoulder. That left Max to manhandle a soused Ben out to the horses, unless...

Just as he thought to ask, the drifter rose and moseyed around the table. A low-slung gun rode his lean hip, but he seemed friendly enough.

"Need some help with your friend?"

"Obliged."

With the two more or less dragging Ben between them, Max asked, "What's your name?"

"Parks," the man said curtly.

"Parks what?"

"Parks'll do."

Between them, they hoisted Ben into the saddle, where he promptly slid toward the other side. Max grabbed his belt as Parks strode around and loosened Ben's rope. In a few deft loops, he had Ben secured in his saddle.

Max slipped their horses' reins from the rail. As he swung up on his mount, he glanced at Parks, who still stood in the dirt street. "You need work?"

"I might."

"Well, we're 'bout to start brandin' and dippin'. You can hire on for a spell if you're a mind to."

"Who's we?"

Even in the dark, Max could see the man's eerily pale eyes. "My boss, Ward Kelly. I honcho the Broken Spur for 'im."

"I'm paid above stairs tonight. Might look you up tomorrow."

Max saluted, backed his horse, and started for home, leading Ben's mount. *Lord have mercy.* He hoped the man would wait to show up until after Ward Kelly had vented his anger at Ben.

While he didn't often get mad, Ward was a sight to behold once he got wound up.

Sure as God sat on high, if the townsfolk got wind of what had happened, they'd be hankerin' for Ward to do somethin' 'bout the Indians on the ranch. Their fault or not, the Indians'd be blamed for stealin' Miss Mariah's rifle. And for hurtin' her.

Chapter Thirteen

"The word got out in town about somebody stealin' Mariah's rifle. I'm mighty sorry, Sil," Tanner said. "If we're lucky, maybe nobody will come nosin' around askin' questions."

Resignation settled heavily in his chest as Silver Eagle shook his head. "Sheriff Tate no bother ask question, Tanner. Run my people off land." He added grimly, "He try."

Seated on a fallen tree beside the stream, Tanner scooped up a rock and skipped it across the water. "Not if me and Pa have anythin' to say about it. Folks ain't welcome on the Broken Spur if they're lookin' for trouble."

Silver Eagle absently played with the feathers attached to his mount's forelock. The stallion blew, then buried his nose in the water, swallowing several times. When he lifted his head, water dripped from his whiskered muzzle.

Silver Eagle sighed. "Is good my father return from buffalo hunt. Village maybe need all warriors before many suns set."

The morning of the second day Silver Eagle heard cantering hoof beats long before horsemen came into view. He counted one, two...four...ten men as each, one by one, materialized from the woods. Sheriff Tate rode among them. Every warrior in the village who had heard the drumming hooves gathered in the central clearing to await his chief's orders. The womenfolk quickly herded their children into the tipis.

Silver Eagle stood beside his father. When he felt a tug on his sleeve, he glanced over his shoulder. Quiet Bird, eyes enormous in her striking face, motioned a question regarding what was happening. He patted her trembling hand.

"Stay out of sight, *nï nami?*." Then he told a reassuring lie. "All will be well."

She slipped away just as Sheriff Tate dismounted.

Silver Eagle looked from grim face to grim face—Mr. Crabapple, Barney, Elmer Hawkins, Jessup McCallister and his twin sons, Horace and Henry, Carl Pickett, the rancher he had done work for from time to time when things were slow on the Broken Spur. Even Preacher Sandborn was there, leaving two riders Silver Eagle did not know by name. Not a single person from the Broken Spur among them.

He was not surprised to see the McCallister men, even though he had surmised Henry wasn't as disposed to hate Indians as his father. And Horace had always seemed indifferent to him and his people's presence.

More than anyone else, Silver Eagle gazed upon Mr. Pickett with disappointment. The older man's face reddened.

Sheriff Tate removed his hat and spoke directly to Falcon Wing. "Mighty sorry about this, Chief, but we've come to search for a rifle that's gone missing."

Out of the corner of his eye, Silver Eagle saw his father straighten his shoulders. He did not respond to Sheriff Tate.

Silver Eagle spoke up. "Miss Kelly attack mourned by my people, Sheriff. Thank gods she no grievous hurt."

He longed to deny that anyone in the village could be involved in that attack and theft, but in good conscience he could not. His gaze flicked to

Howling Coyote, who lurked on the far side of the clearing. Silver Eagle itched to wipe the smirk off the warrior's face.

Walks the Prairie and Gray Squirrel stood with Howling Coyote, unaware he was the cause of this invasion. All three clasped bows. Behind their shoulders, arrows jutted from quivers.

Sheriff Tate cleared his throat and persisted in addressing Falcon Wing. Like the Kellys, he knew well enough that the Comanche chief understood and spoke the white man's tongue.

Tate also understood the Comanche belief that all whites should leave this land to those who had roamed here since the time of darkness. But because many white men had died claiming this land, Tate and his companions considered it theirs.

"Don't want no trouble, Chief, but you need to know we're prepared to use force if necessary."

Out of the corner of his eye, Silver Eagle saw Quiet Bird crouched in the scrub. As she began crab walking backward, he looked directly at her. What unsettled him, was the determined set of her mouth when she ducked her head, and lifted her chin in a defiant manner. She spun around and leaped away to disappear in the trees.

Silver Eagle's heart constricted. He knew as well as he knew the band was in trouble that his mute sister was headed to the Broken Spur. While she knew the general direction, she did not know exactly where the main ranch was.

He turned back to face the trouble at hand, praying silently that the Spirits would protect Quiet Bird.

****

Mariah wasn't worth the price of a .45 shell today. Seated on the back step, she stared gloomily across the clearing at Pa and Tanner as they exited the barn. Both had been out on the range today, but she had been relegated to grooming horses left in the barn.

She glanced past the barn at a small dust cloud, undoubtedly kicked up by a rider. She watched him approach. Perplexed, she rose when she saw it was Parks and he carried someone. She walked forward and said, "Pa, Tanner, Parks is carrying— Oh, for heaven's sake, it's Quiet Bird!"

Pa and Tanner turned around and faced Parks as he brought his mount to a halt. "This girl bailed off a running horse. Damnedest thing I ever saw."

"What are you doing here, Quiet Bird?" Pa asked.

Before she could respond, Parks said, "Near as I can tell, no broken bones, but she's got a sprained ankle." He slipped his hands beneath her arms and lifted her into Tanner's arms.

"Quiet Bird?" Mariah questioned, anxious to know why she was here. Quiet Bird had never been one to ride a horse. It had to be something dire to have her even attempt it.

The girl signed frantically. Pa grabbed her hands. "Slow down. We can't understand you."

Mariah watched her every move.

First, Quiet Bird clasped the air next to her head, extended the hand toward Pa, and swung back to clamp her hand atop her head. She splayed five fingers against her chest. Next, she bounced her hand up and down. She extended the fingers of both hands, and counted all ten. She extended her arm and sighted down it, and pointed at Mariah.

"Pa, do you understand her?" Mariah asked.

"Jehoshaphat! Near as I can tell, the sheriff and a posse have showed up in the village to search for Mariah's rifle."

"What?" Ma said as she arrived beside Mariah. "Oh, Ward, what is Sheriff Tate thinking?"

"Glory!" Mariah said. "He knows better than

that!"

Max and Samuel walked up behind Tanner.

"Tell that to the neighbors," Tanner said, his voice bitter sounding.

Pa glanced around at everyone, stopping at Parks. "You willin' to ride with us, Parks?"

"And do what? You ain't plannin' to draw against white men, are you?"

"Not unless I have to," Pa said. "Harley Tate is a reasonable man. But I can't say that about all the townsfolk or the neighbors. Them Indians is as peacable as the day is long, and I intend to remind the sheriff about that."

"Yeah, I guess I'll join you. But unless they do somethin' I think is unfittin', I won't be drawin' on the sheriff or his men."

"Fair enough," Pa said, and turned to his hired men. "'Spect y'all will ride along, and Tanner. You take Quiet Bird into the house for your ma and sister to tend."

"I'm going with you, Pa."

"Now, that ain't happenin', daughter."

"It was my rifle that was taken. I—"

"Yep, and it's *my* responsibility to get it back. Besides, it won't be found, so you march yourself into the house and help tend to Quiet Bird."

"Oh, for—" Spinning around, she stomped behind Ma and Tanner. While she knew she wouldn't go against her father's command before the men, she still left Pa with her displeasure evident for all to see.

Chapter Fourteen

"Silas!" Sheriff Tate, his face reddened, took a step toward his quarry, "Take your hands off that woman."

"She was sittin' in her hovel like the Queen o' Sheba." Still clasping her frail arm, Silas Carpenter glared at Wings of a Dove. "She didn't come out like you said."

Tate tipped his hat to the shaman. "She's respected in these parts, Silas. And you damn well know that. Don't make me tell you again."

Silas released her, but gave her a little shove.

Silver Eagle strained against his father's fingers cutting into his upper arm. "He has no right." Silver Eagle gritted his teeth.

"No, he does not, but your *cáco* can take care of herself."

Even so, it was not right. Over the years, Wings of a Dove had helped and even cured many whites of debilitating infirmities, and these men were more than anxious for her attentions when they *needed* her. Silver Eagle did not know this Silas and had no wish to. This white man showed no respect to his elder.

As the stout man ducked back into her tipi to further search, Wings of a Dove gave him a once over that should have leveled him to the ground.

While still a child, when his grandmother had sent that look his way, Silver Eagle worried himself into a sweat, believing netherworld Spirits were about to carry him away to the world of darkness, a world from which he would never return.

"Hey!"

The muffled voice came from *his* tipi. Silver Eagle narrowed his eyes when Crabapple stepped out and waved a rifle.

He tapped a finger on the stock. "Got a *K* engraved here."

Everything happened quickly. His father started, his hand seeking his medicine bag beneath his breechclout. At the same time, Silver Eagle glanced at Howling Coyote, who smirked at him from across the clearing.

And Sheriff Tate paused before him, brow wrinkled. "Silver Eagle, I'd never have believed you'd steal from Miss Kelly."

Barney grabbed his hands from behind and tied his wrists with a piece of rawhide.

He did not resist. What was the point? "I no steal rifle."

"I'd sure like to believe you, Silver Eagle." Tate's blue eyes clouded. "But then, what's it doin' in your lodge? How'd it get there?"

Indeed. His glance flicked to Howling Coyote again, just as Barney gave him a not so gentle shove. "Let's go, Sheriff. We got our man. I'm flummoxed that this here Indian would lay a hand on Miss Mariah. Tarnation, he coulda killed her."

I would cut off my hands before I would harm Mariah.

Silver Eagle gazed at his father for a long moment, then resigned himself to the reality. Not even to champion his own son would his chief break his long-standing refusal to converse with white men. Perhaps rightly so. Sheriff Tate would not believe Falcon Wing's denial any more readily than his own.

"Where's your horse?" Sheriff Tate asked.

Hands tied behind him, Silver Eagle hiked his

chin toward the back of his tipi. Not only his stallion but a hundred or more horses belonging to his father and other tribesmen grazed unfettered.

"Come on, men," Tate ordered. "We're done here."

A tall, lanky fellow asked, "You think they's more rifles here?"

"Two that I know of. Lawful purchases by Ward Kelly. Used for hunting purposes."

At least the sheriff was honoring the arrangement struck long ago by Mr. Kelly with Falcon Wing and the townsfolk.

Startled, the stranger took a backward step. "You're joshin' me. These here redskins have rifles? And you let 'em keep 'em?"

Even though few could understand the words, every warrior in the clearing was tense, including Falcon Wing and Uncle Crow Dog. Silver Eagle kept telling himself that Tate was a fair man. Surely he would see that The People kept their rifles and that Silver Eagle received a fair trial.

He hoped.

Suddenly, pounding hooves shook the ground. Moments later, Mr. Kelly, Tanner, Max Stoddard, Samuel, and the Broken Spur's new hand, Parks, reined their horses to plunging halts.

"What the blazes is goin' on, Harley?" Mr. Kelly shouted.

Looking up at the mounted newcomers, Sheriff Tate's men appeared a bit intimidated by the Kellys and their hands. The posse cast furtive glances at their own horses.

But Harley Tate, not the least bit buffaloed by Ward Kelly, doffed his hat and scratched his head. "Well, we got wind of the attack on your daughter. Figured we'd ride out here to see if one of these Indians stole her rifle."

"You immediately blamed an Indian?" Tanner's

green eyes blazed.

Silver Eagle suppressed a smile. Tanner Kelly was nothing if not loyal to him and his people.

"No, I didn't." Tate clamped his hat back on sweat-soaked gray hair. "Figured we'd just come by here to check. Me and the boys were heading to McCallister's spread and then on over to Pickett's place. Ever'body has recent hires. They all need to be questioned."

"I'll just bet," Tanner challenged. "And you can explain why you bypassed the Broken Spur?"

"Son." Sober faced, Mr. Kelly shook his head.

Tate ignored Tanner's leading question and motioned to Crabapple. "Hand it here." He grabbed the rifle from the saloon owner and held it high, so Tanner and his father could see it clearly.

"This belong to Miss Kelly?"

"Jehoshaphat! Where'd you get that?"

"Sorry to say, we found it in Silver Eagle's lodge."

Mr. Kelly pinned Silver Eagle with disbelieving eyes. His heart warmed, but not for long.

His boss scowled. "How'd my girl's rifle get in your lodge, Silver Eagle?"

He shrugged, choosing to remain quiet. As sure as the sun would set on Mother Earth this day, Sheriff Tate would take him to the white man's jail no matter what he said.

"Oh, for Christ's sake!" Tanner dismounted. He ripped the rifle from the sheriff's hand and pushed it toward Silver Eagle. "Tell 'em you don't know how the devil it got there. 'Cause you don't! You were with me."

"All morning?" Tate asked.

At Tanner's hesitation, Tate said, "That's what I thought. Until we sort this out, Tanner, we'll just be taking Silver Eagle to jail."

It helped that Tanner believed in him

unconditionally, but not one of the men who rode with the sheriff today would. Not without evidence otherwise. The problem was, how would he prove Howling Coyote's guilt?

Still, he said nothing. His words would fall on deaf ears. The circuit judge would hold a hearing. Until then... He closed his eyes briefly. How would he survive in a cell?

For the first time, his heart wavered with doubt. Would he be able to convince the good sheriff of his innocence?

****

"What do you mean the sheriff took Silver Eagle to jail?" Faced off in the kitchen, Mariah flipped an indignant glance from her father to her brother. "You let Sheriff Tate take Silver Eagle from his village? I can't believe—"

"Climb down off your high horse, daughter. We don't like it either, but the fact is your rifle was found in his lodge."

"That's—"

"Knock it off, sis. We couldn't interfere with the sheriff doin' his job."

Fists planted on her hips, Mariah *tsk*ed and glanced at her mother seated at the kitchen table. "Can you believe this? Silver Eagle would no more bonk me on the head and steal my rifle than would Tanner."

"Mariah." Her father's long suffering tone insisted on forbearance. "Under the circumstances, Harley had no choice but to arrest Silver Eagle." When she opened her mouth, he whipped up a forestalling hand. "As soon as he gets it straightened out, Silver Eagle will be released."

"Released, schlemeased! Pa, don't you know how difficult, how soul shattering being locked behind bars will be for him? It's like...like..." She searched for the right words. "Like capturing an eagle in your hands!"

Tanner squeezed her shoulder, but she was having none of it. She batted his hand away.

"Pa," she beseeched, "go talk to Sheriff Tate. Convince him that Silver Eagle won't run off. Dear God, you've got to get him out of that jail."

"Stop, Mariah. Just stop." Her mother beckoned and pulled out a chair. "Come here. Sit down, and cool down, too. Outrage won't help Silver Eagle."

Tanner swept his hand toward the chair in invitation. "Yeah, sit and talk it out with Ma. God knows, you won't listen to me or Pa."

As she took the chair, he said, "All this yellin' and carryin' on will only upset Quiet Bird. Is she restin' in Mariah's room?"

"She wanted to go home," Ma said. "When Ben got back he harnessed the buggy and drove her."

"We didn't see 'em on the trail."

Ma smiled at Tanner. "You rode home on the regular trail? That would be a first."

He grinned sheepishly. "We cut through the woods."

"Ma," Mariah broke in impatiently, "can't we all head into town? Talk to Sheriff Tate? There's got to be something we can do to help Silver Eagle."

"Short of breaking him out? No, hon." She laid her fingers on Mariah's arm. "I know this will be upsetting for Silver Eagle, but I also know he's a strong man. He'll survive."

Her father brushed a wide hand over Mariah's hair. "Harley's probably already sent word that he needs Judge Rogers in town. We just have to hope he'll be here soon."

Eyes bleak, Mariah shook her head. "No telling how long until Judge Rogers gets here from," she flipped her hand, "wherever." Though it was pointless, she cried, "He could be on the moon, for all we know."

****

Two hours later, still awake and tossing, Mariah sat up and listened. All was quiet and had been for a while. Dark as a cave outside with no moon. She slid carefully from bed, stilling when the springs protested, the squeak sounding like a thunderclap in the stillness. She stood and listened again. The house remained quiet.

She donned a clean shirtwaist and trousers and pulled on socks. Carrying her boots, she tiptoed down the hall to the kitchen, where she collected her jacket.

Barely breathing, she inched open the back door. After one protest from the hinges, she squeezed through. Sliding her arms into the jacket, she sat on the step to tug on her tall boots.

Eyes adjusted to night-dark grays and black, she found all the needed tack and in short order had Nutmeg saddled and walked from the barn. She dared not pound away for fear someone would hear. When she figured she'd walked far enough from the house to ride without alerting anyone, she mounted and set Nutmeg to a collected canter.

It was a fairly straight shot to Burnett Station, and even though it was dark, her night vision adjusted quickly enough. The well-used dirt track that passed for a road was fairly smooth and actually a bit easier to see than tacking up inside the barn had been. There was no real danger.

Nearing town, not certain exactly how late it was, she slowed and swung behind the church. Few lantern-lit windows cast but feeble light onto the town's only street. Though the back of Crabapple's saloon stood dark, raucous laughter and the tinkle of a badly out of tune piano disturbed the night.

Thankfully, the racket covered Nutmeg's plodding hooves. She dismounted, palmed the reins, and approached the lone window at the back of the jail. It looked out over a dusty clearing. Long ago, Sheriff Tate had cleared away the brush where culprits bent on mischief might hide.

"What you do here, woman?" a quiet voice asked. The voice, the man sent chills of anticipation drifting through her. Had since his kiss.

Seeing his fingers wrapped tight around the window bars, her heart ached for his spirit chained behind iron bars and solid wood walls.

"I came to help you escape from this dadgum jail," she whispered. "I can't believe you let them lock you up."

She had to go up on her toes and crane her neck to see past him into the dark cell. Beyond him, a short hall the length of two facing cells led to a closed door that opened into the front office. Though smaller than the Broken Spur's bunkhouse, the structure was sturdily built.

Silver Eagle grimaced. "If accept harebrained idea, how expect carry out scheme?" He eased his fingers from the bars and patted them. "These no move."

"It's not harebrained!" Having spoke louder than she'd intended, Mariah quieted. "Is anyone in the office?"

He nodded. "One man. Not know his name."

"You think he's asleep?"

He shook his head. "Not know. He no snore if that what you ask."

Itchy from nervous tension, Mariah glanced from side to side. Glory, if someone caught her here... Didn't bear thinking about.

"You shouldn't be in there!"

He shrugged. "I am. Will be until white man's judge come. Perhaps no get out even then."

She didn't buy his nonchalance for one blamed minute. His white-knuckled grasp told the true tale. Anxiety gnawed at his vitals.

Crying would do no good. She bit her lip. What had she thought to accomplish by coming? Even if she could figure a way to get Silver Eagle out of that cell, he'd be a fugitive from the law. And if she helped him, she'd certainly be a fugitive, too.

She gave herself a mental shake. Anything was possible. Even though jail breaking was a federal offense, if caught, at least she'd get a fair hearing. She might be able to talk her way out of going to jail. But Silver Eagle... No fair hearing was assured for him. If she were a gambler, she'd bet against it.

"Go home," he said, interrupting her muddled thoughts.

She gazed into his face, unable to read the depths of his eyes. Those two words sounded rough with hidden emotion.

What emotion?

"Silver Eagle—"

"Go." He jutted his chin forward. "Before make situation worse."

That stung.

Without warning, he reached between the bars, curled his fingers around her nape, and pulled her close. His warm lips crushed hers in a kiss that sent butterflies swarming into her stomach.

Releasing her, his fingers trailed across her cheek. He pressed his thumb against her bottom lip. When her lips parted, his finger slipped inside and swept across her tongue.

Startled, she watched him rub the moist finger across his own lips. Then he licked them and smiled.

"Taste good. Keep with me."

Heat shot through her, all the way to her core.

He stepped back. "Go." He turned his back and disappeared below the window.

Dropping down on her heels, Mariah leaned her forehead against the rough planking and drew in deep breaths. This must be what hot lust felt like.

She was sure smoke curled skyward from the top of her head.

She searched the darkness beyond the bars, and whispered, "Silver Eagle?"

Blast him to Hades. He refused to answer. Why had his voice sounded so raw? His kiss... Her lips still tingled.

She wanted more.

Chapter Fifteen

Hours later, never having returned to bed, Mariah sat atop a corral fence and watched the sun rise. Her heart bled when she thought of Silver Eagle cooped up in that small cell, its solitary window facing northwest. He couldn't see the sun rise over this land that he loved as much as she did.

She put fingers to her mouth and relived the sensations Silver Eagle had awakened in her. Somehow it made her feel close to him.

When boots crunched on the ground, she didn't turn around. Instead, she quickly rubbed a hand over her eyes. Earlier, she'd felt something on her cheek, and when she brushed at it, discovered a tear. She hadn't even realized she was crying.

"Mariah?"

She heard bewilderment in Tanner's voice.

"What the *H* you doin' out here this time of day? Squirt ain't even out of bed yet."

Despite herself, Mariah chuckled. "One of these days you're going to slip and call Ma that in her hearing. She'll pin back your ears."

Tanner shrugged and hoisted himself up beside her. He curled his boot toes behind a fence rung as Mariah's were, and balanced next to her.

"He can't see the sun come up," she said, ignoring his question.

"I know."

That's all he said. All he needed to say. Perfectly in tune with her sorrow, probably much like his own. Silver Eagle was as much a brother to Tanner as if they had come from the same womb.

She cast him a sidelong glance, then returned her intense gaze to Father Sun, as Silver Eagle called it. Golden rays raced across the heavens ahead of its face peeking over the horizon.

"Glory, Tanner, we've got to get him out of there."

"We will, as soon as Judge Rogers gets to town. Pa said Sheriff Tate wired the judge in Austin, Waco, San Antonio, Houston and Fort Worth. He's bound to be in one of those places."

"I mean now," she said, unable to keep testiness from her voice. "It could be days before—"

"And it could be tomorrow if Judge Rogers is makin' his rounds."

"If!" She frowned. "Dadburnit, Tanner, can't you help me get him out today? Tonight?"

"Come on, sis, have a heart. You know I'd do anything for Silver Eagle—within reason. But I ain't breakin' the law. He wouldn't expect me to."

She sucked in a shaky breath. "I know. I don't either, not really. It's just that..." Defeat crowded her mind. "Glory, it's so hard to see him behind those bars."

"See him." Tanner scowled. "When did you see him?"

That wasn't smart.

When she failed to answer, did her best to ignore the query, Tanner leaned to look beneath her ducked head. "You rode into town alone. Didn't you?"

Rather than answer, she blew out a breath and nodded.

"Honest to God, Mariah, if you don't watch yourself, Pa will lock you up tighter'n Silver Eagle."

"But we have to *do* something. Now, Tanner, not days, maybe weeks from now! Dang it, you know what will happen if Silver Eagle ends up in prison."

The statement required nothing from her

brother, and he didn't respond. Tanner's imagination was as vivid as hers. Both knew death would be Silver Eagle's escape. And he'd undoubtedly welcome it.

Brooding, Mariah stared into the brightening day, envisioning that God-be-damned moment when Silver Eagle must have allowed Sheriff Tate to lead him away.

She wished to heaven she'd been there. Surely Tanner and Pa had known what was coming, as had Falcon Wing.

Seated beside her, Tanner gazed into the distance, his thumb rubbing back and forth on a scabbed knuckle. She wondered if he'd abide by Pa's peace-at-any-price restraint. Allow himself to hear those bars clang shut.

Probably not.

While yet a whippersnapper in Pa's eyes, Tanner had scrapped and played often in the Indian village, and he'd picked up a lot of Comanche. Maybe she could talk him into asking Silver Eagle's father—

A door slammed.

Before she could discuss this further, Tanner unhooked his feet and jumped to the ground. He turned to her and gripped the rail either side of her hips. "We can best serve Sil by doin' our jobs, sis. You want to ride with me today?"

His green eyes mirrored her own sorrow-shot heart, but she nodded and let it go for now.

"Guess you're right, but it's..." Her voice hitched. "Well, yes, I'll watch your back today."

Tanner clasped her around the waist and lifted her down. He pulled her into a hug. "It'll be all right, sis. It's got to be."

****

When Tanner failed to appear for supper that evening, Mariah noticed her mother frowning at his empty chair.

"You worked with your brother today. Where's he gotten off to?"

Though they'd worked together most of the day, after they returned home late this afternoon Tanner had disappeared. She hoped he was talking to Silver Eagle's folks right now, but she chose to play dumb, fearing Pa's reaction. Maybe he wouldn't be upset, but she was taking no chances.

Unable to look her mother in the eye while uttering a bald-faced lie, she busied herself forking a slice of the rare treat, pork, onto her plate. "Uh, I don't know, Ma. I finished settling Nutmeg while Tanner was still discussing something with Max. He should be here shortly, I'd think."

She felt her mother's scrutiny but refused to look up. Instead, she plopped a huge daub of mashed potatoes on her plate and smothered it in gravy. Lord, she loved this stuff.

If she didn't stop gorging on Ma's cooking every night of the world, Nutmeg would soon protest the tub of lard on her back. Her evasion worked. Ma turned to Pa to discuss his day's activities. Which left Mariah to sink back into the funk she'd dwelt in the live-long day.

As soon as they finished eating, she jumped up and helped her mother clear the table. Once she had dried and put away the last pan, Mariah excused herself and went to her room. No way could she sit in the parlor and carry on pleasant conversation with her parents. Uh-uh.

She visualized Silver Eagle peering out through the bars. God in heaven, how his heart must ache. His heart and his spirit should soar free like the wind. Instead, they were locked behind bars.

God, how could You allow Sheriff Tate to capture an eagle?

****

147

For three days Mariah worked with her brother and consoled herself with the fact that Tanner had spoken with Silver Eagle's menfolk. Though Tanner couldn't assure her the Chief would act on his plea, she prayed Falcon Wing would find the culprit who'd stolen her rifle. Preferably someone outside the camp.

She didn't give a rip about the bump on her head. Truth be told, the townsfolk didn't either. It was the stolen rifle they would not abide. If evidence against the real thief was not found, Judge Rogers would have no choice but to send Silver Eagle to prison.

That meant Arizona.

Mariah shivered at thoughts she couldn't forestall of all the stories that had circulated over the years about that hellhole in the middle of nowhere. No matter how long the sentence, few men survived incarceration there.

As Mariah crawled out of troubled sleep the fourth morning Silver Eagle had been locked up, she wondered if she dared sneak into town again. That thought had barely flitted through her mind when a knock sounded on her door. Her mother walked right in without waiting for leave to do so.

Mariah frowned at the determined expression on Ma's face. Quickly, she scanned through the last few days. Hmm. She couldn't think of a thing she had done to upset or anger her mother. At least nothing that Ma knew about.

Her mother shut the door and dragged the chair from the corner of the room to beside Mariah's bed. Ma seated herself on the quilted cushion she'd made so long ago and pinned Mariah with troubled eyes.

"We need an undisturbed talk, hon. Better now than later, I'm thinking, although I may already be too late." She jerked up her chin. "Be that as it may, I'm saying my piece."

Mariah leaned against the headboard, apprehension shortening her breath. "What's wrong, Ma?"

"I hope nothing."

Mariah waited for her mother to continue.

"Hon, infatuation with Silver Eagle will find you a broken heart. For both of you if Silver Eagle has feelings for you as well."

"Ma, what makes you think—"

Her mother raised an admonishing finger. "Stop right there. I have eyes in my head. I see how you follow your brother around. It's not necessarily to help him out on the range."

"But I do want to help Tanner. Besides, I think I should keep an eye on him now that Silver Eagle is locked up."

"My hearing is fine, too, Mariah. Your anguish for that young man comes through in your speech."

"He's behind bars! For something he didn't do!" She leaned forward. "That's got to be agony for a man like Silver Eagle." Eyes burning bright, she asked, "Don't you care? Don't you want to see him free?"

"You know I do. And my regard for Silver Eagle and his people began long before you were born, young lady. You can't evade my concerns by making me the guilty party."

"Your concerns are misplaced." Mariah flopped back against the headboard and crossed her arms over her chest.

Ma's lips lifted in a smile. "Your behavior is quite similar to your actions as a child. Though times change, amazingly, people more or less stay the same."

She chose not to respond, and Ma placed her hand on Mariah's leg covered by the lone star quilt she'd made for Mariah. She had one for Tanner, too.

In fact, she'd saved Tanner's and Mariah's baby

clothes she'd painstakingly made. God knew Mariah would be all thumbs if she tried to sew a dress or little trousers.

"Mariah, I'm not sure what your father would do if he got wind of your infatuation with Silver Eagle."

"Oh, Ma, you're making a mountain out of a prairie dog's hill."

She sat back and contemplated Mariah. "Lord, girl, you're headed for more heartache than you can fathom. Does Silver Eagle return your regard?"

Mariah ducked her head and fiddled with her sleeves. "I'm not sure."

"Lord help us! The truth, young lady. Have you and Silver Eagle engaged in—inappropriate behavior?"

"What's inappropriate?"

"Mariah!"

"All right!" She lifted her chin. "If you mean have we slept together, then, no. Silver Eagle would never do such a thing unless we were married."

"And that isn't about to happen." Ma sighed. "Mariah, your phrasing intimates that if he asked you'd sleep with him."

Her cheeks warmed. Ma was certainly hitting on Mariah's desire. Though she didn't respond, her mother wasn't finished.

"Hon, before you go past the point of no return, think about Silver Eagle. Think about his parents, his grandmother. I'm sure they would be alarmed for Silver Eagle and you, too." She leaned forward and cupped the side of Mariah's face. "Please, think before you act."

"I told you, Ma. Silver Eagle would never do anything that might hurt me."

"Sarah!" Pa called. "Where are you?"

She gave Mariah's cheek a caress, rose, and returned the chair to the corner. Opening the door, she said, "Coming, Ward."

"Ma." Mariah stopped her as she started into the hallway.

"Don't worry. I know what everyone would say. I'll be careful. Besides," she said with a wry smile, "I don't know that Silver Eagle cares for me. Not the way you mean."

As her mother closed the door, Mariah allowed, yes, he'd kissed her. But she'd bet Tanner kissed willing women whenever the opportunity arose. Were Indians any different? Not likely.

As much as she wanted to see Silver Eagle, Mariah would force herself to stay away from town. If she were caught sneaking in to see him, there'd be hell to pay. And the chaos that ensued would not only come from her folks.

Besides, her mother had raised a niggling question. What *did* Silver Eagle really think of her? Was this *infatuation*, to use Ma's description, one sided?

She touched fingertips to her lips. Might help if she were more experienced in kissing. Maybe then she'd know if his kisses were as soul-rocking for him as they had been for her. *Intimacy with Silver Eagle is unlikely to happen—ever.*

Ma was right. If Pa ever found out how she felt, he'd go off like a shooting star. It would be awe inspiring, all right, but not of the glorious kind.

Knock, knock.

Dadburnit. Was her room the Baltimore and Ohio Station this morning?

"Sis? You still in there?"

"Yes. Come in." She pulled the cover up to her waist.

Tanner pushed open the door, but rather than walk in, he propped a shoulder on the doorjamb. "Hey, lazy bones, you gonna stay abed all day?"

She beckoned. "Come in, and shut the door."

He quirked his mouth as if irritated but did as

she bid. "What?"

"I haven't been able to get you alone for days, but I know you, brother dear. You went to the village. What did Falcon Wing and Wings of a Dove say? Are they going to investigate the charge against Silver Eagle?"

He rolled his hat around by the brim. "I spoke with Falcon Wing and Crow Dog. Never saw Wings of a Dove. They didn't say anythin'." He shrugged. "Never do. I told them what I thought needed doin', but your guess is as good as mine if they'll do anythin' about it."

"He's their kin, Tanner. Surely they won't let him go to prison without a fight."

He scowled. "Let's hope not. But if Pa doesn't step in, I doubt the Chief will."

"Tanner—"

He put up a hand. "Look, Mariah, you know how careful Pa is about keepin' his word to the tribe. Falcon Wing's no different. He promised Pa there'd be no trouble, and by gum, he's kept that promise."

"Well, he didn't start this. Sheriff Tate did by going out there and hauling Silver Eagle off to jail."

"Actually, the varmint that took your rifle did." He sighed and tunneled fingers through his hair. "Mariah, like it or not, we have to play this out. That's what Silver Eagle wants, and that's what his people need."

****

Seated on the cot, back propped against the wall, Silver Eagle clamped down on the unfamiliar claustrophobia gripping his guts more tightly with each passing day. From the first, Sheriff Tate had treated him with a measure of respect. Even so, after they arrived at the jail, Silver Eagle had been surprised.

"I'm mighty sorry about this, Silver Eagle." Although Tate apologized, he'd clamped leg shackles on him and only then removed the rawhide from his wrists. "If I don't treat you like all the other inmates I've held in my jail, folks will question my authority."

Jaw set, he'd continued, "I've always had the town behind me for the way I handle my job. Sure as hell don't want to lose their goodwill now." He shrugged. "Never know when folks will take the law into their own hands."

Silver Eagle understood. Necktie party. Still, none of it made the shackles any easier to endure.

Thankfully, Mariah Kelly had not realized he was chained, he'd moved his feet as little as possible while she stood tantalizingly close on the other side of the window bars.

Thoughts wandering, he touched his fingers to his lips, ran his tongue over them. He could still feel hers, soft and responsive beneath his. Could still taste the sweetness. He lowered his hand to his lap and stared at his fingers. Mere illusion, yet quite real.

He heard the rumble of voices in the front office from behind the closed door. Two, no, three men. His heart stuttered. Perhaps the judge had finally arrived. His fate might only be a few hours away.

He craned his neck to gaze at the bars above the cot. Would the Spirits condemn him to live the rest of his days on Mother Earth behind such as those? He shuddered.

Spirits, I would rather hang.

The door opened. Sheriff Tate and an officious-looking man strode in. Though thin and as weathered as a defoliated tree limb, the stranger wore one of the well-cut suits some white men favored. His stiff collar reminded Silver Eagle of the noose that might circle his own neck before long.

"Silver Eagle, this here is Judge Rogers. He's gonna preside over your hearing."

Eyes as dark as his own gave Silver Eagle a thorough once over, from the feather in his hair down to the moccasins on his feet. "You've landed yourself in a passel of trouble, young man."

Silver Eagle wanted to say, no, he had not gotten himself into this situation. But his word would not convince white men otherwise. Likewise, accusing Howling Coyote would gain him nothing.

So that is what he said—nothing; he merely returned the judge's assessing look.

Rogers turned to the sheriff. "Does he understand English so that I can begin proceedings tomorrow?"

"Sure. He works for Ward Kelly on the Silver Spur."

"Ward Kelly," the judge said thoughtfully. "Seems I remember him from somewhere."

"Maybe," Tate said. "He's a mighty fine man." The sheriff gave Silver Eagle a meaningful glance. "Ward doesn't give his friendship lightly. Only to those he trusts."

The judge frowned at Tate and gestured to Silver Eagle. "You saying there's some mistake here?"

Silver Eagle stared at the sheriff. Was it possible the man thought him innocent? Of course, finding the rifle in his tipi was a compelling argument.

"I ain't saying anything. Just want the hearing to be fair."

"You doubting I'll conduct an impartial court, Sheriff?" the judge said testily.

Tate harrumphed. "Don't put words in my mouth."

As Silver Eagle listened to the exchange, he did not think the hearing boded well for him. Not well at all.

"Tomorrow might be a little too soon to get all

the parties rounded up, Judge. How about the day after?"

Two more nights behind bars, Silver Eagle thought. And then only time would tell if there would be an endless sameness to his days.

If he would even exist on Mother Earth.

Chapter Sixteen

The only place in Burnett Station large enough to accommodate the crowd gathered for the proceedings was the saloon. Ironic, Mariah thought. It was bigger than the town's one and only church.

Just proved where folks' priorities lay. Some folks, anyway, she thought dourly, and wished with all her heart that Silver Eagle's nightmare were over. That he was on his way back to his village.

Seated in the first row of chairs in the saloon, Mariah scanned the smiling faces, heard the occasional laugh. This hearing to decide a man's fate, an incredible man's fate, provided entertainment for them.

Pa, with Ma beside him, sat in the chair closest to the center aisle. Her mother and brother flanked her. Max had wanted to be here, too, but someone had to keep things working smoothly at the ranch. Nervous, Mariah unconsciously picked at the cuticle on one thumb.

Tanner clamped a hand over hers. "Stop it," he ordered softly. "You're makin' me nuts with your fidgetin'."

Mr. Curtis, one of the town's leading citizens, had been picked to serve at the judge's pleasure. He stood at the back door of the saloon and directed in a loud voice, "Ever'body get up."

Chairs creaked and boots scraped on the plank floor as folks came to their feet. Judge Rogers strutted in carrying a gavel and a black book.

Bible, Mariah thought. The magistrate could

pass for a preacher in his severe black suit. But if he intended all who spoke to place a hand on the Book and swear to be truthful, she figured more trouble brewed. She doubted Silver Eagle would. He didn't believe in the white man's God, but held his own gods close to his heart.

Tears pricked behind her eyes, and her throat constricted when Silver Eagle proudly strode in. Into the wolf's den. Head high, hands tied before him, his fierce gaze unerringly locked on hers.

The sheriff followed him in and caught his arm before Silver Eagle got too far ahead of him. "Over here." He steered his prisoner to one of two chairs set behind a small table, cattycorner to the audience.

Everyone remained standing until Judge Rogers seated himself behind a longer table that faced the crowd.

"Sit," he ordered shortly.

Collectively, all sank into their seats, a murmur of voices passing through the crowd like a wave.

It was then Mariah noticed another chair at the other end of the judge's makeshift bench. The witness chair.

Judge Rogers cleared his throat. "Mr. Curtis, would you now call six of Silver Eagle's peers to serve on the jury?"

Mariah started. "Peers?" she blurted, though she hadn't intended to voice the question aloud. Ducking her head, she whispered to Tanner, "What peers? He doesn't have any here. His people are—"

"Young lady!"

She glanced up. The judge glared at her, every eye trained on her. She blinked, astonished at the volume of the voice resounding from such a narrow chest. "Uh, are you speaking to me?"

"You want to share with this court what's so all-fired important that you'd interrupt these proceedings?"

"She didn't mean to—"

Mariah jabbed Tanner in the side with her elbow. "Yes, I did!"

"Daughter," her father warned as Judge Rogers pounded the table once with his gavel.

"Order!" His gimlet stare pinned each Kelly before continuing. "What were you saying?"

"I just wondered, aloud, whether—"

"Stand at your seat so everyone can hear you."

Brow creased, she looked first at her mother, then at Tanner. "Is his hearing bad?"

"Are you the Kelly girl?" the judge asked, color deepening in his face.

"Yes. Mariah Kelly."

"Well then, why don't you come up here and take the witness seat now rather than later?"

Tanner whispered, "You've stepped in a pile of shit now, Mariah."

She scowled at her brother, then rose and glanced at Silver Eagle as she walked to the ladder-back chair.

Astonishingly, a faint smile turned up a corner of Silver Eagle's mouth. She gave him a quick nod and squared her shoulders.

To appease Ma, who'd insisted she wear a skirt today, she had donned a pale green day dress that she thought she'd never have to wear again after escaping the East. And since she really did know how to conduct herself like a prim and proper lady, she sank decorously onto the chair and made a production of straightening her skirts. Which, thankfully, hid her boots. Under no circumstances would she ever again wear those ghastly, uncomfortable high-button shoes.

"Mr. Curtis, if you please." The judge handed Andy Curtis the Bible.

"Place your right hand—"

"Mr. Curtis," Rogers interrupted, "a witness

must stand to swear the oath."

Without thinking, Mariah said, "But I just got seated."

"And quite a performance it was," the judge said dryly. He waved a dismissive hand, silencing a few titters. "Nevertheless, you'll stand to swear before Almighty God, Miss Kelly."

"Oh, all right." She sprang up and laid her hand on the Bible. "I swear to tell the whole truth, nothing but the truth, so help me God." This time she plopped down.

Mr. Curtis looked nonplussed. "Judge Rogers, wasn't I supposed to ask her if she—"

"Never mind. Just sit down."

Mariah's gaze found Silver Eagle again. Glory be, he was actually smiling. Cheekily, she winked at him, and Tanner groaned.

"Miss Kelly, if I may have your attention?"

She swiveled her head, tucking stray hair behind her ear as she did. Thank God she had won the war about not wearing a bonnet. "Yes, sir?"

The judge looked away for a moment. "Sheriff, bring the rifle in question here, please."

Dutifully, the lawman laid it on the table. The judge promptly picked it up for closer inspection. "A fine piece," he said absently, before turning his attention to Mariah. "Is this your rifle?"

Mariah leaned over so she could see the stock. "Yes, sir. Pa gave it to me when I was, oh, ten years old, I think." She cast a quick smile at her parent. "To add to the surprise, he had that *K* engraved on the stock."

"Have you ever had cause to fire it?"

"What does that have to do with anything?"

Twitters and a few chuckles erupted. Mariah scowled at the gathering.

The judge sighed. "Miss Kelly, I'll ask the questions. You'll answer them."

"Well, if you insist. But I still don't know what me firing my rifle has to do with why we're here today."

"Humor me," the judge said.

"Then, yes, I have. I'm a darn good shot, too."

"Your language, Miss Kelly."

She gazed at the judge, utterly confused. "What about it?"

"I don't allow swearing in my court, missy."

Mariah's eyes rounded. "Swear... You mean 'darn'? Oh, for heaven's sake. That's not swearing. If you want swearing—"

"Mariah!" her father admonished from his seat.

She swiveled to him. "What?" Then she saw all the spectators' smiles and heard the chuckling.

"Miss Kelly," the judge said, "don't say anything except to answer my questions. Do you think you can you manage that?"

"Sure. Be happy to."

He rolled his eyes, then pounded the gavel once again for quiet. "Miss Kelly, you do not have to understand why I ask these question. You *do* have to answer them."

"I said I would." She turned to her father. "Didn't I just say that, Pa?"

Guffaws and shrieks of laughter made a shambles of the makeshift courtroom. Judge Rogers propped his elbow on the table and buried his forehead in his hand.

Glory. I've done it now. Mariah looked around at all the townsfolk she knew and those she didn't. Pa's face was red, Ma looked dazed and Tanner... Well, hardly a surprise, mangy-hided Tanner laughed right along with everyone else.

She frowned. No. Tanner was laughing at *her*. She surely couldn't lump him together with the townsfolk. So many seemed to look upon these proceedings as nothing more than a show. A man's life was at stake, and yet they clamored for entertainment.

Lastly, Mariah sought Silver Eagle. He sat impassive as a stone, watching her. But amusement glinted in the depths of his dark, dark eyes. She spread her hands, shrugged and mouthed, *What is so all-fired funny?*

He wagged his head, mouth twitching.

More laughter ensued from those who had seen her silent question.

Bang, bang, bang!

Mariah jumped as the gavel thumped on the table.

"Order! Order!"

It took several minutes for the judge to regain control. Once he had, he regarded Mariah sternly.

Before he could say a word, she raised her hand as if wanting the teacher to call upon her. "Sir, before you get back to your questions, I'd really like to tell you what I said earlier to my brother. I think it's kind of important."

"Why am I not surprised?"

"What do you mean?"

"I *mean*, Miss Kelly, we are *not* going off on another merry-go-round of your making. Not in my court. Not again! But I will listen to what you wanted to say. At the *beginning*, if you please."

"Peers."

He scowled. "What about them?"

"None of Silver Eagle's are here." She swept her arm. "No Indians."

Incredulous, Rogers asked, "Indians?"

"Well, yes, sir. Silver Eagle is a Comanche. There are none here to sit on his jury. Correct me if I'm wrong, but I believe we're supposed to have *peers* judging us when we are accused of a crime?"

Judge Rogers sat back and blew out a breath.

Mariah stressed her point before he could say a

word. "That's what you called for, sir. Six of Silver Eagle's *peers.*"

Judge Rogers cleared his throat and leaned forward. "Mr. Kelly, was she like this before she was hit on the head?"

"Like what?"

The official waved a dismissive hand. "Never mind. Do you understand Texas law and the law of these United States?"

Pa straightened. He frowned before answering. "I believe I do. Yes."

Rogers sighed. "Well then, would you escort your daughter from this court and explain the law to her? And while you're at it, be sure she understands she can't disrupt a court of law."

Surprisingly, her father sat still for a long moment before he spoke. "Actually, Judge, Mariah might be right. Silver Eagle has no peers in this room."

"Mr. Kelly!"

Her father raised a confrontational hand. "I paid a bundle of hard earned cash to send my girl to a young ladies' school in Maryland. They taught her right well. You saw for yourself how well she can..." He looked at her ma. "Sarah, what's that word?"

"Comport. I think *comport* is what you want to say, Ward."

He swung back to the judge. "That's it. My girl comports herself right well. Her ma taught her some common sense, and I'm thinkin' she prob'ly learned a thing or two about the law while she was studyin' in that school."

"Stop! Stop right there, Mr. Kelly. You and—" He threw a telling glance at Mariah. "She may know *something* of the law, but here in Texas, Indians do not serve on juries. In fact, they don't serve on juries anywhere in these United States. So either direct your daughter to stop disrupting these proceedings and simply answer my questions, or you may take your entire family from my court."

Mariah held her breath while her pa assessed the judge. And when he spoke, she wanted to shout her approval. 'Cause Pa was right as a badly needed soaking rain.

"I take it you ain't been blessed with a daughter, Judge Rogers." He went on, even in the face of the judge's scowl. "I *am* blessed with one, and she's got a good mind of her own. *You* can explain to her about your rules for this farce. I'm confident she'll understand you."

Mariah smiled at this man she loved unconditionally. With a that's-telling-him nod, she turned her attention to the judge.

He had put the noose around his own neck, and then Pa had tightened it, neat as could be. The official would either have to back down from his ultimatum or bar the Kellys from the court. How in blazes could he do the latter? The jury needed to hear her and Tanner's testimony.

Rather than admit Ward Kelly had him between a rattler and a cactus thorn, Judge Rogers leveled a quelling look at her. "Young lady, take your seat beside your mother. Remember that you are still under oath." Looking none too happy at the prospect, he added, "I will call on you again when necessary."

"But I didn't—"

"Return to your chair."

Mariah rose and walked toward her seat. On the way, her back to the judge, she scrunched her eyes and stuck out her tongue for Tanner's benefit.

Not only he but all the spectators who saw her erupted into laughter. It wasn't until she turned and sat that she saw Judge Rogers' mottled face. He used his favored gavel with enough force to send a nail through wood, or *her* head. *Bang, bang, bang!*

"Order! I'll have order, or I'll clear this court!"

Chapter Seventeen

Grieving, Wings of a Dove gazed off to the west. Behind the white man's barred walls her grandson was dying a slow death. Could he see Father Sun's face? Could he watch hawks and hear birds sing?

Before her tipi, seated upon a blanket in front of the small fire she had kindled as homage to Father Sun, Wings of a Dove passed a wrinkled hand over her eyes. Eyes dimmed by many suns. Then she picked up the eagle feather lying beside her and waved it over the smoke curling skyward.

Voice just above a whisper and in cadence with a drumbeat from somewhere in the village, she prayed, "Hear me, Father Sun, Mother Earth, Spirit of the Wolf, of the Buffalo. All living things, hear me. Spare Silver Eagle that he might walk free once more, that the future I have seen for him is indeed truth."

She fanned the feather back and forth, back and forth and repeated her chant. Eyes closed, she inhaled deeply of the smoke. Long moments passed before she laid the feather aside and raised both arms to the sky. "Hear me, Great Father of the skies. I beseech you, send Silver Eagle home to me."

****

It was dark, the drums long since silenced when Falcon Wing approached. "You should seek your blankets, *nï pia*. The night grows damp."

"I will, *nï tua?*." She nodded, not ready to retire. "Have you heard anything from the white man called Kelly?"

"The young one came here an hour past. *Nï tua?* is once again locked up for the night. Today, the important man who wears the black suit decided nothing."

"Sit, *nï tua?*."

Her son sank onto the edge of her blanket, and drew his own buffalo robe closer.

"You have searched our brethrens' tipis?"

He shook his head. "How can I justify such an act? There is no evidence to incriminate another. The white girl's rifle in Silver Eagle's lodge tells the tale."

"Bah!" She dismissed the accusation with a quick wave of her skeletal hand. "For the white man, perhaps. Surely you do not believe that."

"What I believe, what I know to be truth, has no bearing on the white man's justice. I know not how to prove *nï tua?'s* innocence."

"Perhaps there is a way."

She stuck her hand inside the blanket enveloping her frail body. After a moment's fishing, she withdrew a length of shiny ribbon the color of a clear summer sky.

He scowled. "Where did you get that?"

"Painted Woman had it tied around her wrist."

"That is a white woman's adornment. Did Mariah Kelly or her mother gift it to Painted Woman when they visited?"

Wings of a Dove rubbed the slick material between her fingers, and shook her head. "No, *nï tua?*." She looked directly into her son's questioning eyes. "Howling Coyote gave it to her."

Falcon Wing straightened. "No one but Silver Eagle enters the white man's town. He might purchase a gift such as that for *ma nami?,* or *ma pia,* but where would Howling Coyote get a white woman's treasure?"

"Where, indeed?" Wings of a Dove asked.

****

Silver Eagle often chafed at the length of time it took his father, Uncle Crow Dog, or Grandmother to make a decision when considering things of momentous importance. But Spirits of the Gods, they galloped as fast as stampeding buffalo in comparison to the deliberations in the white man's court.

He had been led into the saloon for the third day. The only one left to speak on his behalf was Tanner.

"I will hear from Tanner Kelly at this time," the judge said.

Tanner walked to the witness chair. His brother-friend smiled at him, then turned his attention to the sheriff, who rose to stand in front of him.

Judge Rogers had long since dispensed with the formality of swearing in each person. Silver Eagle suspected he feared another runaround like Mariah's if he allowed Mr. Curtis to take control for a single moment.

"Your name's Tanner Kelly, correct?"

"Come on, Sheriff, you know who I am."

"Please answer the questions for the record, Mr. Kelly," Judge Rogers said.

Tanner frowned. "What record?" He glanced at the designated jurors in the front row and then at the audience. As his gaze made the circle and came back to the judge, he scrunched his face. "What record? I don't see anyone writin'."

Red crept up the magistrate's face. "Although we don't have a clerk, young man, everything must be spoken aloud to provide a record. An oral record. There will be no question as to a fair hearing."

Tanner snorted.

Silver Eagle sighed. Tanner was not making it easy for his trial to proceed.

The judge pounded the gavel once. "There will be none of that! Answer the sheriff, young man."

"Yeah, I'm Tanner Kelly. And for all intent and purpose, and for the record, Silver Eagle is my brother. That makes him kin to Mariah, too!"

Certainly, my feelings are not like those of a brother.

Laughter and shouts erupted throughout the room, which fueled the judge's ire as he again hammered his gavel. After what seemed forever to Silver Eagle, the people quieted, only to be subjected to another lecture from Rogers about proper conduct in a courtroom. Finally, the stern man gave the sheriff leave to continue.

"On the day you found your sister unconscious, what were you doing?"

"We'd been roundin' up cattle to take to the ranch. We're in the middle of dippin' and brandin'."

"We?"

"Me and Silver Eagle. We was ridin' together. So he couldn't've hurt Mariah."

Another rumble, but the judge gaveled the townspeople down in short order.

The sheriff scowled at Tanner. "I didn't ask that question. But since you're so all-fired anxious to pursue that point, I'll ask what I already know. Did Silver Eagle ride with you the *entire* morning?"

Tanner stared right back at the lawman. "No, but we'd been searchin' for a couple hours."

"So, your sister could have been attacked long before you came upon her. Correct?"

"I don't think so."

"What you *think* doesn't matter, Tanner." Doggedly, the sheriff pursued the point he intended to make. "Might it have happened?"

Silver Eagle had a sinking feeling that those men eyeing him from the front row had already made their decisions. He sighed again when Tanner went on, probably in vain.

"Well, sure. She coulda lost her rifle on the trail somewhere, too. And since we're supposin'," Tanner said in his own stubborn manner, "somebody might've found it and hid it in Silver Eagle's lodge."

"Yes!" Mariah yelled from her seat, which led to a disruptive outburst from the crowd.

After another round of gavel pounding and defiant shouts from many, the magistrate once again regained the quiet he sought. "Sheriff Tate, you and Mr. Kelly please return to your seats. I shall finish this up."

In spite of the gravity of the moment, Silver Eagle smiled at Tanner's blink when he realized that *he* was the *Mr.* Kelly the circuit judge was speaking to. He rose and slowly walked back to sit beside Mariah.

Rogers sent a glare over the townsfolk before focusing on Silver Eagle. "It seems we can't get reliable testimony on your behalf from anyone, so I'm forced to go with the evidence we have.

"First, Miss Kelly's rifle was found in your tipi. Second, you have offered no denial of your guilt." He paused to clear his throat.

"I am going to give the case to the jury. But before I do, I want you to understand you are entitled to respond to the charges. Now is that time, Mr. Silver Eagle."

There was no way to prove his innocence other than his word. Silver Eagle considered maintaining his silence, but decided to deny the charges. He could do nothing else.

Without having to be told by the judge to stand, he rose and faced the entire town, head high, shoulders squared.

"I no steal Miss Kelly's rifle." He shrugged. "No need gun my work." His gaze trailed over the Kellys, falling lastly on Mariah. "I no hurt her. Lady never need fear me."

For a long moment, he held Mariah's green-eyed gaze, and knew with certainty he was not imagining it. There was love and longing in those depths. His heart constricted, so heavy in his chest he could hardly breathe.

"Matter not what I say, Judge Rogers. You come, send me white man's prison."

"No!" Mariah jumped to her feet.

Mrs. Kelly grabbed her arm.

Tanner also leaped up and pointed an accusing finger at the judge. "He's right! There's no justice here. Not for an Indian!"

Mr. Kelly bellowed, "Sit down, both of you! We'll hear this out before we decide what's to be done." He turned fierce eyes on Sheriff Tate and Judge Rogers. "It remains to be seen *if* somethin' else needs doin'."

"Mr. Kelly, are you threatening this court?" the judge asked in an icy voice.

A Spirit's tread could have been heard in the large room. All heads turned to hear Mr. Kelly's response.

"You take my determination to have a fair hearin' for Silver Eagle as a threat, Judge Rogers?"

"It's how you *phrase* your concern," the judge said.

Mr. Kelly gave him a humorless smile. "Folks'll tell you, no need to wonder about me. I take care of my own, sir. And I mean every word I say."

The two faced off for long seconds, Judge Rogers finally shaking his head. "Everyone, take your seats."

Mr. Kelly cast a speaking glance at Tanner and Mariah, who had not heeded his earlier demand that they sit. With mutinous expressions, both sank into their chairs.

"Now then." Rogers laced his fingers together and looked toward the front row of jurors. Men he had chosen simply because they sat in forward seats. "Gentlemen, since we aren't apt to hear anything new, it's up to you to study everything that's been brought before you. You *will* give the Indian in question the benefit of a studied verdict."

"The Indian in question" Silver Eagle thought. He knew the judge gave him little credit as a human being.

The stiff-backed judge gave Mr. Kelly a sour-faced smile, then turned back to the jurors. "Do I make myself clear?"

All nodded.

Elmer Hawkins, owner of the general store, and Preacher Sandborn were the only men on his jury Silver Eagle knew well enough to speak to. He had seen three of the others in town at different times. The last man wore work-worn ranch clothes. Silver Eagle figured he might be the sodbuster who recently bought a spread outside of town.

Hawkins, who sat in the chair nearest to the center aisle, rose and spoke for the others. "Uh, Judge Rogers, you want us to talk this out right here?"

"Well—" Rogers scratched his bearded chin. "Don't think you can discuss much with all these folks listening in." He looked out into the audience. "Mr. Crabapple, are you here?"

About halfway back in the seating, Luther Crabapple sprang up. A short man, he waved his hand to be sure he was seen. "Yessir. Right here."

"Is there a room in this establishment where these gentlemen can confer in private?"

The owner pointed to a door at the opposite end of the long bar. "My office is right over yonder. It ain't much bigger than a closet, but the men can meet in there if'n they're of a mind to."

The judge motioned the jurors in that direction and at the same time addressed the audience. "Until the jury has reached a decision, these proceedings are adjourned."

Again, scuffing boots and scraping chairs echoed in the big room, along with a shout. "How long they gonna be, ya think?"

"I have no idea. But the sheriff will send someone to ring the church bell when the jury's done talking," Judge Rogers said.

Mariah Kelly rushed over and accosted Sheriff Tate before he could say a word to Silver Eagle.

"Sheriff, Silver Eagle isn't going anywhere. Why don't you let him come along with my family for lunch at Granville's Cafe?"

Before she even finished the request, Tate was shaking his head. Which came as no surprise to Silver Eagle.

"I can't do that, Miss Mariah. He's my prisoner until the jury says otherwise. The town would be down on me like a flock of vultures if I let him wander loose."

"Not with Tanner and Pa to—"

"No." He shook his head. "Sorry." "That just ain't the way things are done according to the justice system."

"Well, justice is stupid!"

Her mother intervened. "I think it's called blind, Mariah, not stupid. Although I'm not sure how blind it is. Seems to see color just fine." Mrs. Kelly cast a weak smile at Silver Eagle. "I'm sorry for this. You don't deserve to be locked up."

Hands tied before him, Silver Eagle merely nodded, unable to speak without betraying the emotion clutching his heart. While he appreciated her faith in him, he knew "sorry" would not get him released. "Sorry" was no defense and would more than likely send him to prison.

I would rather hang.

Tanner reached toward Silver Eagle, but Sheriff

Tate stepped between them. "No. You can't lay hands on my prisoner."

Though quietly said, the lawman left no doubt he meant it.

Tanner scowled. "You know I don't plan to do my friend harm. But that ultimatum of yours better extend to anyone who does threaten my *brother*, Sheriff."

Mouth tight, Tate clasped Silver Eagle's arm. Ignoring Tanner, he touched his hat brim and dipped his chin. "Ladies, Ward, excuse us."

Silver Eagle remained planted when the shorter man tugged on his upper arm. "A moment."

Tate looked hard into his eyes, then relented.

Though most people had already filed from the large room, a few hangers-on sat in chairs, visiting. Silver Eagle turned his back to them to speak to Mr. Kelly.

"No men believe me, but want you know, sir, I no steal Miss Mariah's rifle. I no hurt her. Never."

Mr. Kelly jerked his head back. "Jehoshaphat! I know that. But some varmint did, then put my girl's rifle in your lodge. We're gonna search him out, and he's gonna pay for it."

While he did not wish the white man's justice on anyone, not even his arch enemy, Silver Eagle prayed to the gods that the truth would be discovered long before he was sent to the prison where men died for no apparent reason.

"We're gonna find out who did this, Sil," Tanner said.

Mrs. Kelly laid her small hand on his arm. Sheriff Tate's mouth tightened, but he did not stop her.

"Take heart. We will do everything in our power to see justice done. I promise you that."

He dipped his head deferentially. "I grateful."

At her mother's shoulder, Mariah gazed at him

with crystalline eyes, the green pools swimming with unshed tears.

The intensity of her emotion was like a kick to his midsection. Still, Silver Eagle stoically gazed back, refusing to show his own longing. Would that he could kiss her one more time. Just once more. To hold in his heart for a lifetime.

Perhaps his boldness at having done so was the reason this white man's punishment was upon him.

Chapter Eighteen

Supper came and went, and still no summons to return to the saloon to learn his fate. Silver Eagle stood gazing out at the vast night sky. Stars glittered, cold and aloof, as if winking at the wretched probability of his freedom forever lost. The office door opened behind him.

"Silver Eagle?"

He glanced over his shoulder. *Chink, chink.* No matter how little he moved, his ankle chains never let him forget.

Tate didn't come any farther into the short hallway. "Curtis came by and said everybody has gone home for the night." He shrugged. "If they reached a verdict, they didn't say anything."

No surprise, Silver Eagle thought. Perhaps this lesson in patience was a prelude to how his life would unfold in the years to come.

"Judge Rogers said I'm supposed to take you back to court in the morning. Nine o'clock."

The information required no response, so he dipped his chin and swung back to contemplate the quiet night. As the door clicked shut, his fingers clenched the bars. Another long sleepless night.

****

Early the next day, Mariah watched as each member of the jury took his seat. She knew every single one except the new rancher, Mr. Conrad. A dirt farmer, not a cattleman, Conrad would not be welcomed by many in the area.

Tanner said he'd bought the old Bond spread

174

southwest of McCallister's. Jessup McCallister was not the neighborly sort. He and Pa only got along because her pa was amiable—and had settled onto the Broken Spur, a section larger than Jessup's, five years prior to McCallister's move from Pennsylvania.

She'd always thought that fortuitous. For the Comanche, in particular. There had been more than a few head buttings between the two ranchers over the years, several because of Falcon Wing and his people.

The speaking glance between Jessup and Mr. Conrad made Mariah wonder if they'd already had a run in. Jessup was the big, blustery type. But Mr. Conrad, though older and more care worn, was probably tough as a leather quirt. She'd always thought a person had to really love farming, a back-breaking way to survive if there ever was one.

Judge Rogers waited until everyone had taken a seat before raising his sonorous voice. It could surely be heard all the way to Waco, Mariah thought.

"All right, gentlemen, have you come to a decision?"

Mr. Hawkins rose and cleared his throat. "Yeah, we have." He scanned each of his fellow jurors, then returned his attention to Rogers. "We think Silver Eagle is—"

"You can't come in here!" Jessup McCallister's voice boomed from the back.

Every head turned toward the commotion. Judge Rogers shouted, "What's the meaning of this?"

Mariah and her whole family jumped to their feet. A collective gasp sounded as Falcon Wing, Wings of a Dove, Crow Dog, and that horrible Indian who had hurt Painted Woman stopped into the room.

More than one Burnett Station citizen clamored for removal of the unwelcome Indians in their midst.

"Out!" Someone yelled.

Another cried, "No redskins allowed!"

Jessup McCallister stepped directly in front of Wings of a Dove, effectively blocking her from taking another step.

Outraged that he would do such a thing, Mariah started forward, but her brother grabbed her upper arm.

"Leave it be, sis. Wings of a Dove wouldn't welcome your interference."

"But she's so little, so frail! He has no right—"

"Leave it, I said."

BOOM!

The deafening gun report along with the acrid smell of gunpowder silenced all as if throats had been cut. Many ducked, then everyone's attention swung to the bar.

Reflected in the smoke-hazed mirror, J.D. Parks stood atop the mahogany bar, six shooter smoking in his left hand, muzzle pointed at the ceiling.

His stance relaxed but solid, Stetson tipped low on his brow, Parks spoke quietly into the startled silence. "Y'all believe you have the right to charge an Indian with a crime. If that's the case, it's only fair his people be here to listen." He waved his gun. "Folks, I suggest you set yourselves down and shut your mouths."

Murmurs rose like a wave as people scraped chairs and boots, clothes rustling as they took their seats. More than a few wary glances shot toward J.D., but no one contradicted him.

Mr. McCallister stood a moment longer, Wings of a Dove completely hidden behind his bulk.

Mariah glanced at Silver Eagle, who'd risen, dark eyes on his people. While Falcon Wing and the others had not advanced another step, neither had they retreated. If the gun report had startled them, they remained astonishingly stoic, giving nothing

176

away.

J.D. stared down Jessup for several seconds. Finally, the older man reluctantly took his seat. But if looks could kill... Whew. Parks would be a dead man where he stood!

After all was again orderly, J.D. holstered his gun and hiked his chin at Rogers. "Okay, Judge, have at it."

Mariah hid a smile behind her hand. She didn't know J.D., not at all, but he certainly knew how to gain attention—and respect, by gum. Or by gun.

"What's—" Judge Rogers's voice cracked. He paused and cleared his throat as color flooded past his stiff collar.

"What's the meaning of this, uh..." He floundered, undoubtedly unsure how he should address Falcon Wing.

"Chief!" Tanner said.

"Yes," Mariah added. "He's Silver Eagle's father."

"Chief, then," Rogers said, irritation rife in his voice. "Indians aren't permitted in my court. Guns are always forbidden." He threw a glance at J.D., who still stood at hip-shot ease on the bar, arms crossed over his chest.

J.D.'s response was a thin, humorless smile that said, *You think you're man enough to take my gun?*

Judge Rogers swung back to Falcon Wing. "There are no extra seats, Chief."

"J.D. is right," Pa said. "If an Indian can be here as a defendant, his family can be here, too."

"I don't make the rules," Rogers snapped.

"Sure you do," J.D. said.

The judge's color heightened.

When Falcon Wing spoke to his son in Comanche, Mariah fretted, wishing she had learned the language. The chief stepped aside as Crow Dog pushed the other warrior forward. It was then everyone saw the rawhide lashed around the younger Indian's wrists. One or two women cupped their own cheeks, taken aback by his ghostly white face. Another murmur spread through the audience. Some half rose in their seats, craning their necks to get a better view, but no disorder this time.

"Howling Coyote has at last spoken the truth, *nï tua?*. He stole the rifle from Miss Kelly. He will be punished according to our custom."

****

Silver Eagle narrowed his eyes at Howling Coyote. Stone faced, his enemy returned his steady gaze. Say what one would about the warrior, he was ready to fight. And Silver Eagle would like nothing better than to be allowed hand-to-hand combat against the coward, but in his gut he did not believe that would happen. In his gut, neither did he believe his father's wishes would prevail here.

Would these white men even listen to an Indian? Particularly if he refused to speak their tongue? Would his father at long last relent? While townsfolk were unaware Chief Falcon Wing understood the white man's tongue, the Kellys knew better.

But their defense of him had not helped his situation. Proof must be provided. Silver Eagle despaired that more evidence would be found.

"What did he say?" Rogers asked no one in particular. His attention finally settled on Silver Eagle. He waved a hand at Howling Coyote. "Why is that man fettered?" Before Silver Eagle could respond to the first question, the judge asked another. "Does your father speak English?"

Tanner jumped in. "No."

Expression showing nothing of his emotions churning inside, Silver Eagle looked at his friend. Why would Tanner say that? He knew Falcon Wing spoke English.

Ah. Comprehension dawned. Tanner would not

allow the judge to feel superior to Falcon Wing because he could not express himself fluently in the white man's tongue.

"I understand Comanche well enough, Judge Rogers," Tanner said. "Falcon Wing is a proud chief, and he has brought a guilty man to this court."

"Guilty of what?" a voice shouted.

Another took up the cry. "They don't belong here! They don't belong in Burnett Station."

Many nodded agreement.

Tanner ignored all of it. "Howling Coyote has confessed to takin' Mariah's rifle. That's good enough for me."

As Tanner spoke, Falcon Wing extended his hand. A blue ribbon dangled from his fingers.

"Hey!" Mariah brushed a hand over her hair and stepped into the aisle. "That's mine. Where did—" Her gaze flipped to Howling Coyote. "*You* took it from my hair that day, didn't you?"

For the first time, hope stirred in Silver Eagle.

Mariah wasn't finished with Howling Coyote. She shook her finger at him. "You're a no-account sidewinder! And a coward, to boot!"

A couple women snickered; the men said nothing. Instead, their troubled eyes traveled from her to the stoic Indians, then to J.D., who remained deceptively patient, watching the proceedings from his high perch.

Silver Eagle had to admit J.D. Parks was a daunting specimen. Everything about him spoke of power—height, massive hands, impressively wide shoulders. It was no wonder the Comanche had died by the hundreds at the hands of men like Parks.

Amusement lurked within Silver Eagle, though, because no one in this room, other than the Kellys, knew his father and uncle were not a threat. They would not raise a hand in anger to these white people.

A vow to Ward Kelly was a vow never to be broken.

The next voice nearly sent Silver Eagle spinning backward in astonishment.

"Hear me!" The woman spoke in English.

Her best blanket wrapped around narrow shoulders, Wings of a Dove took the ribbon from his father's hand and walked halfway up the aisle, back as straight as her frail form would allow. Her penetrating, dark eyes leveled first upon Judge Rogers, then on Sheriff Tate.

Most of the spectators on either side of the aisle had never seen Wings of a Dove, and now eyed her with curiosity. Others with obvious distaste. But everyone listened with avid attention when she spoke.

"You come my village, take away my heart. That is no right. You judge my grandson. That is no right. My people judge and punish man who break covenant between my son and Mr. Kelly."

"Madam," Judge Rogers interrupted. "Who are you?"

Laughter spread through the room. Face red, the judge again pounded that infernal gavel several times.

"Order! Order! I'll have order in my court!"

Silver Eagle couldn't hear what Tate said to the judge, but of a sudden, Mrs. Kelly rose and strode to Silver Eagle's side. Tate scowled, but remained silent.

However, the judge was not tongue tied. "Good God Almighty, what do you think you're doing, Mrs. Kelly? This court is already a shambles. I'll not have it!"

"You," Mrs. Kelly pointed an admonishing finger at the man, "may be quiet for five seconds while a saner voice is heard."

Silver Eagle had always prided himself on

hiding his feelings. But now, his own face creased in a grin at Judge Rogers's expression. Even more amazing, the judge clamped his mouth shut.

"Now," Mrs. Kelly said, turning to the townsfolk. "I have listened to enough drivel about the discovery of Mariah's rifle in Silver Eagle's lodge. It was there, no doubt, but I know, and," she swept her finger over the crowd, stopping at the jury, "*every single person sitting in this room knows*, other than Judge Rogers, Silver Eagle would not and did not steal that rifle."

She turned so she could direct her next statement to him. "Silver Eagle and his entire family are as dear to me as my own. They have been these twenty-eight years since Tanner's birth."

Her gaze scanned the crowd. "Most of you know Silver Eagle. He would not lie. He would not steal so much as a crust of bread from us. From any of you!"

For the first time in his life, Silver Eagle knew the meaning of humble. His heart turned over in his chest. He would cherish these precious words uttered by Mrs. Kelly about him and his family.

Still not finished, she directed her next attack at the six men who had been deliberating his fate. "Gentlemen, I don't know what conclusion you came to before you had all the facts, but you *will* listen to Silver Eagle's honorable people, and you *will* respect their integrity." She tilted her head imperiously. "Have I made myself clear?"

When no one responded, when no one moved, she turned to the bench. "Now, Judge Rogers, Wings of a Dove, Falcon Wing, and Silver Eagle's uncle, Crow Dog, have come here in good faith. They investigated this crime, better than some." She cast a quelling look at Sheriff Tate. "They are now presenting to this court the guilty party.

"You complained about *your* court being a shambles. Well, the fault lies at your own doorstep, sir." She gave his honor no chance to respond.

Instead, she gestured toward the bar. "Mr. Parks is correct. If you and this town believe you have the right to judge an Indian, then, by heaven, you will listen to this wise Indian's testimony."

Pausing, she tilted her head respectfully and extended her hand to Wings of a Dove. "This way, please. Take *this* empty seat." Mrs. Kelly smiled. "You can hear and see the proceedings quite well from here."

Though the men of his band stayed where they were, Silver Eagle's grandmother straightened her frail shoulders and walked to the witness chair.

Once grandmother was settled, Mrs. Kelly returned to her place in the front row. She nodded at the judge, effectively giving him permission to continue.

Chapter Nineteen

Though obviously uncomfortable before this assemblage, his grandmother's voice did not waver. "Crow Dog, bring Howling Coyote forward."

Unable to understand her tongue, the white people glanced at each other, then guardedly watched Howling Coyote march up the aisle. His defiant demeanor was not lost on anyone, least of all Grandmother and Judge Rogers.

Pointing at Howling Coyote, Wings of a Dove again spoke in English, wisely understanding it was necessary. "Is warrior destroy band's peace oath. Is warrior steal weapon that kill." Lifting the ribbon for all to see, she said, "Howling Coyote steal adornment. Gift to mate." She laid the ribbon on the table before the judge, then folded her hands in her lap. "That is all."

Not enough, Cáco.

Judge Rogers's skeptical expression said as much. He was not ready to accept her simple explanation as fact. And glancing at others in the room, it was clear few were.

"Madam, I fear your conjecture does not negate the fact that Miss Kelly's rifle was found in your grandson's tipi. Your word is not—"

Unaware that she was out of order in a white man's court, Grandmother scowled and interrupted the judge. "What mean word, con-jec-ture, ne-gate?"

"Conjecture is your story, and negate means to deny truth."

"I speak truth!"

183

Silver Eagle hid a smile as he watched his grandmother ready herself to add more. One did not rile a shaman. Not if one wished to remain unscathed.

But before she could continue, Rogers again stepped in too deep. "Women do not testify in this court unless they are directly involved." He glanced at Mariah, Mrs. Kelly, then back at Grandmother. "As far as this court is concerned, it has heard quite enough from the women of this town."

"Is that right?" Mr. Kelly asked in a quiet voice. He stood, eyes darkened like storm clouds. "Maybe if you listened to women more often, mister, you'd earn the respect a judge is supposed to have."

"Mr. Kelly—"

"Hold it!" Sheriff Tate stepped forward, hand raised for quiet. "That includes you, Judge Rogers," he said, expression tired looking. "Seems to me I know these folks as well as anyone." He looked pointedly at Ward Kelly, a challenge to nay-say him. "I ain't never had reason to doubt Falcon Wing's word."

He glanced over the crowd. "And not one of you've had cause to fear the band. They've been peaceful and stuck to themselves." His attention returned to the bench. "You don't know them, Judge, so it makes sense you'd question Wings of a Dove's word." Soberly, he stared at Silver Eagle's grandmother. "Personally, I believe she'd burn at the stake before she'd tell a falsehood." He gestured at Howling Coyote. "If she says this warrior stole Mariah's rifle and the ribbon she's presented that Miss Kelly says was taken from her that day, then, by gum, Howling Coyote did!"

Undoubtedly, no one else saw the subtle change in his grandmother's expression. Surprised by Sheriff Tate's defense and praise of her family, Wings of a Dove was nevertheless pleased.

184

The sheriff had no idea, nor would he ever know that his words had invoked a shaman's honor, that this shaman would, when he was called from this earth, usher him through the in-between time.

There was no higher praise for any man than her prayer that he should ride the winds of eternity on a white stallion.

Judge Rogers's voice jolted Silver Eagle back to the present. "It still remains for the jury to—"

"What remains is to drop the charges against Silver Eagle and bring charges against Howling Coyote," J.D. Parks said.

Everyone's attention shifted to the white man still atop the bar, hand resting on his gun butt. A humorless smile on his lips, his gray eyes pinned each juror and then Rogers. "Simple enough for you?"

Silver Eagle looked from one to another, then another and another, astonished that Sheriff Tate would speak up for his people, for his grandmother, even more taken aback by Parks's defense. The man had only worked for Mr. Kelly a short time.

He did not believe J.D. Parks cared one way or another about Indians. But he apparently knew the white man's justice system. And intended the proceedings to be fair.

"He's right," Sheriff Tate said. "And since I wrote out the charges, I hereby recall them. But before I arrest this here other man, I have a few more questions for Wings of a Dove." He walked to Silver Eagle and removed the shackles from his wrists. "Y'all are free to go as soon as the judge says so."

Silver Eagle could not help but rub at the phantom irons still encircling his wrists. For the first time in days, he was able to draw a deep breath. Tonight he would stand beneath the star-spangled sky without bars before his eyes, feel the breeze on his face. He searched out Mariah and saw triumph in her eyes.

She smiled, sending his heart racing like crazed Beelzebub.

Judge Rogers once again rapped the gavel. "It seems the court has no choice but to dismiss the charges against Silver Eagle, Sheriff." He threw a sour smile at Parks, then stared at Sheriff Tate. "Your questions of this woman," he flicked a dismissive hand at Wings of a Dove, "can better be asked when this Mr. Howling Coyote is charged. We shall adjourn long enough for you to write up charges against him." He flapped an equally dismissive hand at the still defiant warrior.

"I'll ask Wings of a Dove those questions now if you don't mind, and that ought to do it," Tate said.

The judge relented and shrugged his assent.

Silver Eagle stepped toward Howling Coyote, and even though Tanner was the only white man in the room who could understand him, he spoke in a low voice for the warrior's ears alone. "You will now learn what it means to defy my father's word."

"I do not understand what has been said here, and I care not." Smirking at Silver Eagle's unfettered hands, he taunted his enemy. "Chief Falcon Wing will doubtless banish me, but not before we do battle. I will yet defeat you, reduce you to offal, Silver Eagle, to be thrown to the wolves."

Howling Coyote did not yet comprehend that his punishment no longer rested with the band, with the chief. Silver Eagle swung around. "Judge Rogers."

"Yes?"

"Is truth man must understand charge against him, what say in court?"

"Of course. Wasn't everything explained to you?"

"Yes." He nodded at the warrior he had come to hate. "Howling Coyote no understand white man's tongue. You wish it so, I translate."

"This is most irregular." When Ward Kelly surged to his feet, Rogers put up his hand. "However, if Sheriff Tate has no objection, I don't either."

Despite the uncomfortable heat in the large room, not a soul left the saloon. The low hum of conversations spun through the spectators as Sheriff Tate pulled out a stub of pencil and leaned on the table to write on a frayed piece of paper.

Silver Eagle squatted beside Wings of a Dove, still seated in the witness chair. "Thank you, *nï cáco*," he said quietly.

Rather than acknowledge his thanks, she complained. "I do not like this chair, Silver Eagle. I do not like many white people so close. I would go now."

He smiled. "As would I, but we must remain a short while longer, until the white man has his say about Howling Coyote."

The warrior stood alone, eyes straight ahead, expression revealing nothing. Crow Dog had retreated to stand beside his brother just inside the door. Silver Eagle knew his people weren't comfortable in the confines of the saloon.

"I know Falcon Wing," his grandmother said. "He will cast Howling Coyote from our village, leave only with what he arrived. Nothing. Painted Woman will be cared for by another warrior who accepts a second wife. He will adopt the children."

Silver Eagle did not contradict her, did not try to explain that Howling Coyote's punishment was no longer his father's to impose. The tribe's laws were of no import in the white man's court. In the white man's world.

He glanced up at Howling Coyote. Even though he had come to hate him, Silver Eagle cringed at the suffering the warrior would endure locked behind bars. And though he abused his mate, Howling

Coyote cherished his children. Children he would doubtless never see again.

Had Howling Coyote's attack been against him only, Silver Eagle would work to see the man released to the tribe. Then he might get his wish to fight hand-to-hand. But had that been the case, the white men would not have cared, would not have involved themselves in this affair.

Silver Eagle's glance skimmed his grandmother, then his father, who, to him at least, appeared uncomfortable. His family did not belong here.

Then his attention focused on Mariah. Her eyes shone with...what? Relief? Regard? More than simple regard? Even though it was unwise, he wanted to believe she loved him as fiercely as he loved her.

Silver Eagle fought the bleak expression threatening his own countenance. No, as sure as the turn of seasons would continue on this earth, he and Mariah could never be together. Her people *and* his would oppose them.

****

As the sun sank to the horizon, the Kellys moved with the crowd from the saloon. Thank God, Mariah thought, sucking in the cooler evening air. It was over. That despicable Howling Coyote was on his way to jail, and Silver Eagle was free. He walked ahead with his people, his hand cupping his grandmother's elbow, steadying her as she stepped off the boardwalk.

When Mariah started to join them, her mother's fingers clamped around her upper arm. "No," she said for Mariah's ears alone.

Mariah's brow creased. "What?"

"You will not follow him. You will come home with us."

"I wasn't—"

"Yes, you were. Or you wanted to," Ma amended.

188

No way could she disregard her mother's order. Not before Pa and Tanner. Not before the entire town. Especially not before Silver Eagle's people.

Besides, along with her family, she had already offered congratulations to Silver Eagle in the saloon. He'd given no indication he wanted her near him, wanted her riding at his side.

Ezra Newcomb, the blacksmith, led Silver Eagle's horse from his stable, where Sheriff Tate had undoubtedly boarded the stallion all these days Silver Eagle had spent in jail.

Mariah watched him lift his grandmother into the saddle, a woman no larger than a young girl, who held the respect of her people in her wise heart.

Now, the town had been given reason to extend respect to her as well. And if they didn't, they'd answer to Sarah Kelly. Mariah smiled.

Wings of a Dove rode beside Falcon Wing. Silver Eagle mounted and led another paint. Probably Howling Coyote's gelding, which he wouldn't need for a long time to come, if ever. Crow Dog reined in beside Silver Eagle as, with dignity, the Indians unhurriedly rode out of town.

A pace or so ahead of her, Mr. McCallister intercepted her father, Tanner by his side. Her mother clasped her upper arm, stopping to hear what their neighbor had to say, but not close enough to intrude.

Standing toe to toe, he challenged her pa. "For years I've told you them redskins is nothin' but trouble, Ward. You need to run 'em off your land. Will you listen?" He shook his grizzled head. "Naw."

Spying Mariah, he motioned toward her. "You gonna wait until one of 'em rapes her or your wife before you do the right thing?"

She could only see her father's face in profile, but it and his whole body had tensed. "You weren't listenin' either, Jessup. Silver Eagle didn't hurt

Mariah; Howling Coyote did. And he'll rot in prison."

"Still—"

"Father." Henry McCallister walked up, leading his and his father's mounts. "Let's head home."

Mr. McCallister never took his eyes off Pa. It was as if his son had never spoken.

"One of these days I'll have a run in with one of 'em, and I sure as hell won't get the law involved."

"You best watch your back, Jessup, if you come on the Broken Spur bent on causin' trouble."

"Mr. McCallister." Her mother spoke brightly and walked forward, interrupting Pa. "We don't see much of you. How is your dear wife?"

Biting back a laugh, Mariah watched the older man gather what manners he had as he moved back from her father. Eyes narrowed, he understood she was defusing the confrontation, and he was forced to acknowledge Ma. He had no choice.

He touched his hat brim and dipped his head. "Not doin' so good, Miz Sarah. I thank you for askin'."

Her mother had written last year that Mrs. McCallister was surely dying of cancer. While Mariah didn't like Mr. McCallister or Horace, Henry had always been cordial to her family, and she remembered Jenny McCallister as a motherly type. Even more so than Ma.

The woman had to be a saint to have lived with this grizzled man and two strapping sons. Mariah felt a bit of guilt. Since her return, she hadn't even asked after the neighbor's health.

But she had to give Jessup McCallister his due, though. He had always doted on his wife, and now, when he spoke of her, his expression was haunted.

"I should probably stop in and see her."

He shook his head. "That's kindly of you, Miz Sarah, but my Jenny is too weak to receive visitors."

Just behind his father, Henry cast him a

seething glance, his mouth flattened in a line. But he didn't say anything.

Mariah wondered what that was all about.

"Oh, dear. I'm sorry to hear that, Mr. McCallister. Do give Jenny my best, will you?"

He nodded.

Before anyone could say anything more, Ma slipped her hand around Pa's arm and forcibly took him forward with her. "We need to head home, dear."

Mariah followed her mother to the buggy. As she passed the two men, Henry saluted her with a finger to his hat brim. His smile could not be misconstrued as one of humor.

Now she remembered seeing Henry, Horace, too, sporting black eyes and cut lips when they were younger. At the time she'd thought it was brothers scrapping a bit more than intended. Now she thought it might have been run ins with their father.

As Mariah drove the buggy toward the ranch, flanked by Pa and Tanner, J.D. Parks rode a pace or two behind her brother. Mariah's thoughts returned to Silver Eagle. Maybe tomorrow she could steal away for a few minutes alone with him. She longed to learn whether the man cared a fig about her. Or not.

****

Entering his lodge for the first time since Sheriff Tate had led him from the village, Silver Eagle found his belongings in disarray. His clothes were tumbled and falling over the side of the trunk. Mariah's hat lay flattened beneath his spare whip.

He sighed, then proceeded to restore order to his dwelling. None of the villagers would invade his tipi, so it had to have happened when the rifle was found. His mouth thinned. Howling Coyote was the exception to invading another man's privacy, when he had tried and almost succeeded in putting the blame for the theft on his archenemy.

As Silver Eagle gathered a few belongings from his tipi, he ignored Quiet Bird watching with troubled eyes from outside. When he knelt inside the dim lodge to stuff jerky and other food staples into his saddle bags, without permission, she ducked inside and pulled on his sleeve.

Pausing, he searched her sober countenance. "What troubles you, *nï nami*?"

She walked fingers, swept her arm down, splaying those fingers at the same time. *You travel far, for many moons?*

"I go for a time to commune with the Spirits, to the wide river near the cedars. Not far."

One, maybe two suns?

He shook his head. "I do not know. Wings of a Dove understands my desire to be one with the Earth, the stars, the sky."

Will Tanner-friend know where you are?

Her question fueled another's countenance; Tanner's sister leaped to mind. Silver Eagle busied himself buckling the saddlebags, hiding the turmoil within from his sister.

That was one decision he must make.

Should he, could he, claim Mariah Kelly for his own?

Schooling his features into a smile, he stood and ushered Quiet Bird from his tipi. Securing the rawhide ties on the tipi entrance flap, he answered her question. "Tanner need not know. I shall return to work when my time with The Spirits is done." He cupped his sister's cheek. "Do not fret, Quiet Bird. I will return."

Other questions churned within.

How long could he remain in this village, so close yet so far from his heart's desire?

How long could he work on the Silver Spur, tantalizingly near, yet unable to claim Mariah?

Burying those painful thoughts, he again spoke to his caring sister.

"Now, I must bid Mother Sparrow and Wings of a Dove good bye."

Chapter Twenty

Having shed his buckskin shirt, Silver Eagle sat crosslegged beside the fire. Coffee boiled in the pot Tanner had gifted him when they exchanged tokens marking twenty years since birth. A slight breeze rustled tree leaves and from time to time soughed mournfully.

He stared at the bright flames, troubled thoughts beating steadily in his head. What would his father and Mr. Kelly say if he made his desires known?

Silver Eagle had encountered half-breeds, many of whom were outcasts from both societies. Some had been born after raids by his people, or following the plundering of Indian villages by white men.

Though a rare occurrence, what of Indians and whites who chose each other? Like their offspring, were those men and women also outcasts from either world—or both?

One day he wanted sons. What man did not? Would Mariah mate with him and bring half-breeds into this world? Though their sons would be born of love, she knew as well as he how difficult life would be for them.

Mariah's face rose like a specter dancing before the firelight. Upon her return from school far to the east, she had made it perfectly clear that she held her family and the Broken Spur dear to her heart. As dear as his people were to him.

Those truths settled inside like a rock, and he rubbed his bare chest. Mariah would not leave her family again. Not for him. Not for anyone or anything. And could he abandon *his* life?

Running his tongue across his lips, the haunting taste of her teased his senses. She had not avoided him when he kissed her.

He tilted back his head, closed his eyes, and waited a moment before opening them again. No moon this night dimmed the distant stars aflicker in the Great Spirit's world of darkness.

"There are no answers easily attained."

His voice sounded hollow to his ears. Time, he reminded himself. Time would bring the answers. Answers that might send him far from those he cherished.

****

Standing in the yawning mouth of the barn as the sun crested the horizon, Mariah's father nodded at Max, then glanced at Tanner, J.D., and her. His roundup crew had just crawled out of bed, and except for J.D., all looked like it. She felt sluggish, but Parks managed to appear ready to wrestle a bear no matter the time of day.

"I want y'all to do a sweep as far as you can comfortably ride afore noon, then turn for home and bring back the mavericks you find." Sticking the butt end of a match in his mouth, Pa talked around it. "Don't expect many strays. Max counted sixty-four-hundred head pastured between here and McCallister's spread. I ain't surprised the herd's down. Water as scarce as it's been in years, just wasn't enough grass to feed a big bunch."

J.D. settled his Stetson and swung aboard his stallion. "I'll sweep along the east fence and meet Tanner at the windmill in the north section. Okay with you, Tanner?"

Tanner nodded.

Here it comes, she thought when her father looked pointedly at her. "You ride with your brother, missy. Don't stray."

She rolled her eyes. "Don't worry about me, Pa. I'm not apt to come upon a rogue."

"Humor me, daughter."

Mariah rose on her toes to buss her father's cheek. "I have a choice?"

Her smart-britches remark tempered with a smile, she wondered if she'd ever be allowed to strike out on her own like Parks would today. Pa sure didn't have much of a say over him.

Moments later, all scattered, leaving Samuel and Ben inside the barn, well started on mucking stalls.

Mariah kept Nutmeg abreast of Tanner's mount as they headed west. They'd turn long before they reached Silver Eagle's village, then circle around north until they met up with Parks. Max and Pa would crisscross between.

Riding at a comfortable gait and seeing nothing, they finally came to the narrow river. Just east was a dense stand of cedar. Tanner reined back, allowing his horse to mosey through the brittle grass to drink at the slow-moving water's edge. Mariah did the same.

Not even seven o'clock, yet heat was on the rise. Fall would be here before long, bringing weather that could change overnight. She'd better enjoy the warmth while it lasted. Ma had written that last winter had been the coldest she could remember in all her years in Texas.

"Maybe we should split up around the cedars, Mariah. It's only a couple miles to the other end. If you see any critters you can't handle, shoot in the air. I'll hear."

"Fine with me. We can cover more territory that way."

He studied her for a long moment. "Then again, Pa might not like it if I let you ride alone, even for a little while."

Mariah laughed. "I'm sure you know what I think of that, brother dear."

In the end, they agreed. Mariah, a good shot, had her rifle back in the scabbard where it belonged. Tanner rode along the bank while Mariah crossed over and headed farther west.

As she recalled, this stand of cedar was thick enough to be impenetrable by anything bigger than a coyote. Cautious but confident, she scanned the terrain. She'd ridden less than a mile when she thought she caught a whiff of smoke. Reining in, she lifted her chin, sniffed, and frowned.

Dang, smoke for sure. Possibly a disaster in the making out here on the prairie. Flames could take hold and whip across the land in two shakes. But a search all around yielded nothing.

"Hup," she urged softly, and Nutmeg splashed through a shallow tributary that flowed out of the cedar break. Following the trees' perimeter, Mariah searched for a telltale column. The scent grew stronger. She rode around a dozen trees growing as close together as stacked cordwood.

And there he was.

Silver Eagle, the man who had sneaked in and stolen her heart. If she admitted the truth, she'd loved him for years. She hadn't realized it until sent away. In Baltimore she'd pined for him and for this land they both loved.

Seated crosslegged on a spread blanket, back straight, Silver Eagle looked to the horizon. Didn't acknowledge her presence in any way. Hoping she would ride on?

Beneath a tree, his horse munched oats spilled over the ground. Though not his black and white stallion, it was a handsome white on brown paint gelding. She dismounted and sent Nutmeg to join the other horse, then turned back to inspect Silver

Eagle more thoroughly.

He wore only buckskin trousers, his wide, bronzed shoulders bare to the sun. A beautiful specimen of manhood. What little breeze stirred the air at this time of day flung strands of glossy midnight hair across his chiseled lips. His eyes were closed.

She found a rock and sat down to simply take in the quiet, the peace. And to savor looking at him. She didn't kid herself into thinking he didn't know she was there. He'd heard her approach long before she saw him. But he chose to ignore her for now.

That didn't bother her. She instinctively knew that even that short time behind bars had undoubtedly taken a heavy toll on a man born to run free as a high flying eagle. He'd need this time to gather his sense of wellbeing, to again feel one with his world.

She watched a bird high, high in the cerulean sky, soar and dip on air currents. Not a cloud marred the painfully bright wide arch of blue. In a short while, heat would force many creatures to find shade.

"Hawk."

At his utterance, she glanced at him. Still seated stone still, his dark eyes held steady on the redtail hawk as it sailed lower to the ground. She admired the bird's graceful swaying, unsurpassed in hunting skills when it swooped down, barely slowing, and rose again, a rodent clutched in its talons.

"What you do here, woman?"

She didn't move as Silver Eagle rose and walked toward her. His light gait reminded her of a soft-stepping wolf.

Collecting her wits, she said, "Scouting for strays."

"Strays no here."

"Well, no. But I split from Tanner a ways back

198

and we'll meet up on the north end of the cedar break."

"You no find cattle here."

"No," she agreed. From her seat on the rock, she looked up when he stopped in front of her.

He leaned over, never breaking eye contact, clasped her upper arms and lifted her up and against his warm, naked chest.

His actions contradicted his words. "You no should be here."

She nodded, unable to speak, her heart fluttering in anticipation as he slowly lowered his head, his heated gaze now on her lips.

And then his touched hers, forcefully claiming, as if he'd thrown a rope around her and cinched her to him. Her hands slid up his sleek, deliciously warm chest, into his black hair, and hung on for dear life as his tongue plundered her mouth.

Ah, God. She'd come home. At last.

His fingers tangled in her hair, knocking her hat to the ground. He tugged her head back. Slowly, she opened her eyes and stared into the black, fathomless depths of his.

He shook his head ever so slightly. "No should do this."

"You've said that before, yet you kiss me again."

"No can help myself. I want you, Mariah." His raspy voice and the reluctance in his expression said he questioned his own sanity. "No should, but very much want you."

A frisson of heat shimmered through her body, settling low in her stomach. His kisses took her to heights where she'd never been. Made her yearn for more, much more.

She wanted to experience lovemaking with him, too, but she wanted more than a hot few minutes on a blanket under God's wide sky.

She wanted forever. But that was—

"You people no want me around if know my desire." His hands dropped away.

She immediately felt adrift. "You can't be sure of that. And what of yours? They would accept me in their midst?"

"Many moons on this I think. Maybe accept you, but you no like live in my village."

"Why not?"

Be honest, she remonstrated herself. Undoubtedly, she would feel cramped in a tipi and might ask that Silver Eagle build a house. Not a big house, mind you. A couple of rooms and a roof over her head would do. And then, as the children arrived...

His expressive lips curved in a rare smile. "You no keep mouth shut. My father no you father. My father no think same."

"There is that."

More important, were Silver Eagle's beliefs the same as his father's? No time like the present to find out. "Are you of a mind like your pa? Do you allow abuse of women?"

His brow creased. "My father no hurt women."

"Yet he did nothing when Howling Coyote slapped his wife to the ground."

Silver Eagle was shaking his head before she finished. "My father no interfere. Another time tell Howling Coyote of displeasure."

"Why didn't he step in *then*? Dang, she had no defense against that brute."

A glimmer of a smile reappeared in his eyes. "She have you. Sometime grandmother, too. No man challenge shaman."

"So I've heard. But none of that has anything to do with you and me." She hesitated, and then went for broke. "You could live on the Silver Spur, you know."

That suggestion had him pausing for another

moment of contemplation, leaving her to wonder if he cared enough for her or just wanted lusty, quick satisfaction.

"Come." He extended his hand. "We sit."

Her heart soared when he brushed unruly hair off her cheek. With nothing more than kisses, he made her body hum with desire. Her attention snagged by pounding hoof beats, Mariah glanced north.

She and Silver Eagle rose and merely held hands by the time Tanner closed in and leaped from the saddle. His hat sailed off as his body hit Silver Eagle, and sent him to the dirt, to sprawl on his back.

The momentum tore Silver Eagle's hand from hers.

"Damn you! Damn you to hell!" Tanner dealt a knuckle buster to the jaw, snapping Silver Eagle's head sideways. Knees planted on either side of Silver Eagle's prone body, her brother continued yelling, "Damn you!" The impact of his left fist whipped the defenseless man's head the other direction.

"Stop it!" Mariah shouted. "Are you crazy, Tanner? Stop!" She slammed her weight against his back.

"Stop! He's not fighting back! Tanner, for God's sake, you'll kill him!" She pummeled his head and shoulders with each desperate word.

Tanner finally heard her. He sat back, and dumped Mariah to the dirt beside his knee.

She scrambled to her feet, tears freely running down her cheeks as she surveyed the damage Tanner had inflicted.

Silver Eagle lay motionless. He'd absorbed each blow, hadn't even tried to protect his face. Blood oozed from a split in his lower lip. Bruising already evident on his cheek, he'd have a shiner so severe, he wouldn't see out of that eye for a week.

When he slowly turned his head, Mariah saw swelling beginning around the other eye as well. But what made her own vision blur with tears was his impelling eyes. Eyes that mirrored the same heartbreak that sliced her own heart. He knew as well as she that his and Tanner's friendship, their brotherhood, would never be the same.

And could her proud Indian that she had come to love so desperately even work on the Broken Spur after this?

"Dammit, Tanner, move. Let him up." Mariah tugged on his arm as if she could lift his weight. "What in tarnation were you thinking?"

He jerked out of her grasp and pushed to his feet. "Me? Christ, Mariah, what I'm thinkin' don't hold a candle to what you and Sil were doin'!"

As he extended a hand to help Silver Eagle rise, Mariah shoved him aside. Falling to her knees, she brushed trembling fingers over her beloved's forehead.

"Look what he's done to you," she cried.

Chapter Twenty-One

"Get up, woman," Silver Eagle muttered through swelling lips.

Despite the beating he'd taken, like the warrior he was, he nimbly rose to his feet. Mariah watched him kneel at water's edge to bathe his face with cool liquid. That wouldn't stop the swelling, but it would at least remove some of the blood before it caked on his dark skin.

He ducked his head all the way into the water to wash away dirt ground into his hair. Finished, he threw back his head, hair gleaming like an otter's wet fur, and rose to face Tanner.

"I sorry. Know this no good."

Mariah planted fists on her hips. "*You're* sorry? He beats your face bloody and *you're* sorry?"

Angrily confronting her brother, she noticed tears in his eyes. *What the devil does* he *have to cry about*? "What do you have to say for yourself?"

"Mariah, from this moment, nothin' will ever be the same. Nothin' can ever come of this, either. If you can't see that, you're blind, deaf, and dumb."

"Excuse me?"

"Tanner, he right. Many time tell myself same. I try tell you, Mariah."

Well, hallelujah, he finally calls me by name before one of my family. And isn't his timing just peachy?

"So you were saying." She cast Tanner a fulminating glare. "When we were so rudely interrupted. Maybe it would be hard."

203

Tanner snorted.

"All right, it *will* be hard for us to be together." She glared at Tanner, and then refocused on the man she loved despite all the heartache it might bring. "But are you willing to give it a try, Silver Eagle? Don't you care enough for me to *try*?"

"Maybe care *too* much. No can put you in danger. White men maybe come. Maybe punish you."

Frowning, Mariah gazed into the dying fire. Then she looked back into Silver Eagle's face. "Do I understand correctly? We could be together, you would marry me if not for what white men might think or do?"

He nodded.

She couldn't stop her own snort. "Well, that's a load of bull. Pa wouldn't let any man lay a hand on me."

Silver Eagle said, "You be my woman, *my* job protect you."

Good grief, men take offense at the darndest things!

"Dammit, Mariah," Tanner said. "Pa might be the very one to slap sense into you. He might even send you east again."

"Don't be stupid, Tanner. That's never going to—"

"Prove it. Go home right now and talk to Ma and Pa. See what they have to say about this insanity."

Mariah glanced from her brother to Silver Eagle. Before she could speak, Silver Eagle took the decision from her.

"No see Mr. Kelly like this." He touched his swollen eye, winced. "Few days, I come. Ask for Mariah, like white man do."

Voice flat, Tanner looked resigned. "In other words, you want to be kicked off the Broken Spur for good."

"No!"

204

Her outburst sent birds flying from nearby trees.

She would not let Pa send Silver Eagle packing. Somehow she must convince her parents that she loved Silver Eagle enough to bear the barbed remarks and outright snubs from some neighbors and townsfolk.

"It won't come to that, Tanner," she said.

He scooped up his hat and plopped it on his tousled hair. "We'll find out soon enough. Let's go."

She shook her head. "I'm staying. I'll clean up Silver Eagle's face."

"No."

She rounded on this man she had come to cherish no matter what. "Yes! I'm not riding home with Tanner. Not after he..." She shook her head. "Not now."

She did her best to ignore the long studied look from her brother. Resignation, hurt, and despair shone in his eyes. Her stomach sank. Could he be right? Maybe Ma and Pa *would* be dead set against them.

"You won't ride with me?"

She heard the hurt in his voice, saw the pain on his face, but she didn't relent. Though worry nibbled at her, she hardened her heart.

By gum, if Silver Eagle would have her, she'd go with him even if it meant leaving this land they had both grown up on and loved. Even if forced to leave their loved ones.

Tanner challenged her no further. Turning on his heel, he marched to Dandy, mounted, and rode off. Not once did he look back.

She drew in a deep breath and prayed her brother's reaction wasn't a prelude to how Ma and Pa would view the situation. Situation? Huh! A mild word for these few moments that would no doubt prove life changing for all.

Silver Eagle's steady regard made her nervous. Silence settled around them, so profound it was as if the world stopped turning.

She knew, glory, did she know, he would deny their feelings, deny their desire to be together—all to spare her.

Before he could speak, she walked to him and raised a hand to slick back wet hair from his temple. "I'll wash your cuts."

"No need."

He started to step away, but she grasped his forearm.

"Don't turn from me, Silver Eagle. Let me do this. If you care for me, let me do this."

"Care for you?" Eyes intense, his hand cupped the side of her face. "You in every heartbeat, every breath Spirits give my body."

"Ah, God." She swayed toward him and again felt that I'm home feeling when he took her in his arms, held her close. Breathing in his wild scent, she felt the depths of his emotions. The same emotions that coursed through her. "What are we going to do, Silver Eagle? What can we do?"

"This day? Nothing. I think on it. You think on it." He slipped a finger beneath her chin, lifted, and gazed into her eyes. "Need Mr. Mrs. Kelly say yes. You no happy otherwise."

She wanted to refute it, but could not deny the truth. Her heart would crack if Ma and Pa disowned her because she followed that same heart to the man she loved. Had yearned for since she was twelve.

Stepping away from him, she clasped his hand, and turned toward the campfire. It had burned down to mere embers. "I have a clean bandanna in my saddlebag. I'll use it to bathe your cuts."

He didn't argue this time, but sank to the blanket. Stirring the fire to life, he tossed in a few small sticks. Mariah picked up a tin cup, filled it with river water, and set it to boil.

After collecting the bandanna and finding some ointment in her saddle bag, she squatted next to Silver Eagle, examined the bruises on his face, the split on his lower lip, another on one cheek, and a longer tear on his left temple. That eye had almost swollen shut.

"I'd like to horsewhip that brother of mine for this."

Silver Eagle smiled and, amazingly, didn't wince. His swollen lip had to pull on the split near the corner of his mouth.

"You bang him on back already, pretty good. Protect me like protect Painted Woman. You make strong warrior."

His words sang through her head, took on a sexual tone. Oh, yes, she'd love to make another strong warrior—with him! She looked away to hide the blush that raced over her face.

Moments later, the water boiled and Mariah began washing away dirt and tiny gravel embedded in his cheek. She had done this many times at the hospital for soldiers who, if conscious, were grateful for the attention. Some of the wounds had been so bloody, so severe, she had the eerie feeling death hovered close. Oftentimes it did. No doubt her ministrations hurt like fire licking their skin, but not a one complained. And now, neither did Silver Eagle.

Unnerved after awhile by his steady regard, she finally finished and asked, "What are you staring at?"

"No believe Spirits answer prayer."

She settled back on her haunches. "What prayer?"

"We mate."

A storm of butterflies fluttered in her belly. Her eyes widened. "Now?"

"You wish it so."

"You mean make love—here—in broad daylight?" Her heart pounded as if she had run a foot race. "I didn't know. People make love during the day?"

He shrugged. "Why not?"

"Um... Well, I just, um... Ma and Pa..." She scowled at her own disjointed words and thoughts.

He brushed his fingers down her arm, all the way to her hand. Taking it to his mouth, he pressed a kiss in her palm. All thought fled. She shivered as he leaned forward, forcing her back until she lay on his blanket.

He came over her on his hands and knees, his still wet hair streaming down either side of his battered face. Ever so slowly, he lowered his mouth to hers—and stole her breath.

His lips caressed hers as lightly as those butterfly wings she'd imagined, seducing her mouth. She opened to him. His lips curved at her little start of surprise when his tongue slipped inside.

Lord have mercy! No wonder Ma looked dazed after Pa— The kisses the soldiers had stolen were nothing compared to this. How could he kiss so expertly with swollen lips?

She tasted blood. Not even realizing she had placed her hand against his chest, he pulled away when she pressed ever so slightly.

"No like kiss?"

"You're joshing, right?"

A chuckle rumbled in his chest. A drop of blood oozed from his lower lip.

"Doesn't it hurt your mouth?"

Flicking away the bead of blood with his tongue, he said nothing, only shook his head and proceeded to take her to places she had never been. His hands stroked areas on her body she hadn't known could leap to quivering anticipation from tender caresses.

She arched into his touch when his thumb brushed her nipple.

And then his hot mouth closed over that sensitive flesh.

Cotton rasped against the nipple, bringing it to a hard peak. She sucked in a breath as her eyes drifted shut, and her body responded of its own volition.

Unable to remain still as inner fires blazed, her fingers tangled in his hair. She gave back as good as she got, exploring his coffee-flavored mouth, tongues dueling. She started when his callused fingers brushed her bare skin.

Releasing her mouth, his kisses branded a path down her throat, teeth nipping at the top of her breast. Heat pooled in her center when his magic lips took her bare nipples. First one, then the other.

She couldn't think as her trousers were pulled down and Silver Eagle feasted on parts of her that had her breath jammed in her chest. His fingers roused sensations in her nether region that had her gasping. Her hips lifted of their own accord, meeting his finger as it slipped inside.

Moments later, slick, ready for—for? She wasn't sure, but when he probed for entrance, she opened, accepting him as naturally as if they'd made love for years, yet with the innocence and incredulity of a virgin.

Her passage contracted against his fullness. He waited for her to relax. Waited while she absorbed the invasion that didn't hurt, exactly, but was foreign to her body.

They moved together in a dance as old as creation. She caressed his hard-muscled back and drew him closer. Something delicious built inside. Indescribable.

"Silver Eagle," she sighed as her eyes glazed and she could no longer see this man she loved.

Only feel.

****

"He's not here."

Mariah jumped, spinning to face Tanner. Her cheeks flushed. Shrugging, she hooked a stirrup on the saddle horn and began loosening the cinch. "I'm not sure when he'll be here, brother dear, but that's when we'll speak to the folks."

"Puttin' it off—"

"We aren't! I'm not sure he's ready to have anything to do with white men for a while. Glory, Tanner, on top of the pummeling you gave him, he was locked up for days. Can't you appreciate what that did to him? How unsettling that was for a man like Silver Eagle?"

"Hell yes, I can understand it. Maybe better than you, sister dear," he added with a sneer.

"But the sooner y'all face the folks, the sooner you'll realize how impossible the situation is."

He rubbed the back of his neck with his hand, sighing. "This will hurt him and me in ways you'll never understand, never feel, sis. Hell, it might end Silver Eagle's association with all of us. But better to get it over with, better to know rather'n drag out to the inevitable."

"Tanner, I won't believe that. Nothing is inevitable. Besides, he doesn't want Ma and Pa to see what you did to him. He's not one to lie. So how could he explain it to them? No matter what the folks decide, he loves you like a brother and always will."

"Yeah? Then why did you two kiss? He said hisself that nothin' could come of it."

"*I* pushed him to it! Dadburnit, this has nothing to do with you. I hope to marry him!"

"Oh, God, Mariah, you can't—"

"Why not? It's about time people realize Silver Eagle is not much different than they are. That his people are peaceful and no threat to anyone."

"You won't change the way folks think, sis. Not in this lifetime."

"Starting with you, Tanner? You won't accept Silver Eagle as an equal?"

"Don't throw this on me, Mariah. I've always considered Sil a brother, and you know it."

She flung the saddle up on the cross fence. "Prove it!"

After pulling the bridle from Nutmeg's head, she draped it over her shoulder, stepped out of the stall, and planted fists on her hips. "Stand with us, Tanner, when we tell Ma and Pa."

"Your desire to fight worries the shit outta me, but maybe I can talk sense into Sil."

"You're barking up the wrong tree. Silver Eagle loves me as much as I love him. So, I'll ask you again. Will you accept Silver Eagle as a brother in fact, Tanner? Are you willing to accept children we might be blessed with as your kin?"

"Dammit! This is not about me, not about anyone but you and Silver Eagle. Stop tryin' to saddle me with your problems!" He pulled off his hat and tunneled fingers through damp hair. "I'm not the one that needs convincin'."

"Oh, really?" She thrust her chin at him, closing the distance between them. "Then why did you fly into him?"

"Because I know how futile a relationship between you two is. And not only from Ma and Pa's way of thinkin'. Hell, if the neighbors find out, they'll probably lynch Sil. You know as well as me that McCallister would string 'em all up if he could."

"Glory! I don't care about the neighbors! The only ones who matter to me are Ma, Pa and you. Everyone on the ranch will accept Silver Eagle as my husband as readily as they've been willing to work beside him."

"Parks ain't too happy about it."

"Ain't happy about what?"

"Speak of the devil," Tanner muttered just loud enough for Mariah to hear.

Both turned to face the man who carried a gun, and knew how to use it. Mariah had seen him draw. He could strike as lightning fast as a rattler. Parks wore the characteristics of a gunfighter as comfortably as his gun rode against his hip. Yet he was cool headed, as reliable as Max.

Studying him, Mariah thought, no help for it. Just spit it out. "From what I've seen, you don't cotton to working beside Silver Eagle."

Parks sauntered through the wide doors, his horse trailing a pace behind. Both brought the smell of dust and wild sage with them. "Ain't had a row with him, but I keep my eyes peeled. That's a fact."

He opened a stall gate and motioned Skeeter in same as he'd usher a person ahead of him. The well-trained horse moseyed directly to the manger, which Samuel kept full of alfalfa or oats.

"Glory, Mr. Parks, Silver Eagle is trustworthy."

He dipped his head, finger to his hat brim, respectful-like. "I ain't arguin' with you, Miss Mariah. Have no reason to. Yet."

He tempered the last word with a grin that didn't quite reach his gray eyes.

Mariah let the subject drop. She wasn't about to air her concerns before a hand, and arguing with her brother accomplished not one blessed thing. All she could do was hope disaster wouldn't follow in her wake.

Chapter Twenty-Two

Silver Eagle failed to show the next week. As Mariah went about her chores half heartedly, two weeks more slid by and still no word from him. The days came and went, and she grew more agitated. Maybe Tanner was right. Maybe Silver Eagle's people had raised a ruckus he couldn't surmount. Or maybe he hadn't spoken to them about her.

Or didn't want to.

Toward the end of the fourth week, she woke and sat up in bed. Before she could throw back the cover and hang her legs over the edge of the mattress, the room did a quick spin. She clamped her hand against a queasy stomach.

"Beans," she muttered and forced herself out of bed. She'd made a pig of herself last night on butterbeans and cornbread.

By the time she had washed her face and pulled on a clean shirtwaist and trousers, her stomach had settled and she felt almost herself. She clipped her hat off the half horseshoe mounted on the wall beside the door and started for the kitchen.

Ma, as usual, bustled about as though fearing a whipping if she failed to have breakfast on the table by the time her family arrived. This morning, Mariah was the last.

Tanner hunched over a steaming cup, glumly staring at the coffee. He hated getting up before dawn, and yet he'd never think of shirking his share of the labor. For the past three weeks they had worked long days to get the dipping and branding

213

done. They'd go through the same thing again come spring. At least there wouldn't be as many then, only new birthed.

Of course, work wasn't the only reason he was down in the mouth. He'd probably be as prickly as a burr under a saddle until she and Silver Eagle faced their problems.

Pa, shock painting his features, looked up from the one-sheet *Bulletin* Cyril Stokes printed biweekly. "Jehoshaphat! Howling Coyote went and killed hisself."

Holding a skillet of fried potatoes, Ma swung around, the astonishment on her face as profound as that on her brother's, and undoubtedly her own.

"Damn! How?" Tanner asked.

Pa read a moment longer. "Says here he grabbed the sheriff's wrist when he handed him his supper. Yanked him against the bars and got his gun. Blew the side of his own head off afore Tate could extricate hisself."

"Good Lord! Thank heaven he didn't shoot Sheriff Tate," Ma said as she placed the potatoes on the table. "When did this happen?"

"More'n a week ago." He glanced at Mariah and then at Tanner. "Guess this is the reason we ain't seen nothin' of Silver Eagle."

Mariah and Tanner eyed each other as she took her seat at the table. Neither said a word.

Her mother slid a plate of fried eggs in front of her. Mariah clamped a hand over her mouth and scraped back the chair. "Nothing for me," she mumbled and hastened for the outhouse.

While she hadn't upchucked, she felt shaky and pale when she returned to the kitchen. Her mother gave her a narrow-eyed once over. "Don't tell me you're coming down with something."

Mariah shook her head. Sipped the milk sitting at her place. Thank the Lord, the eggs were gone.

And she knew just who had scarfed them down. Tanner swished a piece of biscuit over his plate, soaked up the last of the yellow and popped it in his mouth.

She shuddered. "I think I overdid the beans last night. I'll be all right, Ma."

Still studying the article, Pa said, "I wonder if we ought to take a ride to the village, Tanner? See if there's anythin' we can do for that little widow of Howling Coyote's."

Again, Tanner exchanged a speaking glance with Mariah. "I don't know if that's a good idea. Sil hasn't been here since he got out of jail. Seems to me, if they wanted us around, he'd've contacted us and told us what Howling Coyote done. He's had plenty of time."

Besides, Mariah thought, it wasn't as though Painted Woman was like a neighbor. One Ma would take comfort food to, as she had to the McCallisters some time ago.

****

"Dang! What is wrong with me?"

Mariah braced her head between her hands. Not only did she have a queasy stomach for the third morning in a row, her head pounded with sharp pain like a blacksmith's hammer on an anvil.

Dragging herself up, she listlessly donned shirtwaist and trousers. When she leaned over the washbowl, her stomach heaved. Gulping back bile, she splashed cool water into her face, then rinsed her sour-tasting mouth.

While drying with the towel, Mariah leaned closer to the mirror over the dresser. Bloodshot eyes stared back at her. The few freckles across her nose stood out against unusually pale skin. She looked as bad as she felt.

By the time she reached the kitchen, Pa and Tanner had already left the house. She eased down on the chair and propped her elbow, resting her head in her hand. "No breakfast for me, Ma. I've got a headache that won't quit."

Her mother frowned as she cleared the dirty plates and cutlery from the table. "Coffee?"

"Um. I guess."

Thank goodness the steaming brew didn't make her stomach roil when she took a sip. In fact, it settled her a little.

Her mother took her usual seat at the oblong table and sipped her coffee. "Am I going to have to give you a dose of castor oil, hon?"

Mariah gagged. "Glory, Ma, don't even mention it!"

Her mother chuckled. "At least the thought put a bit of color in your cheeks." She laid a palm on Mariah's forehead. "Clammy. You don't feel warm enough for a fever, though."

"Dadburnit, I'm not sick. It'll pass. Just like my upset stomach earlier."

"Again?"

"Not for long." She looked into her mother's speculative eyes. "Maybe I should lay off fried meat and potatoes for a while."

"I'm snapping a mess of green beans and roasting a beef haunch for supper."

Mariah nodded, finished her coffee, and went to the stove and sliced off a chunk of her mother's sourdough bread.

As she nibbled, Ma said, "That won't keep a body together until lunch."

She plopped on her hat and mustered a faint smile. "I'm working in the barn today. If I get the hungers, I'll come back for something."

****

Silver Eagle sat on his heels, listening to the elders express opinions regarding a warrior who had, on the one hand, dishonored the band, but on

216

the other had hunted and shared his bounty. His name would forever be banished from utterance, but his hunting exploits could be praised.

And Uncle Crow Dog did so now. "The Gods smile on those who hunt only to feed their people. The warrior shared much, and his generosity will be missed."

"*Haa*," several agreed, though most only nodded.

Silver Eagle did nothing. He was here to honor the band's ritual, not the warrior. The man had taken the coward's way out. There had been no mourning, no wailing, and he had not been given sacred burial rites. Silver Eagle could not, would not believe the Spirits would allow a coward to ride a winged stallion through eternity.

Kill Deer had already taken Painted Woman as a third wife. And within the band, the father of her children would never be mentioned again.

The single ceremonial drum had barely quieted when Silver Eagle rose to his feet, nodded respectfully to his father, his uncle, and the others seated around the small fire. Darkness had descended, and he was anxious to return to the prairie. After gathering fresh supplies from his tipi, he started toward the remuda.

Quiet Bird appeared out of the gloom before him and gestured. "*Ni pabi?.*" She swept her arm toward their grandmother's tipi, and patted her lips. "Wings of a Dove wishes to speak with you."

Though he might wish otherwise, he would never ignore his grandmother's summons. He nodded and followed Quiet Bird, depositing his belongings beside the tipi's entrance before ducking inside.

As usual, his mother sat on the far side of the tipi, hands busy. Reeds filled a basket by her knee. A superior basket weaver, Sparrow supplied baskets of various sizes to all band members. Occasionally she gifted one to Mrs. Kelly.

Silver Eagle paused to admire his mother's intricately woven work, then nodded respectively to his elder. "You wished to speak with me, *nï cáco?*"

She gestured for him to sit. "I will not keep you long."

Behind him, the tipi flap whispered closed as Quiet Bird left. He waited uncomfortably while his revered elder scanned his face and his hands.

"You are healed with no ill effects."

The statement required nothing from him, so he remained quiet. He had long since come to the conclusion that the less said, the better to thwart opening subjects he considered private.

When her eyes narrowed, he sighed inwardly. The ploy did not always work. It appeared she would have her say.

"These few nights past, my dreams have disturbed me, Silver Eagle. You would do well to speak to the woman with fire-lit hair. She has news." Wings of a Dove paused, dark eyes closing. She swayed, muttering unintelligibly.

He cocked his head when she smiled as if she had lapped up all the honey from a comb.

"Tanner Kelly is not anxious for me to speak with his sister."

"When has any man stopped you from your chosen path?"

Never.

He, himself, was the problem. He had not yet decided if he *could* take the path he longed to travel. Truth, he should not have made love to Mariah. It only made him want her more.

"*Cáco,* what is this news of which you speak?"

"That is for the Kelly woman to say." She proceeded to light and puff thoughtfully on her pipe. An enigmatic expression settled on her countenance like a cloak.

Frustrated that he would get nothing more from her, Silver Eagle headed back to his secluded camp. Whether or not he returned to the Broken Spur and Mr. Kelly's employ remained to be seen.

Chapter Twenty-Three

"Glory!" Mariah whispered in astonishment. "I'm pregnant!"

"I feared so. My prayers the past few days have been in vain."

Startled, Mariah looked at her mother's image in the mirror, then turned to face her. Ma closed the door behind her. Thank God. What was Pa going to say?

Searching her mother's expression, Mariah realized it mattered not that the news would trouble her parents.

She put a trembling hand against her flat stomach, a slow smile lighting her features. "I'm glad, Ma. I want this baby more than anything."

"Your father will be very..." Pensive, she *tsk*ed. "I don't know how he will take the news. When did you manage to be alone with Silver Eagle?"

Mariah's brow crinkled. "I haven't said who the father is, Ma. How could you know?"

"Mariah, every time he appears, your feelings for him are written on your face as plainly as a headline in Cyril's *Bulletin*. Even before you left for school, I knew this trouble was headed your way."

"Trouble? Ma, I *want* this baby."

"Of course you do. A daughter of mine would. But what about Silver Eagle? What will his people think? You well know the reason only he goes into town. Comanches are not welcome there, never have been. And a half-breed child..." Sorrow lit her hazel eyes. "God, hon, you may be visiting hell on Earth upon this child."

"Then I will go somewhere—"

"Where, Mariah? Stop. Think, honey. Where could you go that white people wouldn't give you grief? And would Silver Eagle go with you? This is his child, too." She scowled. "You wouldn't think of not telling him."

A tread sounded in the hallway, and their conversation abruptly ceased. Tanner, Mariah thought. Thank goodness he passed by.

Her mother swung around for the door. "I'd best get breakfast on the table." Hand on the doorknob, she paused. "We'll talk again later, Mariah."

****

That night, long after quiet reigned in the house, Mariah stole out of the back door into the starless night. A breeze slapped her face. Good thing she'd worn her coat; the lower temperature heralded fall.

Opting to check Silver Eagle's campsite before visiting the village, she was relieved to find him still there. The fire glowed invitingly as she approached. Gracefully, he rose to his feet and waited.

"What you do here, woman? No safe you travel night shadows." Even as he remonstrated her, he came forward and took Nutmeg's reins, then tethered her near his horse.

While Mariah had remembered her coat, her gloves lay forgotten in the tack room. She extended her chilled hands over the fire.

She felt Silver Eagle's body heat warming her back, and his arms slid around her. His fingers laced with hers as he pulled her against his hard frame.

"You no should be here, but thankful to Spirits you come." His voice rumbled in her ear, sending a shiver of pleasure down her spine.

"I need to talk to you."

He turned her in his arms. Firelight flickered

221

over his face, making dark angles of his cheeks, reflecting in his eyes. Eyes hot with the same desire that pulsed through her veins.

"First I do this." He lowered his head and took her mouth in a searing kiss that turned up her toes. When he finally released her kiss-swollen lips, his arms still circled her. Had he let her go, she probably would've pitched right over on her face. Diabolical, the way the man stole her senses and twisted them into knots.

"Come," he said softly and made her comfortable near the fire.

Following her down, he sat near, too near for her racing pulse to settle. And she needed her wits about her. What would he say? Would he be angry? Would he care?

"Silver Eagle, have you ever considered living away—away from your people?"

"Why you ask? You father no want me work now for him?"

"No. Don't think that, not for a moment. It's..." She fumbled around like a ten-year old. *Spit it out. Find out exactly where you stand with this man. The father of the child growing inside you at this very moment.*

"Do you like children?"

He poked at the small fire. "Why you ask?"

Glory, he wasn't making this easy. "What I mean is, do you want children of your own? Someday?" she added lamely, still meandering around the main issue.

"All man want son of loins."

"Dang it. You! Do *you* want children of your own?"

He didn't answer.

Ever so slowly, his head turned her way. Dark eyes unfathomable in the firelight searched her face. A stick crackled, disintegrating, sending sparks dancing skyward.

Her heart sank. He didn't want children. Now what would she do?

"You carry my son?"

She blinked, wishing she knew what his sober expression meant. "Um. What if it's a girl?"

"You carry my son?" he demanded.

"Yes! But I don't—"

"You no want him? I take him after come forth."

She scrambled to her feet and ran to her horse. As she reached for the reins, his hands clamped around her wrists. She tried in vain to jerk from his grasp.

"Let me go!"

"You no want my son, I take him."

His mouth a flat line, she well understood why some white folks were terrified of Indians. Oddly, she didn't fear him, though his grip was almost bruising.

"Stop it! You won't take *my* son. Or daughter," she added, determined to make him understand she might have a girl child, one not as valued as a boy in his culture.

But maybe that wasn't true in his band. Even though she was mute, Quiet Bird didn't appear ill treated. And it was evident his grandmother was a powerful woman, well respected. Howling Coyote had surely been the exception, she assured herself.

While Silver Eagle didn't release her, his grip eased, and he studied her face. "Breed no welcome in white world."

That was certainly not news. "Would he be in yours?"

"No dare hurt Comanche chief's grandson."

"Or granddaughter," she persisted, and finally saw a glimmer of a smile light his eyes.

His lips softened. "Maybe so. I understand?" He cocked his head. "You want my child?"

223

Are you brave, Mariah? Can you profess your love without assurance of his?

She tugged, and this time he released her wrists.

"Silver Eagle, in my world, when a woman loves a man, she wants to give him children." She laid a hand on her stomach. "I want this child as much as I want his father."

He may as well have been a statue. Not even a breath stirred his chest. Only his intense eyes proved him alive. The silence was so profound, she fancied she heard the flames flicker in the small fire.

She closed her eyes against the pain. He didn't want her, only the child they had made. Then she felt his fingers slide across her cheek, brush her ear, and tangle in her hair.

As she opened her eyes, she found him so close, his breath warmed her face.

"Love in my heart is breath I take. Sound of voice, feel of soft skin make body sing prayer of thanks." He raised his other hand and cupped her cheek. "In dreams see eyes like summer grass, lips that smile." His gaze wandered over her entire face, scanned her hair as he fingered curls. "Hair soft like fawn belly." He leaned closer, feathering a kiss over her eager mouth. "I inside you, feel whole."

She couldn't stop tears from welling in her eyes when she saw such tenderness in his, heard it in his voice. He wrapped his arms around her, nestled her in an embrace that spoke of possession.

"Home," she murmured, and lifted her lips to his.

He led her back to his blanket near the fire. Within moments he had her quivering like a dollop of jelly. Heat raged through her as she offered her body.

Silver Eagle's touch lingered on each sensitive spot he found. Sparks ignited beneath his talented fingers.

"More," she gasped, arching to meet his thrusts. Her hands raced over his broad shoulders; greedy nails scored his back.

His mouth ravaged hers, then, nipping her from throat to collarbone, he paused to lick and soothe. "*Haa! Kamari, nīnī animui*—together."

Sure she soared into the heavens, Mariah didn't know how much time had passed while she blissfully floated back to Earth. Little aftershocks detonated in her belly for long moments while she lay unable to move. She laughed at how much effort it took to simply turn her head.

He had moved from atop her, his head only inches from hers on the blanket. For the first time ever, she saw a full smile on his gorgeous face.

"Why laugh?"

"I'm happy. You are the father of my child. We're together. What more could I want?" She slid one hand protectively over her belly and clasped his with the other. "One day our child may grow up to be— She chuckled again and teased. "A troll."

He sat up, brow furrowed. "What troll is?"

Oh dear. Silver Eagle would take what she said literally. "Um. Truly, I'm only joshing, Silver Eagle. Trolls are found in folklore from across the sea."

He tilted his head. Wouldn't leave it alone. She sat up, too. "All right, I'll tell you, but it's a joke. Don't take what I say as gospel, Silver Eagle." When he looked further confused, she moaned, "Dear Lord."

"Tell me."

"In folklore a troll is another name for a dwarf, sometimes a giant. An ugly one."

He laid his hand on her belly, and serious as Judge Rogers, he said, "He born giant, you suffer much."

She stared at him. Oh for— He *had* taken her

literally. Then he looked up, devilment flashing in his eyes.

"Oh! You, you—"

For the first time, she heard Silver Eagle laugh, really laugh. He left no doubt he knew what a joke was. Pushing her back to the blanket, he covered her. And in moments laughter turned to heat, heat to scorching lovemaking.

****

Sometime later, Mariah stirred. Glory! She'd fallen asleep. Looking up into the star-drenched sky, she searched for the North Star. Maybe they should name their first daughter Star. She smiled at the thought. While she wouldn't give him the satisfaction, like Silver Eagle, she somehow knew this first child born of their love would be the son he predicted.

Silver Eagle leaned over to kiss her belly, then laid his head where he had kissed. Arm curved around her, he held her protectively.

"What was that you said before?"

He stayed where he was, his breath fanning her bare belly.

"When you speak of?"

"A little while ago, just before we…you know. You said *ka—kamari*, or something like that."

"Ah. *Kamari, nïnï animui.*" He caressed her side. "I say, 'Come, we fly.'"

A silly grin blossomed. "We certainly did *that*. Twice."

He sat back on his heels, eyes troubled. "Sun rise soon. Now take home."

"What's wrong, Silver Eagle?" The question had barely left her mouth when she realized she knew the answer. "We will tell them together." Not only her parents but his, too.

****

The sun crested the horizon as Mariah and

Silver Eagle rode into the barn and spied Parks. Already up and preparing for work, Parks paused as he reached for his saddle draped over a crossbar. His expression didn't change as he glanced from Mariah to Silver Eagle and back.

Parks didn't need to say a word. His lack of expression at seeing them ride in together—at dawn—showed clearly that it stuck in his craw, as it would with many of the neighbors.

"Good morning," she said, pushing him to accept the inevitable.

"Mornin'," he said—to her.

Silver Eagle had nothing on this man of few words. The two prideful men stared each other down. Then, surprising her, J.D. Parks inclined his head, acknowledging Silver Eagle.

Although he hid it well, Parks couldn't have missed Silver Eagle's start of surprise. Mariah prayed the hard man's mental shrug was a portent of things to come. After all, Silver Eagle and his people had lived on the Broken Spur longer than any white man had lived in Burnett Station. None of them had ever suffered at the tribe's hands, nor would they.

Max Stoddard walked in, followed by Samuel and Ben Stewart. "You're up early," Max said to her. Seeing Silver Eagle, he said, "Glad you're back. We can use your bullwhip persuasion on a couple cantankerous cows. They ain't happy 'bout given up their younguns."

"Max, we're headed to the house. It'll be a little while before Silver Eagle will be out to work."

Clearly perplexed, he nodded.

When they turned to leave, Silver Eagle's mount dutifully followed him.

"You want I should stable your horse, Silver Eagle?" Samuel called.

"No need, maybe," he said.

Before Mariah got all the way in the back door, her mother started on her. "Honest to God, Mariah, if I hadn't birthed you myself, I'd think you were kin to an idiot. When your father discovers you were out all night—"

Her mother's tirade abruptly halted when Silver Eagle stepped into the house behind Mariah. Ma's hand flew to her chest. "Dear Mother Mary, this will not end well."

Although Mariah feared she was right, she had no more time to figure out how to tell her father. He chose that moment to stride from the hallway into the kitchen, hat in hand. Mariah couldn't get a breath, sure she would suffocate.

Pa halted, clearly surprised to see Silver Eagle there. "Haven't seen you in several weeks, but I'm sure glad you're here."

Understandable, Mariah thought. Silver Eagle could handle cattle like no one else.

Pa's welcoming smile died when he noticed her sober expression, and Ma's. "What's wrong?"

"I speak with you, Mr. Kelly."

"*We*, Silver Eagle," Mariah said.

Pa's brow creased. "I can almost taste the tension in here." He looked down at the table, where a steaming rasher of bacon and a platter of flapjacks grew cold. "Why are y'all standin'? Better eat while the food's hot."

Silver Eagle stood stiff shouldered, one hand resting on the knife hilt at his waist. "Mr. Kelly, I break trust. I—"

"You certainly did not!" Mariah said. "If blame is to be assigned, then I, more than you, caused this."

Still, no one moved.

"No—"

"Hold it!" Pa threw up a hand. "What in tarnation are you two disagreein' about? You're doin' nothin' but confusin' a body."

"Ward, I think you should sit down."

He tunneled fingers through his abundant hair. "Jehoshaphat! Would y'all stop dancin' 'round the campfire and tell me what's goin' on?"

"She wants to marry Silver Eagle," Tanner said in a quiet voice.

Her brother stood in the hall doorway, green eyes stormy.

"Who? What the dickens are you talkin' about, son?"

"Me, Pa. He's talking about me. Silver Eagle and I have fallen in love. We want to marry."

"Good God Almighty, daughter, have you lost your mind? Ain't goin' to happen. Hell's fire, you two are like brother and sister. You know as well as me—"

"I'm pregnant, Pa."

"Is my child," Silver Eagle said.

Her father took a step back. He looked from one to the other, finally settling on practical Ma. "Tell me this is a joke, Sarah." A scowl creased his brow. "A bad one, but a joke."

"Pa, I wouldn't..." Mariah clasped Silver Eagle's hand. "*We* wouldn't josh you about this."

"Is my son," Silver Eagle insisted.

Before she or anyone could say another word, Pa lunged forward and smashed his fist into Silver Eagle's chin, ripping his hand out of Mariah's and sending him crashing into the wall.

Silver Eagle managed to stay on his feet. But instead of defending himself, he rubbed his bruised chin.

Pa reared back to smack him another facer.

Mariah grabbed his arm. "No! Stop it. He won't fight you, Pa!"

His momentum took Mariah off her feet. Still clinging to her pa's arm, her body swung like a pendulum, slamming against the wall just as Silver

Eagle had. "Ah!" she moaned, her breath leaving in a rush.

"Mariah!"

She heard all four chorus as she crumpled to the floor.

"Goddammit!" Pa exclaimed at the same time Ma cried, "Oh, Ward, what have you done?"

Though Pa leaned down to help her up, Silver Eagle was there ahead of him. He tenderly eased her up to half sit, her shoulders resting against his buckskin-clad knee.

Distress clearly painted on his face, Silver Eagle cried, "My heart!"

She forced a reassuring smile. "I'm okay. Help me up."

Her father raised a beseeching hand. "Gawd, daughter, I'm sorry. You gonna be all right?"

"Yes, Pa." Mariah straightened, winced, and brushed a hand on the hip that had banged against the wall.

Her mother pulled out a chair. "Sit here, hon."

****

His arm around Mariah's waist, Silver Eagle started to help her the few feet to the chair, but her father slipped his arm across her back from the other side.

Rather than cause more distress, Silver Eagle stepped away. He backed against the wall and waited. This was not over. He *would* have the woman of his heart. And no man would deny him his son.

Once Mariah was settled in the chair, Mr. Kelly stalked over to confront him again. "I want you out of here, Silver Eagle. Off my land. You had no right touchin' my daughter. The two of you know you can't live together in these parts."

"Then we'll go somewhere else," Mariah said.

Kelly rounded on her. "The hell you will. You

belong right here with us, and that's where you're gonna stay, young lady. Your baby will be raised as a Kelly."

Not so, Mr. Kelly. I will raise my son.

Mrs. Kelly moved toward him and laid her hand on his shoulder. Not only could Silver Eagle *see* the sorrow in her eyes, he could *feel* her anguish in her trembling hand as well.

Quietly, she said, "Go. For now. We will make this right, Silver Eagle. You'll see."

He did not see, but he would not cause Mariah more pain. If necessary, he would steal in during the night and spirit his woman and child from her family. He prayed to the Spirits it would not come to that. But he would if forced to it, he silently vowed.

For a moment, Silver Eagle stood where he was. The woman of his heart was so beautiful.

"I need to get to work," Tanner said and crossed the room. His lifelong friend searched Silver Eagle's own troubled expression. "I warned you. I warned both of you."

"I know." After one lingering glance at Mariah, Silver Eagle walked out the door ahead of Tanner.

Chapter Twenty-Four

Midmorning, Silver Eagle had barely explained his intention before his father called a family council. Now he sat in his grandmother's tipi, surrounded by those he loved and trusted—Father Falcon Wing, Mother Sparrow, sister Quiet Bird, and Uncle Crow Dog. As shaman, Grandmother Wings of a Dove sat in the place of honor.

"Silver Eagle, the Kelly woman will not be happy living amongst The People." Wings of a Dove shrugged. "You know it is our tradition that the warrior live within the maiden's family."

He did not have to be reminded. But his grandmother had neither heard Mr. Kelly's ultimatum nor seen the pain in his eyes. Tanner, Mrs. Kelly—all had suffered shock and sorrow. Sorrow for what each perceived could never be.

"*Cáco*, Mr. Kelly speaks truth. It would be very difficult for me to live openly with Mariah in their home. The entire family would be censured by the townspeople."

"You think that censure would not extend to the band?" Falcon Wing said. "You think the townspeople would not descend upon us, perhaps with guns?"

A possibility, of course. His people had suffered for generations at the hands of white men. The Comanche had fought back. Sometimes viciously. Others learned to endure. Some, like his family, had thrived. However, in truth, this time *he* would be the cause if anyone suffered or died.

"*Nï tua?*, I did not see you give tribute to a father for his daughter's hand," Sparrow said.

"That is not her family's way."

He searched each troubled face. Was it right to put his gentle mother and sister in danger? Grandmother had lived many moons. She had experienced much hardship, but now she was old. How could he justify once again visiting adversity on her head?

"*Nï pabi?*," Crow Dog said, "Silver Eagle is your *tua?*. Do you think he will turn from his chosen mate and the child of his loins?" He sliced the air with his hand. "*You* would not. Your *tua?* will not. The babe will be of our people. He belongs here if the maid's family will not accept Silver Eagle."

Sparrow and Quiet Bird nodded. Even Wings of a Dove reluctantly agreed.

Falcon Wing's expression did not change when he said, "I will think on this. Other warriors must be apprised of possible calamity visiting us. They have the right to voice an opinion, to agree or disagree, before I make my decision."

****

Still awake after a long day of working through one frustration after another, Sarah counted the chimes as they measured ten o'clock. Sitting up, she brushed a hand across the cold sheet next to her and stared into the dark. She'd heard nothing of Ward for over an hour.

Sighing, she reached for the warm wool shawl her father had given her when she turned twenty. Just before all hell broke loose for her and Ward as it had for Mariah and Silver Eagle this morning. Like mother, like daughter?

She pulled on soft leather slippers and left the bedroom. Finding Ward nowhere in the house, she went outside through the rarely used front door.

Folding the wrap closer around her shoulders,

233

Sarah began to circle the house, peering studiously at the ground for fear of disturbing nightcrawlers of the dangerous kind. Surely Ward hadn't left the compound. Not this late. He wouldn't have gone to visit the Indian village at night.

With no moon to spill even faint light, she almost missed him. He sat atop the table beneath the oak, where they sometimes ate the midday meal or supper when the entire kitchen felt like the inside of the woodstove's oven. Booted feet on a bench, he leaned forward, elbows on his spread knees.

He didn't acknowledge her presence until she was close enough to look into his shadowed, troubled face. Even then, he didn't say a word, just reached out and scooped her up and onto his lap. Then he buried his face against her neck.

She slid her arms around his broad torso and waited. Like her, sometimes even more so, Ward was an eminently practical man. He only needed time to sort through his chaotic thoughts. At least, she prayed that would be the case this time.

Long moments passed, his breath whispering against her skin. Cattle moved restlessly in the pen where they'd be branded tomorrow. A pity, she thought, that Silver Eagle would not be here to help. He could, all by himself, take down a steer with the snap of his whip and hold it immobile long enough to brand. He didn't need near the room the wranglers required to rope from horseback.

Ward kissed her throat and lifted his head. "One helluva mess, ain't it, darlin'?"

"Surely you weren't completely surprised."

He gazed into the distance. "Afore Mariah left for the East, I noticed interest for each other in both of 'em. But after two years, I hoped they'd have gotten over it."

She leaned back in the circle of his arms. "Do you recall what you said to my father?"

A sheepish grin turned up his lips. "You mean when he threatened to horsewhip me if I didn't get off his porch?"

"That very time, Ward Kelly." When he looked at her without saying anything, she prompted, "Well?"

"Absence'll only make the heart grow fonder, Mr. Davenport."

She cupped his whisker-stubbled cheek and smiled. "I remember a more personal statement, dear heart."

"Huh?"

"Don't be coy with me, Ward." She chuckled. "You can't pull it off." When he refused to say more, she went on. "'*My*,' you said. 'Will make *my* heart grow fonder.'"

"All right. And it's true. But Mariah's a youngun. She—"

"You can't use that excuse, Ward. Our girl is no longer the apple-cheeked cherub who stole both our hearts from her first gurgling laugh. And I ask you, how old was I when we ran off?"

"We ran here, Sarah. The townspeople could have cared less about us. With Mariah and Silver Eagle, it's different. Where could they go without trouble?"

"Is that what you want? For your daughter to run away?"

"No. And she ain't goin' to. I already told her—"

"*Threatened*. Just like my father threatened me, both of us. And did I listen? Did you?"

He clamped his mouth shut while she looked intently into his stricken gray eyes. "Ward, do you want to lose your daughter? I certainly don't. Mariah grew up while in Baltimore. She was forced to mature, to watch men die, agonizingly sometimes. She didn't run from those horrors. I don't think she will run from verbal abuse by neighbors. She's made of sterner stuff."

"Verbal abuse? That's not what I fear, darlin'."

"Physical violence?" She scoffed. "There's not a white man within a hundred miles who would dare lay a hand on Mariah. Everyone knows you and Tanner would shoot and ask questions later. But, dear heart, we will lose her if you persist in browbeating. You and I both know it."

She shrugged. "Search your heart, dear. Do you really believe Silver Eagle will walk away from his child? From the woman he loves? You heard him. He called her 'my heart.' Does that sound like a man you could easily run off? Just like Mariah, he's made of sterner stuff."

She stroked his cheek, whiskers rasping against her fingers. "Do you really believe our daughter would be in this situation if they loved each other any less than you and I love one another?"

"I ain't sayin' that, darlin'. But both of 'em are sensible. They'll be up against a damn sight more than we were if they live together openly."

"'Sensible' has no bearing on how they feel about each other. My darling, when was love ever measured by common sense?"

Somewhere beyond the cleared compound, coyotes yipped. Sarah turned to listen. Years ago that sound would have sent chills down her spine because raiding Indians mimicked the same sounds before they descended to steal horses or carry off settlers' children or wives, sometimes leaving dead amidst burning homes.

Now, thank God, that yipping really was coyotes running down prey. Even so, lantern light blossomed in the bunkhouse window. Max would be up with rifle in hand to check out things.

She and Ward sat quietly until the light was extinguished again. Laying her head on his shoulder, Sarah sighed. There was nothing more she could say. Ward would do what he thought best. "It's late. We need to seek our bed."

He rubbed her back in a consoling gesture. "Yeah."

As she leaned away to get off his lap, he slipped an arm beneath her knees and rose, lifting her.

"Good Lord, put me down! I'm too heavy."

Laughter rumbled in his chest. "The day I can't carry my slip of a girl is the day I'll be six feet under."

"*Slip* of a girl?" It was her turn to laugh. Over the years she'd only gained five pounds over what she'd weighed when they married. But a one-hundred-twenty-five-pound woman was certainly no featherweight.

Looking at her husband's stubborn jaw as he strode to the back of the house, Sarah argued no further. Truth be known, when Ward held her in his arms, she felt cherished. And she thanked the good Lord every day for that gift.

****

The next morning, stuffing trousers, socks, and shirtwaists into the battered portmanteau she'd lugged across the country, Mariah sniffed. A vain attempt to stop her nose from running. Of course, if she'd control her blubbering, it would take care of itself.

Glory. Why couldn't Pa see that she and Silver Eagle had considered the problems they would face? Besides, no matter what other people thought, if Ward and Sarah Kelly accepted Silver Eagle into their family, the townspeople could flap like wet sheets in the wind for all she cared. They might not like it, but they wouldn't hurt her or her family—or Silver Eagle.

For years Pa had faced them down because he'd given Wings of a Dove his word. In turn, Falcon Wing had given his. Never again would there be raiding or bloodshed between his Comanche band and anyone on the Broken Spur. Though never voiced, the same assurance extended to Burnett Station's residents. That bond had stood unbroken for nearly three decades and would continue to stand.

Once, when she'd been very young, Mariah remembered other Comanche had stormed down from the North, intent on uprooting the white men who'd had the gall to settle on land they'd hunted for centuries. Land that belonged to no man.

Between singing hymns off key, Ma had rocked her to sleep with vaguely remembered tales of Falcon Wing standing at her father's side, determined to kill those of his own blood rather than break his vow to a white man.

Mariah cast a forlorn glance around her room. To never again live in her own haven, a haven she'd longed for during those years in Baltimore, hurt her heart in ways she could not explain. Nor was it likely Silver Eagle's people would accept her in their midst.

She closed and buckled the straps on the soft-sided satchel, then straightened her shoulders. While Pa might try, he couldn't really stop her from going to the man she loved. And by glory, she would do just that.

A rap sounded on the door. She waited for whoever knocked to open the door, but it remained firmly closed. *Not Ma.*

Leaving her travel case in plain sight, she opened the door. Pa filled the wide portal with his larger than life presence. Though she couldn't halt the fresh tears, she lifted her chin, determined to go her own way. She was grown. She'd lived through the resultant horrors of war, taken care of dying men. And Pa would have to accept her decision.

When her father spied the case on her bed, his

gray eyes flickered—with what? Acceptance? Not likely.

"We need to talk, daughter. Don't intend for you to leave the Broken Spur. Not today. Not ever."

Intend? He'd changed his tune a little. "What does that mean, Pa? I'm already Silver Eagle's wife in every way that counts."

He raised a silencing hand. "And that's gonna have to be enough, Mariah. You won't find a preacher man to marry you. You'll just have to cleave to each other like the Bible says."

Hope, a glimmer, kindled in her mind and heart.

He beckoned. "Come on, time for a family powwow in the kitchen. Your ma and Tanner are already there. Your ma brewed a pot of coffee."

Mariah turned back and picked up the case. Before she could grab her hat off the hook, Pa pried the handle from her hand and set the case beside the doorway. Scowling, she searched his unreadable face.

"Let's leave that for now, Mariah. After we talk you'll have plenty of time to retrieve your belongings, if that's what you want."

"Pa—"

"In the kitchen." He pivoted on his heel and walked ahead of her down the narrow hallway.

Chapter Twenty-Five

"How do you think Sil's family will deal with this mess?" Tanner asked Ma as Mariah joined the others.

"I don't appreciate my love for Silver Eagle described as a mess."

"Not talkin' about love, sis. It's the mess you're makin' of your lives." When she opened her mouth, he lifted a finger. "It's true, and you know it."

He didn't soften his statement with a smile. Ma didn't smile, either. Pa scraped back a chair and reached for the enamelware coffeepot. He poured a cup for Mariah and then himself.

Even though she really didn't want it, she took a sip. As always, Ma made open-the-eyes coffee that Mariah swore was strong enough to walk from the cup to her mouth.

"Daughter, your ma and me have talked about this consarned muddy crossin' you and Silver Eagle have stepped into. Looks like you might have to live here on the Broken Spur."

"But you said—"

"I know what I said. I said you'd have a terrible-hard time findin' a place you two can live in peace. White folks don't cotton to Indians, and I'm thinkin' Indians don't much cotton to white folks livin' amongst them, neither. Jessup sure is gonna pitch a fit when he finds out Silver Eagle has moved in here."

"And you know what I think of Mr. McCallister's opinion."

Her cheeky remark earned a longsuffering sigh from her mother.

Mariah backed off her high horse and scored her thumbnail across the oilcloth, following the green and white checked pattern. "Silver Eagle tried, Pa. He really tried his best to hide his feelings for me. It's my fault. He knew, both of us did, that this wouldn't be easy. But you were wrong to take it out on him."

"He should've kept his britches on."

Mariah's face heated. No way was she going to discuss the glorious lovemaking she and Silver Eagle had shared. No sirree, not with her father. Thank goodness he shied from that path, too.

"Sarah, you best have your say."

Her mother gazed at Mariah long enough to have her squirming in her chair. Finally, she turned to Tanner. "Do you think we would be welcome in the village if we all went to speak with Silver Eagle's family?"

"To accomplish what?"

"Don't take that snide tone with me, Tanner Kelly. Silver Eagle is your friend. He's still a man to be reckoned with. And whether you like it or not, he's the father of your sister's unborn child. Boy or girl, it will be your kin."

"That ain't the problem, Ma. It's the fights ahead of us I'm stewin' about." He frowned at Mariah. "Every time he shows his face in Burnett Station, he's gonna be hounded. Dammit, Sil *is* like a brother, and I won't stand idly by and let folks pound on him, neither. Which means both of us will get pounded on." He fiddled with the handle on his enamelware cup. "We'd gotten to where he could ride with me and nobody even glanced our way." He wagged his head. "That sure as shootin' is a thing of the past."

"Like a brother?" Mariah bristled. "You lit into

him pretty good. Brothers don't, or shouldn't, treat each other that way."

"Lit into him when?" Pa asked.

Heat rekindled in her face. "The first time we made love."

"The first?" Pa sputtered. "There's been more than once? Jehoshaphat!" His fingers tunneled through dark-blond hair.

Mariah touched her father's sleeve. "Pa, the reason Silver Eagle didn't show up for work all that time was because Tanner made a mess of his face. Silver Eagle didn't lift a hand in defense."

Her father cut gray eyes to Tanner. "You beat the tar out of him, then kept everythin' to yourself?"

"Yeah, I did. And I'd do it again. If Mariah hadn't gotten pregnant, Sil might've come to his senses."

"Says the young man who has yet to lose his heart to a girl," Ma said.

"I ain't *never* losin' my heart to no woman. No offense, Ma, but skirts give a body nothin' but grief."

Pa guffawed. "My boy, you'd best take that back, or I'm afraid you'll come to know what grief is in this house."

"I said, 'no offense' to Ma. She don't count." He looked at Mariah and shrugged. "Her, too, most of the time. Before now, anyway."

"You think the feelings Silver Eagle and I share will wane if given enough time? Then your life can go on just hunky-dory as before? In one way it will, Tanner. Silver Eagle really will be your brother—in truth, by marriage."

"Didn't you hear Pa?" Clearly exasperated, his voice upped a notch. "No preacher will say words over you two."

"Who said them over Adam and Eve?"

"Christ!"

"Not in this house, Tanner Kelly," her mother

242

admonished.

"Sorry. But—"

"This jawin' ain't gonna solve a thing. Maybe you and me need to take that ride to the Indian village," Pa said. "When we get close, I'll go on ahead and ask if they'll receive us."

Tanner sighed. "I should do that, Pa. They know me better. I'll check it out right now. Back by lunch. If it's okay with 'em, we can ride over this afternoon."

Everything had been taken out of Mariah's hands. For the moment. But at least fists no longer flew. Thank you, God. And Pa was talking now, in a reasonable voice. Which beat shouting by a country mile.

****

Silver Eagle called for another family gathering, well aware his people might reject his choice of a mate. *Might*? His father had not ruled on the matter, so he would try to smooth the way. He did not want Mariah subjected to stony stares.

They gathered in his father's tipi, his grandmother giving up the place of honor to her son. Sparrow also attended to have her say. In their close family, the older women could speak. He knew Quiet Bird would be happy for him. She liked Mariah. But his sister would offer no opinion.

Having finished eating, Falcon Wing picked his teeth with a store-bought match, one of the few luxuries that Silver Eagle regularly brought back from town.

"I assume we owe this calling together of the family to discuss your feelings for the Kelly woman. I must warn you, Silver Eagle, the council does not want a white woman living in our village. Calling attention to our people because she is in our midst is not wise."

"I have mated with the woman of my choice,

Ahpï?. Despite the council's opinions, it is my intention that she live in the village. But first, I need *your* approval."

Silver Eagle glanced around the circle. Except for Wings of a Dove's, faces held curiosity. Hers said she had already seen the trouble headed their way.

Falcon Wing scowled. "Though it grieves me, and without permission from your people, you have mated with the fire-haired woman."

"*Haa*," Silver Eagle said. While he was sorry his father suffered, he knew in his heart he would do it again."

Clasping the medicine bag attached beneath his loin cloth, Falcon Wing closed his eyes. He swayed and chanted just above a whisper. No one uttered a sound while their chief communed with his Medicine Spirits.

His chant had barely faded away when a voice from outside the tipi interrupted. "My chief, a visitor requests entrance."

Falcon Wing motioned to Quiet Bird, who rose and lifted the flap. Behind Kill Deer stood Tanner Kelly, hat respectfully in hand. Falcon Wing gave Kill Deer an imperious nod. The warrior stepped aside and gestured Tanner to enter.

Silver Eagle narrowed his eyes, wishing he had the same gift his grandmother oftentimes possessed, to read others thoughts. No matter the outcome, he knew his own mind and heart. While he and Mariah might have to move from these home grounds, his regard for Tanner and Mr. and Mrs. Kelly would never wane.

Tanner acknowledged each of Silver Eagle's brethren, coming a last to him. His friend's bleak expression surely mirrored his own. As he always had, Tanner stood quietly, extending unfailing courtesy by waiting to be addressed.

Silver Eagle sighed when his father used his

usual ploy to avoid speaking to a white man. He motioned. "Sit, my brother."

Sentiment gripped Silver Eagle's heart. After the beating Tanner had given him, he could see in his friend's eyes that he still valued the friendship forged over two-plus decades.

Tanner knelt on one knee, leaned forward, and crossed forearms on his bent leg. His hat still dangled from his fingers.

"What you do here?"

"The folks and me and Mariah palavered some this mornin'. Pa wants to discuss the, uh, situation with your folks. All of us, this afternoon."

Before Silver Eagle could ask for his father's opinion, Wings of a Dove spoke—in English.

"I commune with Spirit Gods, Silver Eagle. No reason discuss what bones tell me, what Spirits whisper." She tapped her head above an ear.

Tanner respectfully asked, "What did they tell you, ma'am?"

"Mariah Kelly no happy live among The People. Our way no her way."

"That's a fact." He gestured to Silver Eagle. "Is that what you were discussin'?"

Silver Eagle dipped his chin. And then, to his astonishment, his father spoke in English.

"My son commit foolish deed. No can allow white woman in his heart live here. Bring much distress my people."

"*Ni ahpï?—*"

Tanner laid a hand on his shoulder. "That's what Pa said, too." His friend drew in a breath. "He says y'all will probably have to live on the Broken Spur."

Silver Eagle scowled and shook his head. "No bring trouble your people. Take Mariah away."

Matching Mr. Kelly's gestures when disturbed, Tanner slid fingers through dark-blond hair. "Well, see, that's the thing. Y'all got nowhere to go. You can't go north into hostile territory. And in this neck of the woods, anywhere but on the Broken Spur, you're gonna run into a passel of white folks fired up when they see you two together."

"You father say—"

"He's changed his tune." Tanner shook his head. "We ain't hankerin' for Mariah to be mistreated by nobody. Y'all'll be safer on our home ground until folks cotton to the idea."

His father and grandmother closed their eyes and communed with their Medicine Spirits. Time slipped by, and still they sat motionless; their soft humming sounds filled the air.

Silver Eagle sat back to get comfortable, and motioned Tanner to do the same. He knew there was no hurrying them to make a final decision. No hurrying them to say anything. From a young age Silver Eagle had found it difficult to practice patience. But now he must.

****

The sun was heading down, and still Tanner hadn't returned. What did that mean? Mariah wondered as she stood at the kitchen window. Had Silver Eagle's people rejected her before she had a chance to make her case with them? Or maybe Tanner had ruined her chance to be accepted. He wouldn't intentionally do that. Would he?

Surely Silver Eagle would have something to say on behalf of their relationship. "Ah," she moaned in frustration and turned from the window.

"What?" her mother asked. As she did every day at this time, Ma fixed supper. As sure as the clock in the parlor chimed four-thirty, there Sarah Kelly would be in the kitchen.

Mariah pulled out a chair and sat, propping her elbow on the table. "My doubts are slicing me to bits, Ma. Tanner's been gone for hours."

Her mother caught up the little lapel watch given to her by a friend some years past. "He'll be along when something is decided, Mariah." She motioned with the big spoon in her hand. "Set the table. Keeping busy passes the time."

Mariah pulled four plates from the shelf, then paused, narrowing her eyes. Should she set five places? Positive thinking might work. Then again...

Sighing, she stacked one more plate on top of the other four, scattered them around the table, and went to the corner cupboard Pa had built. Its shelves climbed halfway to the ceiling. She counted out five knives and forks and five cups.

Please, Silver Eagle, she prayed. *Be with Tanner.*

****

Tanner finally arrived long after supper. He rode in alone. When he entered the back door, Mariah's heart sank as she scanned her brother's troubled expression.

"What happened?"

Before Tanner could answer, Ma called them into the parlor. She sat in her rocking chair, feet up on a footstool. Though finished with her main chores of the day, her mother was never completely idle. She now pieced on the quilt while Pa read his Bible. Laying it aside, he looked up expectantly.

"What happened?" Mariah asked again, sinking onto the raised hearth.

"Don't think you're gonna be welcome in the village, sis." When she started to sputter, he raised a hand. "That don't mean they ain't acceptin' you as Silver Eagle's woman. They just don't think you'd do well with their laws, their rules, their way of life."

"That's ridiculous. I can get along with anyone." Even as the words left her mouth, Mariah recalled her stormy confrontation with Howling Coyote, her belligerent words to the chief. Mentally, she winced.

247

Maybe they were right. She'd probably be in a passel of trouble before one day waned.

"Where is Silver Eagle?" Ma asked.

"I don't know. He left the tipi and his kin before I did."

Her folks exchanged a look that Mariah couldn't interpret. Rather than ask, she gritted her teeth. She had a sneaking hunch she knew what they thought. Silver Eagle, the man she loved, was long gone, maybe never to be seen again.

Tanner dug in his pocket. He handed Mariah a pitiful-looking piece of paper folded like an envelope and now badly frayed on all four edges.

"What is it?"

He shrugged. "Search me. I met Mr. Pickett out by the gate on his way home. He said Elmer Hawkins sent it on from the post, that it came in on today's stage. Who's T. Witherspoon?"

Mariah's brow crinkled. "Who?"

As she read the faint lettering, Tanner said, "T. Witherspoon, Greensboro, Georgia."

"Glory be!" Mariah tore open the missive, and her gaze raced over the few poorly printed words.

"The Timothy you told me about, Mariah?"

She looked up. "Yes, Ma." She held up the tattered paper. "How did he know where to send this letter?"

"Who's Timothy?" Pa asked.

"A boy I met in Baltimore, Pa." Her cheeks reddened. "He fancied himself sweet on me. And now..." She reread the words. "He wants me to go to Greensboro and marry him."

Her mother took the correspondence from her limp hand and scanned the back. "I'd say he sent it to the school, Mariah, and the matron sent it on to you."

"You had a suitor in Baltimore? Why didn't I hear about it?"

"Oh, Pa, he was a boy! Seventeen, for heaven's sake. I didn't take him seriously."

"Apparently, he did," Tanner said and wagged his head. "Now you're carryin' another man's child. You best let that boy know he hasn't got a prayer of bein' part of your life."

She harrumphed. "I'll do no such thing, Tanner Kelly. I'm not going to answer this. Let him think the letter never found me." She waved it in his face, then glanced at her mother. "If Ma is right, he doesn't know where I live, and I don't think the school would give out that information."

"No, they wouldn't," Pa agreed. "That's one thing we looked into when we decided to send you east, daughter. I'm thinkin' they wouldn't flap their mouths. Your ma called 'em 'discreet,' and seems we was both right." He harrumphed. "They didn't even see fit to tell us you was workin' in that hospital."

Later, restless in her bed, heartache plagued Mariah, Timothy Witherspoon no more than a dim memory. She lay watching the curtain gently billow, pushed inward by a slight breeze, then collapse as the current died, only to come again. Eyes bleak, she refused to cry.

Rubbing a hand on her stomach, she whispered, "I guess it's just you and me, little one."

****

Morning dawned so bright, it hurt Mariah's eyes when she finally dragged herself out to tend to Nutmeg. She strode outside.

Crack!

The sound of Silver Eagle's whip stopped Mariah as though she'd smacked into a wall.

In the corral adjacent to the barn, a cow bellowed as she fell to her side. In a heartbeat Max pressed the sizzling iron on her haunch. That got another bellow from the cow. Silver Eagle flicked his whip, loosening the rawhide around her legs. She scrambled to her feet and scurried as fast as her hooves would take her toward the open gate.

The scene took on a surreal dance as Silver Eagle took down a second steer. *Crack*! Then another. He, Tanner, J.D. Parks, and Ben Stewart worked as smoothly as wheels turning on a coach. One would take down a steer. Max slipped in, branded, turned, shoved the spent iron into the fire and picked up another. Then they went on to the next.

Mariah backed up and sat on the porch step, drinking in the tableau, especially Silver Eagle. He either didn't know she was there, or he was ignoring her. Which, when he was of a mind to, he was very good at. But the thought didn't vex her like it had in the past. Instead, a silly grin curved her lips.

It wasn't until Nutmeg's whinny echoed from the barn that Mariah finally got up to do the chores she'd set out to do but had put aside while engrossed. She walked right past the corral where the men worked. She knew Silver Eagle saw her. Still, he paid her no mind.

It wasn't until she started back to the house to tell her mother he was here that she saw the tipi.

A tipi! Pitched out back near the table where they sometimes ate.

She swung around and found Silver Eagle staring at her across the distance. When he slipped between the slats, she ran, not caring who saw them. And thank God, Silver Eagle didn't, either.

He caught her in mid stride, crushed her in his strong arms, and kissed her right there for everyone to see. Somewhere close enough for her to hear, Samuel said, "Lawd have mercy."

When Silver Eagle finally released her mouth and let her feet touch the ground, Mariah looked into his intense eyes. A slow smile lit his face.

"Home," she whispered.

Epilogue

Broken Spur Ranch, 1885

Mariah rested against the ladder back chair, put a hand to her nonexistent waist and stretched. Her other hand busily worked the churn handle up and down.

"'Oh my darlin', oh my darlin', oh my darlin' Clementine,'" her mother wailed from the kitchen, endearingly off key, as always.

Mariah winced, but not from the discordant sound. The baby was so low now, she could hardly stand.

"'You are lost and gone forever,'" Ellie chimed in, her perfect pitch, sweet soprano not one bit of help to her grandmother's caterwauling.

Mariah looked down when the baby kicked. A bump appeared on her belly. She rubbed it gently and smiled in spite of the discomfort. To think, in her forties, she was pregnant—again!

She smiled, recalling Silver Eagle's bust-his-buttons pride when she told him.

Twenty-year-old Nathan outstripped his father in height. Ellie, just turned eleven, was as tall as Ma, and Bethany...

Well, Mariah didn't know how tall her older daughter had grown. Today, though, she would see her again as she returned home from Miss Pratt's School for Young Ladies in Baltimore. The whole family would celebrate Bethany's nineteenth birthday next month. On the Broken Spur, where

Bethany and all the Eagle family belonged. Right along with the Kellys.

Another smile played on Mariah's lips as she recalled the battle royal waged when Bethany had been sent away for two years. The end of the world was upon her, to hear Bethany tell it.

Mariah wondered if one day Bethany would have to wage a similar battle with her own daughter. From Ma to Mariah, to Bethany and beyond, mothers would send daughters to school. In the hope of teaching them lessons about the wider world.

Today, the two years would come to an end. The menfolk had ridden into town early this morning, long before the train chugged in from El Paso. All were as anxious as she to see Mariah's second born.

How had she changed? For she surely had. But thank goodness, Bethany hadn't been enlisted to work in a hospital as her mother had so many years ago, where men cried, moaned in despair, and died.

No, Bethany had learned from books and from doctors and had become a nurse. She'd chosen to work with orphaned children.

Gus, distant kin to a hound, crawled out from beneath the porch. Propped on his haunches, he scratched behind his ear and whined. Mariah could never figure out if it hurt, if he was in ecstasy relieving an itch, or moving fleas around.

The dog had moseyed in one day about four years ago and stayed. No one ever came calling to claim him, so he'd latched on to Bethany, then Ellie when her sister left for school.

Suddenly, Gus dropped his hind paw and came to all fours, looking down the road toward the gate, his floppy ears canted forward. *Woof, woof.* His tail arced slowly back and forth, and he whined again, though a different sound this time. He opened his mouth, his tongue lolling to one side.

Like he smiled, Mariah always thought.

Woof, woof.

Shading her eyes, more from habit than need, Mariah stared into the distance, trying to make out what had caught Gus's attention. And then she saw the dust cloud. Not big like a storm, but one caused by fast-moving horses or a wagon. It could only be...

"Ma!" She struggled to her feet, the half-churned butter forgotten. "She's here! Bethany's home."

Ma and Ellie rushed right out the screened door, excitement blooming on their faces. These days, Mariah wore her wild mane in a braid much like her mother's. Today she'd left the thick plait hanging down her back. Mariah's hair showed a few silver strands, and Ma's hair was nearly completely white now. Pa's stubbornly remained dark blond, a few gray strands at his temples providing distinction.

The same wild red hair her sister and mother were blessed—or cursed—with, whichever way one assessed her coloring, framed Ellie's sweet face. The girls had, for sure, taken after their mother, green eyes and pale skin.

Nathan, on the other hand, was the image of his pa. Coal-shiny hair that he wore to his shoulders and dark skin like his father's people. His black eyes danced with humor more than his pa's ever had, though. Thank the Lord.

Oh, sure, there'd been times Nathan had returned from the one-room schoolhouse disheveled and sporting black eyes and cut lips, from beatings the white boys gave him. But when he outgrew most of the bullies, those pummelings stopped. However, his father had eased the way, taking more guff than he deserved from folks who ought to know better.

Jessup McCallister had passed on two years past, and the animosity amongst the Kellys, Eagles, and McCallisters had come to a screeching halt. Henry had never agreed with his father's prejudice.

Horace hadn't either, not really. Although he'd never crossed Jessup when the old man got on a tear.

Mariah sat back down, unable to stand too long. The load she carried strained her back. Now she could make out the five horses. She grinned. Though she'd given in to wearing skirts since she now looked like a butterball rolling around the house, Mariah still preferred trousers and would return to them as soon as the baby was born.

A tomboy like her mother, Bethany rode like a man, and her father had not insulted her by taking a wagon to meet her. Instead, he'd led a sorrel filly he'd traded from his father and trained himself for Bethany's homecoming gift.

Old Samuel had offered to drive in and bring back her trunk. Max stood in the shade of the barn, also looking down the road. Ben Stewart had moved on a few years ago. Mr. Parks showed up now and then to help with branding, and for several years he'd ridden left flank on drives to the stockyards up north.

The closer they came, the better Mariah could pick out the riders. Bethany cantered comfortably in the center, flanked on one side by her father and brother, on the other by her grandpa and Uncle Tanner.

Pride surged through Mariah. Pride she'd harbored her entire life. First for her Ma, Pa, and Tanner, then in the man she had married. The man who had overcome so many obstacles. Even the two of them riding into town as a couple had earned Silver Eagle a beating or two early on. Until Tanner and Pa had insisted they go with him, and that put an end to it. Few people would challenge three robust men at one time, even fewer, the Kelly men.

After she and Silver Eagle had settled on the Broken Spur, he built their own two-room place, which had grown room by room until it connected with Pa's original structure. Still, to this day, a tipi stood near the picnic table. It was Silver Eagle's oasis away from others, even from her. And she never begrudged him that solitude.

Ellie leaned against the chair and draped her arm across her mother's shoulders. "You feelin' all right, Mama? You look kinda pale."

Ellie's older-than-her-years perception always took Mariah aback. She sounded more like a woman grown than a girl of eleven. The child had developed a caring, nurturing attitude by the time she was eight years old.

While Bethany, like her mother, had spent all of her time outdoors, Ellie was a homebody and helped her grandma in the house. Oh, she could ride and rope with the best of 'em, but she preferred working indoors. She'd even made several tiny garments for her impending brother's or sister's arrival.

Mariah patted Ellie's chapped hand. Washing dishes and clothes irritated the girl's tender skin something awful.

"I'm fine, sweetheart." Mariah rubbed her belly. "I'll be finer still after this little one makes its presence known."

The little one kicked her good, which made Mariah gasp. "Good grief! He's rambunctious."

"She," Ellie said, grinning. She wanted a little sister to mother.

"Ma, help me up." As Mariah clasped her mother's hand, Ellie helped guide her up by the elbow.

The horses' hooves beat louder and louder, closer and closer. While the men pulled up before they got so close to the house that dust would fly inside, Bethany did not. No, she kept coming at a steady canter, her hair flying behind like flames in the bright sun. She wore a riding skirt, a hot riding skirt, which Mariah knew would come off as soon as possible, to be replaced by trousers and a shirtwaist.

"Oh, dear," Ma mumbled when Bethany barely reined in the sorrel before leaping from the saddle, her feet churning as they hit the ground.

Tears of joy and remembrance sprang to Mariah's eyes. This scene was so much a repeat from years past, when she'd barreled out of a coach and into Tanner's arms.

This time, Bethany managed to stop before plowing into her mother. She encircled her in a hug fit to split Mariah's ribs.

"Oh, Mama! It's sooo wonderful to be home!" She gave her one more squeeze, backed up, and brushed her hand over Mariah's distended belly. Bethany's shining eyes pinned hers.

Then Bethany turned to Grandma Sarah. "Mamaw, how I missed you!" With her other arm, she circled Ellie's neck and pulled her in close. "You, too, sweety." She sniffled.

That started Ellie to blubbering. Mariah backed up a step and took in the sight. Oh, my. Bethany was as tall as she, her hair a shade darker than Mariah's and Ellie's. A beautiful girl, she thought. And it had nothing to do with pride. Simply a fact.

The men dismounted and crowded toward the porch. Gus carried on loud and clear and he danced around the men's feet.

Arms Mariah knew so well encircled her from behind, strong hands cupping her belly. She leaned into her husband's muscular chest and tilted her head back to see his dear face.

She was always surprised to view him up close. Her man had not changed, had not aged at all since their first kiss. No deep age lines, not a gray hair. In some ways it disturbed her. Would he, one day, look for a younger woman?

And then she wondered what made her even think this man was so shallow that only youth could claim his affection. She looked down at his hands rubbing her belly, absently, gently.

Ever so gently.

Silver Eagle's voice rumbled from his broad chest. "The babe, he come soon."

Carrying on with the joke they had shared with each birth, she said, "Yes, any day now *she* should make an appearance. I've been right the past two times. You got your eagle when Nathan was born. I heard two doves cooing."

"Let's go in," Her mother said. "The sun's creeping across the porch."

Her father put his hand on Ma's shoulder. "Be right with you, darlin'. Need to put my horse away."

"I'll do that, Gramps." Nathan scooped up his grandpa's reins.

Tanner gathered his and Silver Eagle's leads. "Back in a minute," he said over his shoulder.

Mariah grinned and shook her head as she watched her brother walk away with Nathan striding by his side. Tanner had, so far, kept to his word. Something to the effect, "I ain't never losin' my heart to no woman. Skirts give a man nothin' but grief."

Silver Eagle leaned to brush a kiss on Mariah's neck. "Why you sigh?"

She turned in his arms, pressing her bulging belly into him. "I was remembering my brother years ago talking about not finding a woman to love." Her brow creased. "He hasn't, and I sort of worry about him. Feel sorry for him, too."

"Sorry? Why say sorry? Tanner, he have plenty women between blankets, I think. He like work horse, cattle. He have warm bed, much good food. No need marry woman if he no want mate."

Mariah squinted at him. "Says the man who married one and sired two girls, along with a strapping son."

"Ah. The Spirits bless me." Silver Eagle swept his arm. "Live free like birds. Take mate on horse and ride where want." He paused, patted her stomach. "Soon."

Smiling, Mariah leaned her head against Silver Eagle's chest and hugged him. Home, she thought as she did each time he held her.

In the next instant, she grimaced and inhaled a sharp breath.

Not one to miss a thing, Silver Eagle slipped his finger beneath her chin. He searched her face. "What trouble you, my heart?"

"Um, I think—" She clamped her hand on the side of her belly. "Oh my, I believe our new little one is ready to make an appearance. Apparently, she wants to welcome her sister home, too."

Silver Eagle scooped her up in his arms and turned to face the descending sun.

Mariah knew he was offering thanks to his gods and to the woman he'd revered all his life. Although he would never utter his grandmother's name now that she had joined the Spirit World.

But Mariah could.

Her gaze searched the wide sky, where a few clouds scudded high and free. Imagining one as a soft seat, she lifted her chin. "Wings of a Dove, the child you predicted is coming today. May it be healthy and strong, be it boy or girl."

A bird crossed the sun, arresting Silver Eagle's intention to go inside. Together, they watched the magnificent bird again swoop across the sky.

"An eagle," Mariah whispered as her husband started into the white man's house he had learned to reside within many moons ago. His home.

Pausing, his dark eyes aglitter, Silver Eagle dipped his head reverently toward the sign from the Spirit World, from his grandmother.

He smiled.

A word about the author...

Visit her at
http:// www.joycehendersonauthor.com

Breinigsville, PA USA
18 February 2011
255893BV00005B/20/P